KNOT IN TIME

KNOT IN TIME

TALES OF UNCERTAINTY • BOOK ONE

BY

ALAN TUCKER

MAD Design, Inc.
Billings, Montana

This book is a work of fiction. The characters, incidents, and dialog are drawn from the author's imagination and are not to be construed as real. Any resemblance to actual events or persons, living or dead, is entirely coincidental.

 For information address MAD Design, Inc., 212 Fair Park Drive, Billings, Montana 59102.

Second Edition

ISBN 978-0-9885047-0-7 (paperback)

This book is dedicated to
all those who have dared to dream.

Acknowledgements

As always, there are many people to thank at the completion of a project like this. I love my beta readers! Linda, Cat, Jenn, Mercedes, Elizabeth, and Jaimie, thank you so much for your time, effort, and valuable input.

Thanks also to my editors and my family for putting up with a new project and all the revisions along the way.

1

I had no idea what was chasing me, but I did not like the look of its tentacles.

Okay, it wasn't just the tentacles, but the whole four-foot amorphous mass that glided effortlessly two or three inches above the ground that really creeped me out.

And the tentacles.

It was late and I had just stopped at Jerry's Cafe, looking for work, or maybe a meal.

Jerry himself had answered my knock at the service door. "Hey, Dare," he said with a tired smile, wiping his hands on his apron-covered belly. "I'm sorry, I don't have anything for you tonight. Been kinda slow lately."

I sighed, but put on a smile for him. "It's okay, thanks." Pickings had been slim recently. Everyone had felt the pinch from a bad economy.

Jerry nodded and closed the door. A chill breeze blew down the alley, taking an old flyer from a local band for a short ride through the light shining from the cafe's back entrance. I wrapped my overshirt tighter around my lean frame and shivered. Autumn nights were often cold in Colorado.

I had walked away from the light, thinking of somewhere else I might try when I saw what I thought was the end of a wet rope, lying near a mound of trash.

The rope moved and I froze.

When the whole trash pile had begun to shake, I yelled and sprinted away into the dark, deserted street.

Somehow, the hideous thing had kept pace.

I turned a corner and jogged down another littered alley, my lungs heaving. Streetlights struggled to penetrate the gloom the farther I went. My foot hit an empty beer bottle, sending it skittering loudly across the pavement. I cursed and looked back at the mouth of the alley. Sure enough, my gelatinous stalker had noted the sound and turned to follow.

Heart pounding and out of breath, I continued blindly onward. I was familiar with many of the back streets in downtown Denver, but darkness and fear had caused confusion. After a sharp turn to the right, I found myself in a dead end with a row of imposing metal dumpsters. I spotted a door to my left, but a sign read, "Exit Only," and I saw no handle.

In the movies, back alleys are usually filled with metal fire escapes and other stuff to climb so the hero can escape danger. My life had never been Hollywood material and modern buildings don't generally come with handy getaway equipment.

I grimaced and contemplated hiding in one of the dumpsters, but then the blob silently slipped into view. Considering the smell emanating from the closest bin, I actually felt some relief my pursuer had found me before I'd mustered up the courage to dive in.

The creature stopped about twenty feet away, floating just above the pavement. Its body the color of moldy cheese, two of its many worm-like tentacles held small metallic devices of indiscernible purposes.

The last thing I expected it to do was talk to me.

"Dare, please stop," it, or rather one of its little machines, said in a neutral tone.

My name is Darius, but my friends call me Dare. I had few friends and I was reasonably sure none of them were giant amoebas. "What are you? And how do you know my name?"

"We work together— or rather, we will. In the future. It's complicated."

"I bet," I said, looking around for cameras and bracing myself for someone to jump out and yell, "You've been punked!"

A ripple passed over the thing's backside. "You told me to be honest with you. I should have listened, but everything in our training instructs us never to do that with lower species."

"Lower species?" I wasn't sure, but I thought I'd just been insulted by a slug.

"Now I've offended you. Again. This is hopeless."

I didn't know what it meant by "again," but something in its tone made me feel sorry for the sack of jello. "Why are you chasing me?"

"My mission is to recruit you to our organization. But, I've failed."

"Failed? How do you know?"

The tentacle carrying the device it used to speak waved spasmodically. "Because, in thirty-seven seconds, another human will come out of that building." It indicated with another appendage the door I'd seen earlier. "If it sees me, this thread could unravel irreparably."

"This door?" I said, pointing. "In thirty-seven seconds?"

"Twenty-nine."

I glanced down at the bottom of the dumpster next to me. It sat on a set of metal wheels. Running to the end, I leaned in with my back and pushed it forward a few feet. Twice more and the heavy bin completely blocked the door. I moved to the side opposite the exit and braced against the dumpster. A handful of seconds later, I heard running footsteps from inside the building and someone slammed forcefully into the door, jarring the bin, but I held it firm. I heard the person inside curse and they tried a second time to push the door open, unsuccessfully. Soon after, the sound of hastily retreating feet reached my ears, followed by silence.

I relaxed and looked at my self-proclaimed recruiter. "Did that buy you some time?" I asked.

It sat impassively for a second before shaking its small machine again. "Yes. Four minutes and eighteen seconds from now, someone will enter the alley to perform biological functions."

I smiled. "Well, then you have four minutes to tell me what the hell's going on."

"Do you have any idea what you just did?"

Puzzled by the question, I answered without a smart remark, which was unusual for me. "I blocked the door so that person wouldn't see you."

"But you gave no consideration to the consequences! You've altered the thread in complete ignorance of what repercussions might occur!"

"Well, you're the genius from the future, and you're still here, so I guess I didn't destroy the world by moving a garbage can."

"That's not the point."

"You're right. The point is you've got less than four minutes to explain to me why I'm in a dark alley talking to a chia pet gone wild."

The tentacled blob looked at me silently. At least, I assumed it was looking at me. Then it said, "Very well. I have no other options since this was the last safe insertion zone. I work with a group of beings that, for lack of a simpler explanation, act as custodians of time. As I mentioned before, I am here to ask you to join us."

"Why me?" I had worked as a janitor in the last steady job I'd been able to find. Did these people need someone to scrape gum from underneath the tables of time?

"I can't answer that directly."

"Why not?"

"Partially because I don't know all the reasons, and partially because any answer I could offer would influence your decision too greatly."

"You're not real good at this recruiting business," I said. "I'm thinking the important part of the job is to convince me to join up."

"Your decision must be made freely, and without knowledge beyond your current thread in the multiverse."

This gave me pause. My current thread in the multiverse? Then I remembered something it had said earlier. "But you told me before that we work together in the future, so obviously I say, 'Yes,' right?"

"More error on my part. That thread can still unravel. No outcome is absolute. There are only probabilities."

That word had plagued me my entire life. Probabilities. I

had been adopted as a baby into a relatively famous— at least in scientific circles— family. My great, great uncle, Werner Heisenberg, had come up with one of the fundamental ideas of modern physics: the Heisenberg Uncertainty Principle. Simply stated, it said that when looking at extremely small things, like electrons in an atom, you can only know for certain one of two things: where it is, or how fast it's moving. If you know one, you cannot know the other. Confusing, I know. The point is, physicists end up working in probabilities rather than certainties. My life was a laundry list of them. Because of my last name, people thought I was probably smart. Because of my grades in school, my teachers thought I was probably lazy. Because I was often in trouble, counselors thought I was probably a delinquent, or on drugs, and I would probably end up in prison, or worse.

And they were all probably right.

"Do you have a name?" I asked the pile of goo.

It hesitated before answering. "Not as such, but you call me Bob."

I smirked. My sense of humor tended to be somewhat less than politically correct. When he said, "Bob," the joke about what you call the boy with no arms or legs in a swimming pool immediately popped into my head. I knew right then the floating paramecium had to be telling the truth.

"Okay, Bob. I'm in."

His tentacles stiffened slightly. "Really? Just like that?"

"Sure, why not?"

"Amazing. Please consider this carefully. Darius Arthur Heisenberg, do you agree to join the Keepers and forsake your current thread in the multiverse for the safeguarding of all others?"

I had few prospects. I was a nineteen-year-old who lived day-to-day on the street, mostly because I was a smart ass punk who had a real problem with authority figures. But I was sure Bob, or his superiors, already knew all that. Beings who were concerned with such a little thing as preventing someone from exiting a random building, in a random city, on a random night wouldn't pluck a person out of their timeline who was destined to do something important in the future, right?

Probably.

"I do." Suddenly, I felt like I should be putting a ring on my finger.

"Thank you," Bob said with relief, obvious even from an alien blob. Then I discovered the purpose of the other device he'd been holding.

He shot me with it.

2

I woke to buzzing, seemingly coming from everywhere. Then I realized it was coming from me.

I had that uncomfortable, prickly, tingling sensation that happens when a leg or arm falls asleep and then feeling returns— only across every inch of my skin. I squeezed my eyes shut as all the nerves I possessed jangled like a fire station during an apocalyptic meteor blast.

Slowly, my body decided the world was not coming to an end at that particular moment and hypersensitivity replaced the tingles. Through my closed eyes, I sensed a bright light shining in my face. I lay stretched out, stark naked, on a hard, flat surface. My fingers and toes responded reluctantly to the very basic inquiries I sent out, but actual movement seemed like such a waste of energy I could scarcely comprehend it. A wave of fatigue washed over me and it took every bit of willpower I had to remain awake.

Distantly, I heard a dispassionate, vaguely female voice say, "The primate is conscious."

"What? Already?" another voice, deeper, with a rough, gravely tone, said.

"His particular physiology was unexpected. Unique. I am still analyzing some of his higher functions."

I took a chance and opened my eyes, instantly regretting it. The light above me burned bright spots into my vision. "Ow," I said without imagination. It came out as barely more than a croak; my throat was dry as the Sahara.

A shadow moved across my vision and the spots faded from orange to green. "Darius Arthur Heisenberg, be at ease," the deep voice intoned. "You are among compatriots and future colleagues."

"Well, that's comforting," I said, still blinking away afterimages.

"Do you require anything, Darius Arthur Heisenberg?"

"Water. And some clothes would be nice."

"Bodily modesty is a hallmark of primitive species," the feminine voice said. I couldn't place a location for it in the room, it seemed to be coming from everywhere.

I tried unsuccessfully to sit up and settled for rolling onto my side. "Who are you people?"

A furry arm appeared in front of me as the last of the colorful spots vanished. It held a packet of clear liquid with a tapered mouth for drinking. I accepted it gratefully and sucked it almost dry. The water had a strange aftertaste. Probably some nutrients or something else to pep me up, I decided. If these people wanted to kill me, they could have done it many times already.

"To answer your question Darius Arthur Heisenberg, I am M'sang Tah," the owner of the furry arm and deep voice said. "I am in charge of this very minor outpost, and your impending training."

I looked up and nearly spit the last of my water in M'sang's face. My first impression of him was hamster, though, to be fair,

M'sang was much more menacing. His fur was mottled in dark colors— grays, blacks, and earth tones— and his eyes were pure obsidian. A short muzzle ended in a dark piece of flesh, which I took for a nose, and I noted a number of sharp-looking teeth when he spoke.

"Is something amiss?" he asked.

I coughed. "No. I just… you're only my second alien. Is Bob here too?"

M'sang cocked his head to one side. "Bob? What is, Bob?"

"He is referring to the operative who brought him in," the bodiless female voice offered.

"Oh! I understand. No. 'Bob' is not here. He had to return to his own thread. The Keepers thought it would ease your adjustment if someone with a relatively similar phylogenic path to your own initiated your training. Thus, I was sent," M'sang said.

"Um, okay," I said, having very little idea what he was talking about. I felt a little stronger and decided to attempt sitting up again, with much better results.

Uniformly light gray, the walls, ceiling, and floor blended together to give the illusion of size, though the room was rather small. I sat on the only real feature in the space, and the table bore the same bland gray color. My feet dangled, not touching the floor, and a wave of vertigo gripped me as I looked down at my toes.

M'sang placed a firm, fuzzy hand on my shoulder. "Take your time, Darius Arthur Heisenberg. Your body has been through a lot."

"Why do you keep using my full name?" I asked once my uneasiness passed.

"What else would I call you?"

"Just Dare is fine. You say the whole thing like that and I feel like I'm six years old after I just finished taking practice swings with my new baseball bat... inside the house." Not one of my finer moments. I hadn't known my mother's skin could turn that shade of purple and it wasn't something I wished to see again.

"All right, Dare," M'sang said. "Wait here while I... find some garments for you. I must admit, you are surprisingly free of hair for a member of the primate family. You must be somewhat chilled."

Before I could respond, the incorporeal woman said, "His body is fully capable of maintaining its temperature. He is quite comfortable."

"And just how do you know that?" I asked, growing irritated at her self-assured tone. "Who are you anyway?"

"I am one of the Keepers' integrated management systems. This insignificant facility is but one of hundreds I oversee and maintain."

I tried to wrap my mangled brain around her response. "So, you're a computer then?"

"I am farther beyond what you consider a 'computer' than you are from the simple algae that once dominated your trivial planet and eventually gave rise to what passes for intelligent life."

She had packed an impressive number of insults into one sentence, I had to admit. "Didn't mean to offend. I'm just trying to get a grip on all this. What should I call you then?"

"Call me? Why would you have need to 'call me' anything? If you have a request, simply state it."

I sighed. "Look, it's just easier for me if you have a name." I thought about what she'd said before. "How about Kim?"

"Kim?"

"Yeah, Keepers' Integrated Management: KIM"

"If it will soothe your simple mind, you may call me whatever you wish."

M'sang made a chuffing sound I took for amusement. "I will return shortly." He took two strides to the corner of the room and part of the wall melted away, revealing a similarly colored hall. He stepped through and the wall reformed.

"You guys aren't much for interior decoration, are you?"

"Superfluous," Kim stated.

"So, how come I can understand you? I can't believe the whole galaxy speaks English."

"You understand because I have made modifications to your cerebral cortex— my apologies, your brain—"

"I know what my cerebral cortex is! Wait. You changed my brain?"

"Yes, that is what I said. I have also corrected your rudimentary biological chemistry to prevent your decomposition."

My decomposition? "I'm sorry. What does that mean?"

"Your body will finish its maturation process, but it will cease to degrade."

"You mean I'm going to live forever?"

"Hardly. Nearly everything is subject to entropy. Your body will, however, enjoy a greatly increased span of meaningful activity."

I mulled this over. It all sounded very promising. If I understood her, I'd stop aging after I quit growing in a couple of years or so. Not a bad trade off for being abducted from a dead end life to work for a bunch of time-guarding aliens.

Kim continued, "Surprisingly, your species' scientists were not terribly far away from a crude duplication of portions of my work on you. Unfortunately, their understanding of physics has lagged behind biology, which will probably lead to massive overpopulation of your planet and likely the destruction of the small semblance of civilization you have managed to create."

Whoa. "You're telling me the human race is going to destroy itself? Can't you do something about it? I mean, what's the point of being able to hop around in time if you let stuff like that happen?"

"Your mind is not ready to comprehend the scope of our work. Be at ease young Darius Arthur Heisenberg."

I flinched at the mention of my full name again. "Please, just call me Dare."

"As you wish. Your preoccupation with your childhood is an unnecessary distraction I must point out."

The wall opened again and M'sang entered with an armload of clothing. "Here you are, Dare. Will these suffice to cover your flesh and appease your sensibilities?"

He placed the clothes on the table. More gray. These people definitely needed an injection of color. I slid off and my feet touched the floor. Softer than I'd expected, it flexed and rebounded under my weight. The clothes were duller than dull, but at least my junk wasn't parading around for the world to see. They fit a little loose, which suited me just fine, and had several pockets in the pants and shirt. There was still something missing though.

"Shoes?" I asked him.

M'sang looked clearly appalled. "You require coverings for your feet as well? How do you gather information about the world around you?"

I shrugged. "I'll admit, the floor feels nice, but assuming I ever leave this place, I'll need some sort of footwear."

"Astounding. Would you care for a blindfold as well?"

I had to chuckle at that. "That's funny. But, you know, for someone who's supposed to be from a highly advanced species, you're not being very accepting of my differences. Shouldn't you be above all that?"

I looked up and M'sang's jet black eyes squinted at me. I couldn't tell if he was offended or considering if I'd be a tasty snack.

Kim interjected, "M'sang Tah's people are scarcely above your own on the societal evolutionary ladder, Dare. It's another reason he was chosen for this posting."

I laughed again. "Kim, you have a real gift for squashing egos."

M'sang scrunched his nose. "Nevertheless, you are both correct. I apologize Darius— Dare. My speech was insensitive."

"Don't sweat it." I started to reach up and give him a friendly clap on the shoulder, then thought better of it. No sense in pushing my luck with a razor-toothed rodent who was a head taller and considerably bulkier than me. Who knew what sort of meaning that gesture might convey? I certainly didn't want to unintentionally initiate some sort of ritual combat or declare my undying love for him. "We'll worry about the shoes later. Got any more of those water packs? I'm thirsty again."

He looked down and pulled another packet of liquid from a large pouch attached to a utilitarian belt he wore. No clothing, but he did at least need pockets. I accepted it with a nod of thanks and drank it straight away.

"Your body will need several days to adjust to the changes made by the management system," M'sang said. "In the meantime, we can begin your training and education by giving you a tour of our modest facility."

"Sounds good. Lead the way."

3

The sheer amount of gray blew me away— well, as much as a copious amount of bland can blow anyone away.

Outside the examination room, a short hallway led to a larger, open area, maybe thirty feet square. The sameness of everything made judging the distances difficult.

"This is our main work space," M'sang said.

Confused, I studied the room again. Gray, gray, and more gray. "What 'work' do you do? There's nothing here."

"The management system provides what we need. Let me show you." He stepped a little closer to one wall and said, "I'd like to sit and study the flora and fauna of Dare's home planet."

As soon as M'sang uttered the words, a comfortable looking, albeit gray, seat formed up from the floor and the wall in front of him burst forth with color and light. Moving scenes of wild animals, jungles, prairie grasslands, fields of flowers, and a hundred other images competed for attention. As I watched, M'sang shifted his gaze from one thing to another, each time the object of his focus leapt to the forefront, projected in three dimensions. The depictions were so crisp and lifelike, I almost thought I could step into them.

"The visuals are accompanied by audio and other sensory information in my mind," M'sang continued. "If I chose, I could restrict the visuals to my perception only, but that can cause confusion in an untrained mind between the construct and reality." He focused on several more scenes, then commented, "Many aspects of your world bear similarities to my own. Enough, thank you."

The wall immediately returned to its former gray self and the unused chair sank back into the floor. "Wow," was all I could muster as a response.

M'sang crossed the room to another wall. Near one corner, a doorway appeared. "Your personal living space is here."

I walked to the entrance and peered inside, only to be greeted by more gray. The empty room was no more than ten feet across.

He gestured to his left. "My quarters are off that wall, and we have two units for visitors over there. Do you have any questions?"

I looked back at him, dumbfounded. "That's it?"

M'sang returned my gaze. "What more do you require?"

I laughed. "I don't know. Where's all the machines? The computers, the engine room, the transporters, for God's sake! Where's all the people?"

"I'm sorry, I don't know what devices you are referring to, Dare. As I've showed you, everything we need is supplied by the management system. You and I are the only beings here."

"Seriously?"

Kim's voice sounded in the room, or in my head, which amounted to the same thing. "M'sang Tah is being truthful, Dare. He is here to instruct you. I am here to provide for your simple needs."

She couldn't say anything without dropping some sort of insult. "Where is 'here' anyway?" I asked.

"That's a bit complicated," M'sang answered. "This facility is rather outside the dimensions you currently understand."

"Uh huh." I'd read a fair share of science fiction during the time I'd spent not being a delinquent, but this was very different from any alien abduction story I'd ever heard of.

"Perhaps a bit more rest would be helpful," M'sang suggested.

I spent the next several days studying— mostly science, and physics specifically, but a lot of it was over my head. M'sang told me to think of the universe as a nearly endless, immense rope. That rope being created by braiding together a large number of smaller ropes, each composed of still thinner strands, and so on. Down at the lowest level was what I had formerly considered to be the universe: one thread of time and space that I happened to exist within. Those threads were so similar, and so tightly bundled, they became nearly indistinguishable from one another. Yet, they were still separate, which was why time paradoxes like going back and killing your grandfather weren't as catastrophic as they sounded. The event that caused the paradox happened only in a single strand; all the rest around it that were virtually identical would remain unchanged.

There was, however, another danger involved and, M'sang told me, the reason why the Keepers existed. If a single thread became altered or damaged severely enough, it could completely unravel and, in doing so, affect its neighboring threads as well, even to the point of destroying them. Multitudes of universes could be wiped out of existence.

Yeah, it was kind of a heavy concept for my second day of school.

During my small bits of downtime, I decorated my room. More precisely, I directed Kim to decorate my room.

I reserved the wall opposite the doorway for video and had her play episodes of *South Park* on continuous loop unless I asked for something else. Above my bed, which I made large enough to almost fill the room, I created a collage of movie posters. Classics like Bruce Lee's *Enter the Dragon* mingled with *Star Wars* and *Avatar*, among many others. The wall with the doorway showed a tropical beach, complete with sound and smell. I had fond memories of the ocean from when I was little, so having a beach in my room seemed pretty cool. Lastly, across from my bed, I had a view of the mountains west of Denver, seen from the tallest buildings of downtown. While there was really nothing specific I missed about my old life, after a few days I found myself feeling somewhat homesick. Looking at that mountainous horizon made the place feel a bit more like home.

All in all though, I had little time to brood about my past. I trained physically, as well as mentally, and found my body more fit, agile, and responsive than ever before. Whatever Kim had done to "correct" my body chemistry had certainly had a positive effect.

One thing I did miss terribly was food. We did eat, of course, but only gelatinous nutrient packets, supplied, like everything else, by Kim. While satisfying from a purely nutritional standpoint, they lacked any real tactile sensation. After a week or so of them, I was ready to do unspeakable things if offered a fat, juicy cheeseburger.

I woke one morning— and I use that term loosely because I had no real sense of time any longer, an irony not lost on me considering what I was training to do— to a long, flat tone, followed by Kim's voice saying, "Insertion detected." All the imagery in my room had vanished, replaced by a pulsing blue light coming from the ceiling.

"What's going on, Kim?" I asked, rubbing sleep from my eyes.

"Join M'sang Tah in the common area and we will explain."

Groaning, I rolled out of bed and picked my clothes up off the floor. Kim somehow managed to keep everything clean and fresh regardless of what I did with them. I tugged them on and padded into the main room. They had still neglected to provide me with footwear, but I had become used to being barefoot. M'sang looked like he always did and I wondered, not for the first time, if he ever slept.

"Greetings, Dare," M'sang said.

I gave him a grunt in response and noticed the same sky-colored light above my head that Kim had produced in my quarters. It pulsed, not quite in time with the throbbing behind my eyes that began growing in intensity. I rubbed them, then squinted at M'sang. "What's with the blue?"

"The management system has detected an insertion in our locale."

"Insertion… yeah. Kim said that, but what does it mean?"

M'sang huffed and his cheeks bulged, a reaction I'd learned

meant he was irritated, and nearly always at me. "Dare, have you processed any of the knowledge I have imparted to you? An 'insertion' is an intrusion on a thread from an outside source. As agents for the Keepers, we are sometimes inserted to perform tasks or correct problems. Occasionally, other parties will insert themselves into a thread with nefarious intentions."

"So, Kim noticed one of these bad guys entering a thread near here?"

"Just so. Although their motives have yet to be determined. You can observe from here while I establish the extent of damage to the thread, if any."

"Negative, M'sang Tah," Kim interjected. "Dare will be inserted if necessary."

I didn't particularly like the sound of that and evidently M'sang didn't either. His black eyes bulged. "What? But he has hardly begun his training! He could do more damage than the initial interloper."

"Nevertheless, the Keepers have instructed me to prepare him rather than you. Dare, please enter the examination chamber."

I glanced at M'sang's still shocked face and shrugged my shoulders before heading down the short hallway. The room I'd first encountered in the facility had a number of purposes, but I thought of it as the "examination" room, so Kim referred to it that way. I stepped inside and saw a short oval platform with two thin pedestals, each a little short of three feet high and separated by about two feet.

"Step up and place your hands on the control rods," Kim instructed.

The platform felt the same under my bare feet as the rest of the place. I stood between the two small pillars and rested my palms on top. The whole apparatus immediately glowed with a soft, warm light, and my skin tingled all over. Soon, my vision of the room began to fade.

"Calibrating sensory input."

An dark scene took shape all around me. I stood in a narrow street or alley with buildings, three to five stories tall, in every direction. The only light came from a handful of curtained windows scattered up and down the constricted lane. The images solidified, but never quite came into focus. I thought I saw a man, crouched in a doorway a few yards ahead of me, but the figure's edges seemed indistinct and jumped around randomly.

"Why is everything so… fuzzy?" I whispered, afraid to disturb the setting.

"You may speak normally, Dare," I heard Kim's voice say. "You are viewing a multitude of close-knit threads simultaneously. Structures and other relatively permanent objects will seem sharper to your perception as they will vary little within the grouping of time-strings. Creatures and other things that are not so static will appear fluid, or 'fuzzy' as you put it, because you are seeing all of the possibilities for their positioning at once. I know it is a difficult concept for your primitive brain to grasp, so just concentrate on what happens."

I scowled and did my best to brush off Kim's insult. The buildings were certainly more solid looking while the man hiding in the shadows looked to be in the middle of an epileptic fit on speed.

"Pay attention. You will witness the insertion in six seconds."

"But, you said it already happened—"

"Four, three, two…"

I noticed a shimmer near a corner of one of the buildings that swiftly materialized into a tall man. He wore a long, canvas overcoat and a wide brimmed hat hid his eyes. After glancing around he strode confidently toward the figure hiding in the doorway.

"Isolating thread."

The crouching man, who no longer appeared to be in several places at once, stood at the approach of the newcomer. Words were exchanged, then Overcoat pulled something from his pocket and pointed it at the first man. Blue light flashed and Overcoat watched his victim slump to the ground. Heartbeats later, he touched his ear, then shimmered out of existence.

"Physical insertion in progress."

"What?"

"Stand still, Dare. The process can be disorienting for organics," Kim said.

"Wait. What are you—" Disorienting was a rather mild term for what I felt next. I fell to my knees on the hard paving stones and deposited my latest meal of nutrient jello on the ground. Sounds of a lively city reached my ears as I tried to get my insides to unclench and get to my feet. The air held a definite chill and I realized I stood barefoot on cold, moist cobblestones.

Silently cursing Kim, I located the fallen man and leaned over him. He had wavy, dark hair and a mustache that curled down past the edges of his mouth. His surprised, lifeless eyes stared back at me.

Something buzzed in my shirt pocket, causing me to jump halfway out of my skin. Collecting my scattered wits, I reached up and felt something about the size of a phone vibrating insistently. I pulled it out and saw a bright screen with recognizable words:

"Insert the listening piece in your ear."

I turned the device over in my hands and saw what looked like an ear bud attached on the back. I pulled it off and fit it snugly in my right ear. Kim's voice immediately said, "Are your aural faculties functioning properly?"

I whispered, "Yes, I can hear you. But would it have killed you to make me a pair of shoes along with the cell phone?"

"Stop whining. I calculate you have one minute and fifty-three seconds before you are discovered in the alley. Check the being's pockets for a set of keys."

Grumbling under my breath, I searched the unfortunate man. I did manage to find a ring with half a dozen keys. I also discovered an old fashioned single-shot pistol and a knife. Who was this guy? "Got the keys. Now what?"

"One of them should open the door in front of you. Take the weapons you found as well."

Reluctantly, I pocketed the gun and knife. The third key I tried unlocked the door. Cautiously, I opened it and peered inside. Before me, a short dark hallway loomed, with another door at the end and two more on the right side.

"The first room is empty. Open the door and drag the body inside," Kim said in my ear.

This Time-Guardian-Agent thing was turning out to be much less fun than I'd anticipated. I checked the knob of the first door. Finding it unlocked, I opened it. Inside I saw several racks of clothing of all different types. Sensing I was running out of time, I moved back to the stoop outside and grabbed the dead man's coat collar, pulling him inside and into the tight garment room. I carefully shut both doors and let out a pent up breath. The only light in the room came from the display on my "phone," for lack of a better word.

"All right, Kim," I said in hushed tones. "What is all this about? And who is the dead guy I'm huddled up with?"

"His name was John Wilkes Booth and, in approximately twenty-eight minutes, he would have killed a man named Abraham Lincoln."

4

I sat in shock and spent the next few seconds trying to wrap my brain around what Kim had said.

"This is the guy who assassinated Abe Lincoln?"

"Would have assassinated him, yes. He will have a difficult time accomplishing that now."

"What the hell? I thought this was the sort of thing we were supposed to prevent happening!"

"Keep your voice low," Kim admonished. "Unfortunately, we had to allow the other entity to believe he had succeeded in his mission."

"Well, considering I'm sitting next to a very dead dude, I'd say he did succeed."

"Only if Abraham Lincoln is still alive in twenty-seven minutes."

The implications of that statement rolled through my mind like a bowling ball powering toward a set of pins. "You want me to kill Abraham Lincoln!"

"If he lives, this thread, and a great number of those around it, will likely unravel and be destroyed. Including your own," Kim said with finality.

Strike.

If what she said was true, my very existence hinged on me

carrying out Booth's heinous murder of one of the greatest men in American history.

It seemed like a lot of pressure for my first day on the job.

"Wouldn't the world have been a better place if he'd lived? I mean, he was one of our best Presidents."

"I have no idea about 'better', but it would be vastly different," Kim said. "So different, I calculate a ninety-two point eight percent chance the thread will cease to exist."

"But, I'm still here. If the thread blows up because of this, wouldn't I already have vanished or something?"

"The thread hasn't been altered significantly. Yet. Yes, John Wilkes Booth is dead, but if Abraham Lincoln still dies at the appropriate time, in a similar manner, this strand and those around it should remain intact."

M'sang had walked me through some mental exercises during my training regarding the apparent paradoxes of time travel, but that didn't make this situation any easier to comprehend. The events we were discussing were over a hundred and fifty years in the past, yet Kim talked about them like they were in the future. Of course, they were in the future from my current position in time. It was enough to make Stephen Hawking reach for a bottle of pain killers. Even with what was essentially my whole universe at stake, I didn't know if I could do what Kim had asked. Could I really walk up behind Abraham freaking Lincoln and shoot him in the head with Booth's gun?

"I think I'm gonna be sick."

"Didn't you already do that outside?"

I swallowed bile. "Thanks for reminding me." Suddenly, a

new thought flounced through my abused brain. "Wait. Why didn't that other guy lose his lunch when he came through? And he looked human!"

"It was a construct. You would call it a robot. They are used sometimes for simple tasks such as this."

I glanced down at the unlucky Mr. Booth in the dim light of the device in my hand. Though, I supposed he wasn't that unlucky. I recalled he died just a few days after killing Lincoln, running from the authorities. "You've been terminated," I said in my best Schwarzenegger.

"Dare, you're wasting time."

I laughed. "Wasting time? Don't we have an infinite supply of that? What's to stop these guys from sending a robot to zap me out of existence in the next five minutes?"

"Energy," Kim stated in her no nonsense manner. "The amount of energy required to physically insert a being, or object, into a thread is incomprehensible to your mind. And the cost increases the farther back in time you go."

"So, why do it at all?"

"The reasons vary wildly. Personal gain, revenge, insanity, all these and more have been the cause of temporal disruptions."

Distantly, through the building's walls, I heard the applause from a large crowd. I dropped my head and sighed. "How long?"

"Nineteen minutes, sixteen seconds."

If I was going to do this, I figured I'd better look the part. Setting my tricorder-phone-doohickey face up on the floor, I unbuttoned Booth's jacket. I took my time, rolling him over carefully to pull one arm out, then the other, under the pretense of being quiet. Really I was just stalling. The whole situation felt so wrong, on so many levels, I couldn't get a grip on it. The coat fit tight across my shoulders, but was manageable. I glanced at my legs and shook my head. No way was I wearing a dead guy's pants. Then I noticed my bare feet once again and let out a long breath. Painstakingly, I unlaced Booth's shoes and removed them. I spent less time considering his socks than I had his pants. I'd happily deal with blisters. Gingerly sliding my foot in the right shoe, it soon became clear Mr. Booth and I were not long lost twins.

"Aw, c'mon. Really?" My feet were flippers compared to his. It appeared I would remain footloose a while longer. I shined my phone light around the room, but didn't see any alternatives. Evidently, the actors provided their own footwear, or it was stored elsewhere.

"Eleven minutes," Kim intoned in my ear.

"Yeah, okay," I whispered, finding a pocket for the phone-thing. Booth's gun and knife I also stowed in the jacket. "Where do I go?"

"The door at the end of the hall leads to the backstage area of the theater. To your left, you will find a ladder. Climb up to the catwalk and I will explain further."

With a nod, I took a deep breath and listened at the door. While I assumed Kim would warn me if the hallway was occupied, I wasn't taking any chances. I opened the door and slipped out, latching it softly behind me. Padding down the short hall, sounds from the theater beyond became more distinct. An actor was delivering his lines, punctuated by intermittent laughter and applause from the audience. I cracked open the door. Some light filtered through from the stage to my right, otherwise it was dark. I passed through and found the ladder Kim had mentioned.

The arches of my feet wailed in protest as I climbed. It had never occurred to me that climbing a ladder barefoot would be so uncomfortable. I bit my cheek to stay silent and finally made it to the top.

"For such a primitive species, you are surprisingly reliant on external accoutrements," Kim said.

"In spite of what you may think, it's been a while since my ancestors were swinging through trees," I whispered while massaging my sore feet. "Where to now?"

"Cross the short walkway to your left. At the end is a doorway that will give you access to the balconies. Lincoln's party is in the first one."

I nodded and made my way across the rickety catwalk. Two rough planks were all that separated me from a painful, noisy fall. A second actor had joined the first on stage and they were engaged in a fast-paced banter that had the crowd howling with laughter. I appreciated the actors' skills; they allowed me to traverse the unsteady framework unnoticed. I opened the small door before me and crouched through to another dark hallway. Sconces on the wall to my left held small oil lamps, which I assumed would be lit when the show ended, allowing folks to see while exiting the theater.

"Booth bored a spy hole in the balcony door earlier in the day. Do you see it?"

I looked to my right and saw a pinpoint of light. I crawled closer and saw the hole just under the door handle. "Got it," I whispered.

I peered through the hole and saw two high backed chairs immediately in front of me. A light colored bonnet poked over the top of the chair on the right. To the left, the dark head and shoulders of a much taller man rose above the finely upholstered furniture.

Abraham Lincoln!

"Less than three minutes, Dare," Kim informed me.

I closed my eyes and swallowed. I was about to play the role of one of the most reviled villains in history. Could I really do this? My hand found Booth's pistol and pulled it from the too-tight jacket pocket.

"You will need the knife as well."

"Why?"

"The firearm has only one round of ammunition. A military man seated on the woman's right will attempt to apprehend you after you shoot Lincoln. You must injure him with the knife, then jump from the balcony to the stage and escape the way you came in."

"Are you kidding me?" I whispered, louder than necessary. Fortunately, the audience was still fully engaged in the performance below.

"Dare, I do not jest. Any deviations will cause instability, increasing the chances the thread will become damaged beyond repair."

I sighed and did my best to suppress my growing feelings of disbelief at the absurdity of my situation. I had a job to do, for the good of the universe. Or, at least some universes. My head began to spin.

Focus! I told myself. Carefully, I undid the latch on the door and pulled it open a few inches. Light from the stage illuminated me and I suddenly felt very exposed. The crowd erupted with laughter again, startling me. My heart raced and my hand shook as I raised the gun to the back of Abraham Lincoln's head. Emotions warred within me and everything felt wrong— out of sync. This had to be done! My very existence was at stake!

"Dare, your window of opportunity is less than ten seconds," Kim said in my ear.

I adjusted my grip on the pistol. My finger tensed on the trigger.

"Five."

I've never shot a gun, much less killed anyone before!

"Four."

He's already dead, I argued with myself. *Booth would be here right now if that robot hadn't come and killed him.*

"Three."

More laughter from the audience echoed through the surreal scene. My eyes were pinned on the dark, curly head of hair in front of me.

"Two."

Was this now my destiny? Doomed to repeating history, regardless of the moral merit of the actions in question?

"One."

I tensed, bracing for the gun's kick.

5

"Insertion detected."

Reality twisted. Dissolved. I found myself standing in the common room of the Keepers' facility, my right arm extended. Blue light emanated from the ceiling.

"Locale?" I heard M'sang ask behind me.

"Uncertain," Kim responded. "The ripple was incredibly small and barely registered on my sensors."

"What the hell is going on?" I straightened and looked around, finding M'sang focused on a display projected from the wall behind me.

"Your simulation was suspended," he answered without shifting his attention in my direction.

"Simulation?"

"Location determined. Please move to the examination chamber," Kim said.

I felt like my day was starting all over again, yet I was still emotionally strung out from my experience in Ford's Theater. I had renewed sympathy and respect for Bill Murray's character in *Groundhog Day*.

I followed M'sang to the exam room. No one objected to my presence. "Are you telling me that whole Abraham Lincoln thing was fake?"

M'sang stepped up on the platform with two vertical rods that I'd seen before that morning— or at least thought I'd seen. "Dare, I will explain later. For now, please be quiet."

Ghostly images formed in the air around the room. A group of children played in a park or large yard. Some of them wore conical party hats, held in place with elastic bands. The scene looked normal. Familiar.

"Pinpointing," Kim announced.

The viewpoint shifted, sweeping past a group of adults, who sat near a table with an expansive umbrella, chatting and watching the children enjoy themselves. A large house appeared and M'sang and I glided straight through its walls to the interior. A woman in a plain dress with an apron tied to her front moved around a long dining room table, putting the finishing touches on more than a dozen place settings. A substantial mound of brightly wrapped boxes dominated the center of the table and our movement slowed to focus on them.

"Only an object was inserted," Kim said. "The small box on the left side of the grouping."

I located the gift in question. Covered in dark purple paper and tied with a red ribbon, it looked no more than six inches long and half that high.

"Can you determine its contents?" M'sang asked.

"Negative."

My feelings of familiarity intensified. "Wait. I know this place. It looks like my grandparents' house in Florida. We spent winters there when I was little."

"Confirmed," Kim said. "Dare, join M'sang Tah on the platform and grasp one of the rods."

M'sang relinquished his grip on the right hand rod and made room for me. After taking hold of the apparatus, my view gained clarity and depth. "Hold on. You're not sending me in there are you?"

"No," Kim answered. "Not until we determine the object's purpose."

Her response wasn't entirely reassuring, but movement distracted me. The children streamed into the room, excitedly taking their places at the table. Memories of squealing laughter filled my mind as I watched the silent play in front of me. Suddenly, a realization struck.

I was witnessing my fifth birthday party.

I looked to my left and saw a wide-eyed boy at the head of the table, gazing in rapture at the pile of presents in front of him. His brown hair was tousled and wild in a style that would have made Einstein proud and a big smile appeared on his face. The experience quickly became surreal as I tried to reconcile what I witnessed with the memory in my head from the eyes of that over-excited little boy.

"I think my head's gonna explode."

"There is nothing abnormal with your physiology. Be quiet and pay attention to the proceedings," Kim admonished.

I watched my younger self blow out candles and enjoy cake and ice cream with all the guests. The flash of a professional photographer's camera punctuated each moment, capturing pieces of time for my parents to cherish later and wonder what had happened to that sweet, precocious five-year-old boy. As I grew, precociousness had morphed into willful irreverence, fueled from impatience with those around me. I discovered early on that my mind worked differently than my friends' and later, in school, many of my teachers struggled to keep me engaged. I became disillusioned and disinterested, acting out more frequently as time progressed. My behavior caused my parents to tighten their control, which only served to anger me. After I turned eleven and discovered I'd been adopted, things had only gotten worse.

I shook my head and refocused on the vision Kim provided. Once the treats were eaten and the plates cleared away, five-year-old me tore into the festive packages. Toys were unwrapped, ogled briefly, then discarded for the next gift. Soon, dark purple paper and red ribbon gave way to my small fingers. Standing next to M'sang on the platform, I tensed. What if someone had sent a bomb back to wipe me and my family out? What would happen to me? Would I simply vanish? Or was this an "alternate" me to be snuffed out of existence? I took some comfort in my companion's passivity. Surely M'sang and Kim would be concerned if they thought there were danger here. Wouldn't they?

The box revealed a model spaceship. Triangular in shape, its design was smooth and sleek. My boy self spent longer admiring this gift than the others before setting it aside as well and moving on to the next wrapped box.

"I remember that toy," I whispered. "I spent hours and hours playing with it. Kim, are you sure that was what you detected?"

"Affirmative."

"But, how can that be? You just sensed the insertion, right? So, why would I already have memories of it as if it had been there all along? Is it because we haven't done something about it?"

"No. Your and M'sang's presence outside the dimensions of time and space, as you understand them, render you immune to vagaries such as this."

Movement caught my attention and my gaze landed on a woman with dark hair that hung loosely around her shoulders. She stood away from the others and looked to be in her late teens or early twenties with fair skin and full lips. Her brown eyes found mine and widened in either surprise or fear. She turned and vanished.

"M'sang, did you see that?"

"All I see is a spoiled child."

"No, not me. There was a girl over there," I pointed in the direction I'd seen her.

"I'm sorry, Dare. I don't see anyone there."

"I know. She… just disappeared. Kim, you still haven't answered my question. If this insertion just happened, why do I have vivid memories of that toy?"

Kim paused before responding, which surprised me nearly as much as her answer.

"I don't know."

6

M'sang and I sat, slurping packets of nutrient mush, in the common room. Kim had been unable to detect any instabilities as a result of the birthday gift insertion, so my furry instructor and I were left to puzzle the situation out on our own.

I swallowed and said, "I still don't understand the whole bazillions of universes thing."

"It's all related to probabilities and possibilities. Let's say you get up on the left side of the bed every morning. The possibility still exists that you will get up on the right side. That possibility is carried in its own thread of time. Its own universe. Threads like that, however, are infinitesimally thin and become absorbed by their close neighbors. The multiverse, as a whole, doesn't care which side of the bed you get up from."

"So, every little thing we do creates a new universe?"

M'sang puffed his cheeks. "Creates isn't exactly the right word. The thread is already there because the possibility existed, but since the difference is insignificant from the other threads around it, they tend to meld together, essentially becoming a single, stronger strand."

I mulled this over. "All right, but what about the Abraham Lincoln problem you cooked up for me? I'm still ticked about that by the way. Not nice."

"We're not here to be nice to you, Dare. We're here to teach you. We also need to learn more about you and how you react and respond to problems and new situations. I have to say I'm disappointed in your extreme reluctance to do what was necessary."

"Kim was asking me to kill one of the greatest leaders in our history!"

"Yes. One who was already dead to your reckoning and who, furthermore, needed to die to preserve the thread. Your thread."

I sighed. "It just didn't feel right. I can't explain it. But, that's not the point. I don't understand how doing things different can cause so much trouble. Wouldn't it just become a new thread and go on about its merry way?"

"No, because that strong thread was already established. Every thread which carries the history of your people has that event within it. All other possibilities have long since been absorbed, making that thread— or braid, we sometimes call it— dominant. Now, if some significant change is made in that well established past, it's like taking a knife and cutting the thread, destroying it."

My head spun, but I thought I grasped what he'd said. "What about the future then? Bob, the amoeba guy who brought me here, said we worked together in the future. Doesn't that mean that all threads are set?"

"The threads of time— or the universes, if you prefer— become thinner and more dispersed the farther into the future you venture. All possibilities still exist, even if some are more probable than others. As the multiverse progresses, the common strands braid together, becoming the accepted reality for the majority of us."

"Kim said it cost more energy the farther back in time you go."

"Right. If you looked at the multiverse as a whole in the far past, it would look like an incredibly thick and strong cable, nearly impossible to penetrate."

I knew I was getting the Dr. Suess version of the physics of time and the multiverse. Questions continued to sprout in my mind, but I tried to focus on more immediate concerns. "So, back to the birthday party. Why would someone waste a bunch of energy to give me a toy? And who was that girl I saw?"

M'sang sighed. I thought it interesting that, of all mannerisms, that particular one seemed to be common between us. "It may have been a failed attempt to alter your life path. Most insertions are not as overt as the simulation the management system created for you. Those are easy to counteract."

I still didn't consider killing the President "easy", but I let that go. "Okay, but how is it that I have the memory of that toy if the insertion just happened? Or, if it happened fourteen some years ago, why did Kim only now pick it up?"

"Unknown, as the system stated. I'm sure it is consulting with other systems and the Keepers as we speak, trying to ascertain the same thing."

"I wonder if the girl had something to do with it."

"I don't understand why you are so fixated on this female. She was probably just a guest at the event."

I shook my head. "No. She saw me. Not little kid me, but me me. And when she left, she didn't just leave the room, she disappeared."

"I'm sorry, Dare," M'sang said. "It was probably just a trick of the light or something. In observation mode, we're still outside the thread. Besides, if she was an interloper, the system would have noted the insertion."

"What if she was just 'observing' too, from somewhere else? Would we be able to see her then?"

M'sang seemed surprised by the idea. "I don't know. I've never heard of such a thing."

I looked up. "What about it, Kim? Could that girl have been someone else looking in on the thread?"

"The probability is astronomically small," Kim's voice responded.

"But it is possible."

"Yes. But nearly everything is possible, Dare, as M'sang Tah has been trying to explain to you."

"Right," I said. "Just not probable." I crumpled up the empty nutrient packet and chucked it at the nearest wall. Kim absorbed it neatly, as if it had never existed. "So, what do we do? What's the next step?"

"I believe you are in need of some physical activity," M'sang said.

I couldn't disagree with him, but I did anyway. "But what about the toy? Shouldn't we go investigate or something?"

Kim answered, "The event itself seems innocuous enough. If further analysis indicates a threat, you will be informed. Until such time, M'sang Tah has much to teach you."

7

Physical training generally consisted of M'sang beating on me with his arms, legs, or other blunt objects. Though I had improved since our workouts began, occasionally landing a blow or two, he was deceptively fast and fought in a style that was definitively un-human. I affectionately dubbed his fighting technique as "Kung Paw." The joke was, of course, completely lost on him.

I faced him, breathing heavy and sweating by the bucket load. "Time out. I need a drink."

His mouth tightened. "An opponent will not relent simply because you are tired, Dare."

"I know that. Kim, water, please." I reached into a small, newly formed alcove in the wall next to me and found a now familiar disposable packet of liquid. I opened it and sucked gratefully as the wall became smooth once again. "Thanks," I said between gulps.

"Your lack of endurance is troubling," M'sang commented.

"How long have we been at it?"

"Less than an hour."

I chuckled. I remembered times when I was younger that getting up to change channels on the TV because I'd lost the remote was considered "strenuous activity." If we'd been sparring for anything remotely close to an hour, then I was in far better shape than I'd ever been before.

I tossed the empty packet behind me. "All right, Sensei M'sang. Come on and kick my ass again if it will make you feel better."

Expelling a calming breath, I settled into my ready stance when the ceiling turned blue.

"Again?" I asked in disbelief.

"Insertion detected," Kim predictably said.

Suddenly, my outfit was clean and free of sweat. Kim might have been the queen of snark, but I had to give her props for her ability to manipulate our environment. M'sang's nose wrinkled and he headed for the examination room. I followed closely behind.

"I'm guessing this is unusual," I said as we entered.

"To say the least," he acknowledged.

The now familiar platform and control rod apparatus sat in the middle of the otherwise barren room. M'sang stepped up and grasped one of the rods. I hesitated until he beckoned me forward with his free hand. I took hold of the free rod, but this time no clear scene greeted me.

"I'm having difficulty pinpointing the insertion," Kim announced.

"How come?" I asked.

"Unknown."

An image formed in front of us, resolving into an urban, nighttime scene, viewed from above. Kim zoomed in, sickeningly fast, to street level. People milled about on the sidewalks and traffic on the street was relatively heavy. We flew past a building and turned up a different street.

"It's Denver," I said as the realization struck.

The view settled in a darkened alley, not unlike the one where I'd encountered Bob when this roller coaster ride began—had it only been a couple of weeks ago?

"I can't refine any further," Kim said. "This point is within fifty meters and seven minutes of the insertion. I can't observe it directly."

"What are our orders?" M'sang asked.

"Unfortunately, we must send Dare in to investigate on site."

"Unfortunately," I parroted. "Why 'unfortunately'?"

"Because, you are not ready for field work," M'sang said. "As evidenced by your exercise earlier today."

"That Lincoln thing wasn't fair! Besides, I did what I needed to do."

"Did you?" M'sang challenged. "The simulation was suspended before you discharged the weapon. At best I'd say the results were inconclusive."

"I was going to," I said sheepishly. In my heart, I knew he was right. I wasn't sure if I would have pulled the trigger or not.

Kim settled the argument. "Regardless of the state of his readiness, Dare is our only option. These people have never seen an offworlder before, and even if I could disguise you successfully, M'sang Tah, you are unfamiliar with the society."

"I understand the obstacles. It doesn't mean I am forced to like the solution."

It surprised me how much the rebuke stung. I hadn't realized how much M'sang's opinion had come to mean to me. "I'll do my best," I said quietly. "What should I be looking for?"

M'sang's eyes narrowed as he studied me. Whether he was cataloging my weaknesses or reassessing my strengths, I had no idea. "An operative. They will almost certainly appear human if they are to carry out anything remotely complex. Don't make contact, but simply follow and observe. It's imperative to gather as much information as you can."

I straightened and met his gaze. "All right. Anything else? Oh, and can I get a pair of shoes this time?"

He chuffed in amusement. "This is not a simulation to test your abilities, Dare. Kim will properly clothe and equip you. Despite my reservations, I want you to succeed. It is important for you to succeed."

I nodded and looked down to see my outfit had transformed around me. Loose fitting jeans sat comfortably on my waist with flared legs mostly covering dark tennis shoes that fit perfectly. A thin, tan, buttoned over-shirt hung open, revealing a black Nirvana T-shirt underneath.

"You will find a communication device similar to the one from your simulation in your left pants pocket," Kim said. "Your right pocket contains a synaptic neutralizer."

I felt in both pockets and pulled out the small device from the right. Dull gray and smooth, it wasn't much larger than a roll of breath mints and had a single button near one end. "Sounds dangerous," I commented. "Can't say it looks like much though."

M'sang reached over and gently took it from my grasp. "Point it at your target, like so, and depress the trigger."

"It induces a soporific effect that can last up to several hours," Kim added.

I looked at M'sang questioningly. "It puts them to sleep," he said helpfully.

Understanding dawned and I replaced the small weapon in my pocket. "What date am I going to?"

"The night of September 12, 1997, according to the calendar you are familiar with," Kim stated.

I took a deep breath. "Okay. I guess I'm ready. Let's do it."

"Place both hands on the control rods as you did in the simulation," Kim instructed.

M'sang stepped back and exited the chamber. I was on my own. The rods glowed with cool energy after I grasped them and my vision whited out.

My Abraham Lincoln simulation really hadn't done the physical sensation of time travel justice. Reality was much worse.

Head spinning, I pitched forward heaved for all I was worth. Blinking tears from my eyes, I was surprised not to see toenails amid the mess I'd left on the dark pavement. I wiped my mouth on my sleeve and sat back against the brick building I'd materialized next to, letting the crisp, early autumn night air clear my rampaging skull.

I had recognized the area from Kim's projection and figured I was somewhere near 15th and either Champa or Curtis Streets. It was a somewhat seedier area of downtown Denver, home to a few "gentlemen's" clubs whose patronage were generally less than gentlemanly. Light cloud cover obscured most of the stars, but I could see well enough from the lights on the nearby street.

Recalling my obligations, I fished Kim's "phone" from my pocket and found the attached earpiece. Her voice tap danced inside my aching head moments later.

"Dare, you're going to have to do a better job of controlling your physiology post-insertion."

I suppressed a groan. "I'll put that on my to do list. Any clue of who or what I should be looking for?"

"Negative. Anything that seems out of the ordinary."

I used the wall for support and managed to stand. Judging by the amount of traffic I saw looking toward the street, I guessed it was Friday or Saturday. "Out of the ordinary" could encompass a lot of things on a pleasant weekend night.

Deeper in the alley behind me, I heard the sounds of someone else whose insides were in severe disagreement with them. Maybe it was our mysterious operative.

"Remember," Kim said in my ear, "observe. Do not confront. We need to find out what changes they seek to make in the thread."

I nodded and cautiously moved toward the sounds. A woman stood up unsteadily from behind a dumpster and looked at me with bleary blue eyes. Her hair was stark white, but her face and other features appeared young, close to my own age. Cappuccino leapt to mind as I considered the color of her smooth skin. Her clothing, if you could call it that, consisted largely of red and black fishnet, layered in such a fashion to protect her decency in public— barely. She tried to compose herself, then gave me a lopsided grin and staggered forward. Still shocked by her unusual appearance, I held my ground.

The woman stumbled after only a couple of steps and I reflexively caught her. "Whoa, take it easy," I said.

She pulled herself up, using my shoulders. Her ocean blue eyes were on a level with my own. "You're cute," she said, taking my head in her hands and kissing me with a high level of enthusiasm.

Normally, this sort of behavior I would not object to from a striking young woman. I would even encourage it. The experience, however, was rather diminished since both of us had been actively reliving past meals only moments before.

After a stunned second, I moved my hands to her shoulders and pushed her away. “Hey, okay. Generally I like to exchange names before body fluids.”

She pouted and I considered retracting my statement. “Aw. You’re no fun,” she said and backed away.

I shrugged. “Guilty as charged.”

She took a few unsteady steps toward the street. “Too bad. You might change your mind later,” she said over her shoulder and continued down the alley.

Watching her slender figure slink away, I thought she stood a good chance of being right about that. I whispered to Kim, “She must be a dancer from one of the clubs around here. Got too drunk and wandered off during a break or something.”

Silence filled my ear when I’d expected a sarcastic remark. “Kim? You there?”

I reached up and felt inside my ear. Empty. Just like my head.

“Hey!” I yelled.

The girl had almost reached the street. She took one look back at my shout, then turned and ran lithely around the corner.

“Shit.” I pulled the phone from my pocket and ran after her. Reaching the alley mouth, I ran into a pack of frat boys out for a night on the town. Luckily, it was still early enough they were in the happy-drunk stage and laughed me off as I bumped into two of them. I searched in the direction fishnet girl had gone, but saw no sign of her.

Glancing down at the phone's screen, I saw, "She stole the earpiece."

I sighed. "Yes. I know. Can you track it? Or her?"

"Yes," the screen replied. "She entered an entertainment establishment two doors down the street."

"Wait. Can't you just form another earpiece?"

The screen flashed. "No. Because the Keepers' monitoring facility exists outside normal space-time, matter behaves differently, allowing me to manipulate it in whatever manner I choose. Once they've been inserted in a thread, the clothes you wear and the devices you carry become just as immutable as the building you're standing next to. Or the people staring at you as they walk past."

I glanced up and saw an older couple giving me some very strange looks. I grinned and took a few steps back into the shadows of the alley. They turned away and kept walking. "What was their problem?" I whispered.

The phone flickered again. "Dare, you must remember not only where you are, but when. Standing on a street corner, talking to a handheld device is likely not a common pastime in this era."

I started to object that people had cell phones in 1997, but realized those were mostly still pretty big and clunky. They certainly had nothing like the smartphone-looking thing I currently held. "Sorry. I'll be more careful."

"Let's just concentrate on retrieving the earpiece so you can keep this unit concealed," I read on the screen. "It has been stationary for the past thirty-two seconds."

"Wait. If she went into one of the clubs, we've got a problem. I'm underage with no ID and no money to boot."

"There must be a rear entrance. We are not without resources, Dare."

I pocketed the phone once more and left the alley. "Okay, Fishnets," I mumbled under my breath. "Time for round two."

8

After surreptitiously consulting with Kim two more times, I located the back door to the building my earpiece thief had entered. Considering her clothing, I had expected it to be one of the stripper bars. It turned out to be a more conventional dance club and I couldn't decide if I was more relieved or disappointed.

The alley was littered with cardboard boxes advertising a plethora of alcoholic beverages, while the building vibrated in time with the bass from the music inside. The place was hopping and, even considering her distinctive looks, finding Fishnets wouldn't be easy.

I crouched next to a stack of boxes and pulled Kim's device from my pocket. "Okay, now what?" I asked.

Her screen flickered. "Wait here. In approximately eighty-seven seconds, a man will open the door to discard more empty containers."

I sighed and looked around. So far, my life as a time traveling agent hadn't been much different than my previous life. I seemed to be spending the majority of my time hiding in unpleasant smelling back alleys. "If you know when some dude is going to take out the trash, why can't we just wait until she comes out and nab her then?"

"The girl is not part of the thread and thus her actions

cannot be predicted with any amount of certainty. She might complete her task and be recalled from the thread without leaving the building. Thirty-two seconds," the screen read.

I adjusted my position and focused on the door. Kim's words reminded me of the job I came to perform. I'd become so concerned about retrieving the earpiece, I'd forgotten the need to discover why the other agent was here. I put Kim back in my pocket and waited.

The door opened with a blast of sound and a burly man leaned out with an armload of boxes. He tossed them in the direction of the dumpster a few feet away, then turned back inside while the door automatically closed behind him. I jumped out from my hiding place and barely managed to shove my fingers in the crack before the heavy metal door shut completely. I stifled a yelp of pain as I grabbed the door with my other hand and pulled it open, slipping inside while I cradled my abused fingers.

I found myself in a short, dark hallway, lit only by the red "exit" sign above the door behind me. Up ahead, the broad back of the box-tosser retreated into the sea of noise and flashing lights where I hoped to find my attractive thief. After flexing my injured digits, I pulled Kim from my pocket once more.

"Can you give me a map of this place, or at least a direction to go?"

Light from the display expanded upward about four inches and formed into a three-dimensional image of the club's interior. Underneath, on the screen proper, Kim wrote, "The structure is composed of two levels: a main floor with an open space in the center, surrounded by seating areas, and a balcony running around the perimeter of the space with more seating. Our missing component is currently on the second level." A tiny red dot appeared in the holographic view.

I studied the image closely. Maybe finding her wouldn't be as difficult as I'd thought. "Thanks," I said and concealed the device.

The music quickly grew to near deafening volume as I neared the end of the hallway. Strobes and laser lights flashed and spun in sync with the beat, which I felt deep in my chest. Smoke of various flavors drifted above and through the extremely substantial crowd.

Any self-respecting fire marshal would have had a heart attack on the spot.

I did my best impression of a sardine and worked my way toward the closest set of stairs to the balcony level. Kim said the girl hadn't moved for several minutes. I hoped that meant she wouldn't move for several more. Making progress through that mob of people was only slightly less difficult than traveling through time.

Finally, after becoming intimately familiar— and not in a good way— with several perfect strangers, I reached the relative open space of the stairs. At least traffic moved up and down; the bouncers at the top and bottom made sure no one loitered. The air on the upper level was marginally clearer and I scanned the tables for a distinctive head of white hair. I suppressed the desire to consult with Kim. Pulling a shiny gadget like that out in a bar full of hip twenty-somethings would have been like lighting a campfire in a darkened room filled with moths. The last thing I needed was to attract attention to myself.

I spotted her just where Kim's map had indicated: about two-thirds of the way along the wide balcony from the staircase I'd ascended. She sat at a tiny table, sharing a beer and talking with a man who looked a few years older than me— mid to late twenties I guessed. He wore his light brown hair almost shoulder length and hadn't shaved in two or three days by the look of it. Wire frame glasses perched uncomfortably on his nose and his skin had the look of someone who spent most of their time indoors. Fishnets kept touching his forearm and laughing like the dude was the next, well, Jim Carrey, if I was going to be time-appropriate. Whoever this guy was, he definitely had something Fishnets wanted.

I'm a firm believer that lots of people operate with more than the conventional five senses. Before I could work out in my head how to approach her, Fishnets suddenly looked back in my direction and our eyes met. I saw recognition flash in them, and maybe even a hint of fear, though that may have been wishful thinking on my part. She turned back to the guy she sat with, leaning in close to him before getting up and weaving her way to the staircase opposite me.

Cursing my luck, I pursued as quickly as the crowd would allow. I passed close to the table where she'd left her friend. On impulse, I sat down in the chair Fishnets had vacated.

"Hey, buddy!" I shouted over the pounding music. "Do you know the girl that was sitting here?"

He looked up from studying his beer bottle in surprise and fear. "No, man! I just met her, honest! Is she your girlfriend?"

Realizing he thought I was a jealous boyfriend, I held up my hands to calm him down. "No, no. It's cool! I just saw her earlier tonight and I think she took something from me."

"Really? What?"

I shook my head. "It's not important. Did she tell you her name?"

He thought for a second and I could tell remembering the girl's name hadn't been a high priority for him. "Lauri, I think." He blushed brightly. "She's sort of exotic, huh? I kinda figured she'd ask me for money before the night was over, but I was just playing along, you know?"

I laughed. "I get it, dude. No harm in having a look, right? My name's Dare, by the way."

He smiled and held out his hand. "Martin. Nice to meet you."

I shook his hand and asked, "Did she say where she was going?"

"Restroom," he said, rolling his eyes.

"Gotcha, thanks man!" I got up and resumed my course for the far staircase. I sensed I didn't have time to chat more with him if I wanted to catch up with Lauri Fishnets and my earpiece. I hoped the closer look and his first name would be enough for Kim to find out more about who he was and what Lauri wanted from the guy.

A sign pointed me to the restrooms down a short hallway near the bottom of the stairs. Lines extended from both doors, but the girls' was considerably longer. Lauri's distinctive white locks were noticeably absent. I looked around, trying to spot her elsewhere on the ground level. I hadn't spent more than a couple of minutes with Martin upstairs. Considering the length of the line, I doubted she had made it inside the restroom.

I moved over near the wall and used it to hide Kim's device as best I could while I took a quick peek.

"The earpiece is moving away at a high rate of speed," the screen read.

I quickly pocketed it again and searched for exits. Had she met someone with a car outside?

A familiar figure, wrapped in racy black and red fabric, emerged from the men's restroom, fluffing her white hair. She garnered many looks of interest and confusion from those waiting in line. I was a bit perplexed myself.

I stepped toward her and called out, "Lauri!"

Her eyes found mine again, but this time with a smile in them. "Hello again, Cutie," she said loudly over the din of the club. "Didn't take you too long to change your mind."

"You were very persuasive. What did you do with it?"

Her blue eyes looked back at me in mock innocence. "Do with what?"

"You know what. The device you plucked from my ear in the alley."

"Oh, that? I might have dropped it somewhere," she said, tilting her head in the direction of the restroom.

Finally catching on, I shouted, "You flushed it?! Why?"

"Well, I'm not about to make things easy on you since you're here to stop me from doing my job," she said. "Even if you are kinda cute."

Then she gave me a quick wink, and screamed.

Heads all around us turned and she screamed again. "Get away from me!"

Stunned by her shift in behavior, I put my hands up. "What

are you doing?"

A strong, meaty hand grabbed my left wrist and spun me around. A heartbeat later, my face forcibly met the wall and my arm wrenched painfully behind my back. "Easy, pal," a deep voice said behind me.

Lauri cried out, "He said he'd kill me if I didn't go with him!"

The wall muffled my response of protest, but no one was the least bit interested in anything I had to say.

9

The next two hours resembled a bad dream. Unfortunately, it was all too real.

Normally, the bouncers would have just thrown me out on my ear and instructed me to get lost, but since Lauri had so thoughtfully decided to include a death threat in the list of my supposed transgressions upon her, the police got involved. Even then, in most cases I'd have likely been released after a bit of questioning, but the fact that I had no identification and the only things I carried were two odd looking pieces of equipment of unknown origin or purpose… yeah, I was in neck deep and sinking.

Newly photographed, printed, and booked, I'd been shown to a cell with a drunk-and-disorderly who was sleeping it off. The door slid closed with a metallic clang that smacked of finality and the guard left me to my thoughts.

The 1997 version of the downtown Denver lockup didn't seem much different, except for a stronger ammonia smell, than the one I remembered from 2009. I was sixteen and I'd gotten hooked up with some undesirables from school. While out with them on a Saturday, we were picked up for shoplifting—for most of us, it was guilt by association. I spent a few hours fuming about the system and all the elitist snobs who wrote the rules— typical teenage angsty stuff— before my parents came down and bailed me out. The charges had eventually been dropped against those of us not directly involved, but the incident caused my adopted parents to first voice their concerns about my biological heritage, feeling that my misbehavior must be rooted in genetics. That one had been a real eye opener for me. I left home and dropped out of school less than a year later.

It took me a while longer to figure out my friends weren't any better for me than my misguided parents. I can be somewhat hard-headed at times, but I'm sure that particular revelation wouldn't shock anyone who knew me at all.

As I sat on the concrete floor in the corner of the cell, reflecting on my past and listening to my overindulgent bunkmate snore, a realization came to me: I was on my own.

Unconsciously, I believed I'd been operating with some sort of safety net. If things went bad, Kim would just pluck me back and we'd start over or something. Yet, there I sat. The police, of course, had confiscated my meager belongings, so I couldn't consult with her to find out what I was supposed to do. Possibly I had to be in close proximity with the devices for Kim to remove me from the thread— neither she, nor M'sang had discussed the real nuts and bolts of the process. If that was the case, I might be looking at an extended stay in 1997.

At least I'd been thinking clearly enough to tell the police my name was Dare Arthur. I could only imagine the hot water I'd be in if they tracked down the Heisenbergs and found five-year-old me. My complete lack of identity, however, presented its own problems. I assumed running my fingerprints would turn up empty since I hadn't committed any crimes as a toddler— beyond stealing cookies and feeding my cauliflower to the dog at the dinner table. I didn't think the police could hold me indefinitely unless Lauri pressed charges, and I was certain she had other, more important, issues to tend to. Plus, she didn't belong here any more than I did, so she'd want to remain under the radar.

My biggest problem was an utter lack of someone in the world to contact for help. I'd had to stifle a laugh when the cops had offered me a telephone to make a call. I'd considered asking for my "phone" to look up a number, then decided it was best if the devices remained a mystery to the police. Kim's screen had been dark when they'd pulled it and the stun gun from my pockets.

I turned my thoughts back to Lauri and her mission. Martin had seemed like a pretty ordinary, inconsequential guy, so what was her interest in him? I recalled M'sang telling me that things were rarely as cut and dried as my Lincoln simulation, so Martin probably wasn't a hugely significant figure in history. But something he had done, or would do, must have had some sort of impact or else why would Lauri waste time with him?

My mind reeled with possibilities. I leaned back against the concrete wall and closed my eyes, trying in vain to puzzle through my situation.

A voice startled me awake some time later. "Arthur, you have a visitor."

I blinked and it took me a few seconds to realize the officer outside the cell was talking to me.

"Arthur," he repeated. "Visitor."

I grunted and levered myself up. The hard, cool walls

and floor had caused my back and legs to stiffen. I stepped unsteadily to the door, which the cop unlocked as I approached. My left leg had gone numb and I probably looked as drunk as my still-unconscious cellmate. I gave the officer a smile as I tried to shake some blood back into my misbehaving leg and wondered who would want to see me. Had Kim sent help? My jailer returned only a frown before closing the door and locking it again once I stumbled out.

Guiding me by the arm, he led me to the visitation area, which I vaguely remembered from my time three years before. It consisted of a long table with chairs on either side and a plexiglass partition about eighteen inches high, running the length of the table. The chairs were empty, save for one on the visitor side.

"Martin?" I asked, recognizing the spectacled, sun-deprived visage looking back at me.

"Five minutes," the officer said, moving to stand by the door.

Martin gave me a thin, hesitant smile as I shuffled over to the chair opposite him.

"It's, Dare, right?" he asked.

I nodded. "Yeah. Not to sound ungrateful, but why are you here?"

Martin chuckled. "Curiosity, I guess. Hopefully, I don't end up like the cat. Anyway, I decided to follow you after you left the table to go look for Lauri. Got there in time to see you getting hauled off by the bouncers. She noticed me standing there and came over to talk some more, but I think she figured out pretty quick that I wasn't buying what she was selling."

"What did she say?"

"Not much, really. Just that she really wanted to get to know me better and maybe we could go someplace quieter—that sort of thing. After what you'd said and the look I saw on her face when they took you away, I didn't figure she was someone I wanted to get involved with, so I left."

I nodded. "But…"

He laughed nervously. "But, I couldn't stop thinking about her. I went back to the club a while later but she'd gone. Then I remembered that you knew her, at least a little, so I asked one of the bouncers about you. He told me you'd been arrested, so I came down to see you, but they said I had to wait until morning. So, here I am."

I paused to collect my thoughts and praise myself for heeding my intuition and stopping to talk to him in the club. "I'd like to help you out, but I can't do it from here."

Martin let out a breath and sat back. "I had a feeling you might say something like that. Do you know how much your bail is?"

I shook my head. "No. And to be perfectly honest with you, I don't know if I can pay you back, whatever it is."

He leaned in again and studied my face. "Everything says I shouldn't, but somehow I still feel I can trust you. Let me see what I can figure out. What's your last name?"

"Arthur," I answered, remembering my fib.

"All right. Hopefully I'll see you soon."

"Thanks for doing this."

He chuckled again. "Don't thank me yet. You're still behind bars."

I smiled and stood, looking back to the officer at the door.

He took the cue and ushered me back to my cell. From my previous experience, I knew it might take an hour or more for Martin to get all the paperwork filled out and for the Denver police bureaucracy to process it. All I could do was wait.

The guards brought breakfast around soon after I returned to my cell and the smell awakened my stomach from some sort of hibernation. I realized the last thing I'd had was a nutrient pack the day before, so I dug into the plate with gusto. The sensation of chewing real food was almost more than my senses could bear. I was convinced those powdered eggs and soy bacon had been prepared by the finest chef in the world.

My cellmate returned to the living as the guards came to retrieve the plates and utensils from breakfast. Another officer arrived a short time later to escort my bunkie off for processing, since he was now at least semi-coherent, and I was left alone with my thoughts.

An hour became two, then three according to the clock mounted above the door that led to the booking area. I wondered if Martin had changed his mind. Maybe my bail had been set so high he decided I wasn't worth the trouble. Depression had made a comfortable home within me by the time keys clanked in the lock of my cell door.

"Arthur, let's go. You made bail," the officer said.

I looked up with renewed hope and eagerly followed him down the hall.

Once past the lockout door, I slowed my pace as we approached the windowed cubicle where I expected to retrieve my belongings. The officer, however, walked right past it.

"What about my stuff?" I asked him.

"Already taken care of," he said over his shoulder. "C'mon."

Confused, I followed him into a quiet waiting area, furnished with several chairs and small tables. A young woman stood as we entered, her dark hair done up in a tight, businesslike bun. She wore a navy blue suit with a bright white blouse and smiled thinly on seeing me.

"Mr. Arthur, I'm Hope Bulova, with the State Department. On behalf of the government, I apologize for any mistreatment you may have received during your stay. My goal is to have you home in a short amount of time," the woman said, putting emphasis on the last word.

Something strange was certainly going on, but as long the strangeness included getting me out of jail, I was willing to play along. "Thanks."

Hope picked up a leather briefcase and turned to the cop. "Officer, if there's nothing else, we'll be on our way."

He shook his head after glancing at me. "Try to remember to carry some identification next time, Mr. Arthur, so we can avoid these kinds of mix ups."

I nodded slowly. "Sure. I'll do that."

The officer gestured toward the doorway behind Ms. Bulova and the three of us left the room and entered the busy Precinct headquarters. I leaned down close to Hope's ear and asked, "What about my equipment?"

She responded without looking at me. "I have your things, Mr. Arthur. Now, please keep quiet. Your questions will be answered soon."

We stepped outside and I shielded my eyes from the bright sunshine. It promised to be a warm autumn day. Hope herded me toward a black limousine parked on the street. She opened the back door and nudged me inside, following close behind.

"Brown Palace, please," she called forward to the driver, then sat in a plush leather seat facing my own as the car pulled away from the curb.

"Spare no expense, huh?" I quipped. "Thanks for bailing me out, by the way."

Hope pursed her lips and glared back with dark, narrowed eyes. I took the hint, which was a big step for me, and kept quiet through the rest of the short ride.

The driver double parked while Hope turned around and reached forward to pay the fare. She was petite, but exuded a confident air of authority. The thought of bolting crossed my mind, but only for a moment. My situation hadn't changed much, only my jailers. As long as someone else had possession of Kim's communication device, I was at their mercy.

The two of us exited the limo and I gazed up at the oddly shaped building, constructed at the intersection of diagonal streets. At least my new cell promised to be an upgrade. I knew the Brown Palace by reputation only: an old, glamorous hotel in the heart of downtown Denver. I was familiar with the streets and alleys around it, but I'd never been inside. The doorman nodded to Hope as we entered.

Opulent wasn't a word I'd had occasion to use much, but it certainly applied to the hotel's interior. Polished, light brown marble adorned the floor and many of the walls. The center of the large lobby was covered in an intricately embroidered carpet and hosted a number of finely appointed tables and chairs, a handful of which were occupied by smartly dressed folks who sipped drinks and chatted. Looking up, I saw the seating area opened all the way to the roof eight or nine stories above. A skylight of stained glass allowed the bright sunlight outside to filter down, creating a warm, inviting glow. All in all, it seemed an appropriate hang out for a time traveler as I got the feeling the place hadn't changed overmuch in the hundred years or so since it had been built.

Dressed in my jeans and T-shirt ensemble, I represented the proverbial sore thumb. It's a role I was pretty familiar with.

10

Hope directed me toward the elevators and we rode in silence to the sixth floor. I had a thousand questions buzzing around my mind, but I was determined to show her I had enough self discipline to remain quiet until she gave the okay to talk.

Puzzled by my own feelings, I paused to examine them in an effort to distract myself from my other trains of thought.

Initially, I decided it was her confident, "I'm in charge" vibe that subdued me. Yet, my usual first reaction to authority was rebellion, so, that reason didn't play. In fact, everything about her attitude and dress annoyed me. It felt like an act. The suit, which hugged her curves, still seemed not to fit, and the overuse of color on her cheeks clashed with the fair, smooth skin underneath.

Then, it hit me. *Oh, crap. I'm attracted to this girl.*

A cute grunt of frustration escaped her lips as Hope jiggled a key in the lock of room 619. The door relented and we moved inside.

I decided a switch back to thought track A, with its confused jumble of questions, was preferable to the one where I considered Hope's grunting "cute".

The latch had barely clicked closed when I said, "Okay, spill it. Who are you and what's going on?"

Ignoring me, Hope set her briefcase on a work table opposite the fashionably appointed king-size bed. She opened the case and removed a smooth, white hemisphere, about the size of her fist. After placing it on the table and depressing a button on the top, she firmly closed and latched her case.

Turning, Hope's fiery brown eyes found mine. "Now you may talk."

"What is that thing?"

"A temporal distorter, for lack of a better term. It's designed to keep observers located outside the thread from eavesdropping."

"So, who are you? I'm assuming 'Bulova' isn't your real name."

"I'm an agent for the Keepers. My name is Hope, but no, my last name is not Bulova. I had to drop as many hints for you as I could to make sure you played along."

"Am I that dense? Why didn't you call yourself Miss Rolex then?"

"Maybe I should have. I wasn't the one who landed myself in jail."

Okay, that one stung. "Hey, I was getting it worked out," I countered. "What happened to Martin anyway?"

Hope looked confused for a second, then made a connection. "Oh, your friend Mr. Nussbaum? Yes, he was in the first stages of bailing you out when I arrived and convinced him he'd be better off walking away and forgetting the whole thing."

"Why did you do that?"

"What were you going to tell him, Dare? What had you already told him?"

"Nothing! Well, nothing important anyway. He just wanted to know more about the girl."

"What girl?" Hope asked.

"What do you mean 'What girl?' The girl. The other agent. The reason I'm here."

"There's another agent?"

"Man, now who's being dense? Didn't Kim tell you anything?"

"Who's Kim? The other agent?"

"No!" I moved farther into the room and sat on the bed. "Kim is the computer that runs everything."

"Oh, your management system? Dare, I'm sorry, but it's been offline for more than a day," Hope said.

"Offline? She was working fine last night. Well, until I got arrested at least…"

Hope shook her head. "It may have been working, but it removed itself from the rest of the network."

"What does that mean?"

"Your management system isn't talking to any of the other multitude of management systems in the universe."

"But, why would she— it, do that?"

Hope threw up her hands. "I don't know. I'm not privy to the inner workings of the Keepers or the management systems. All I know is my system detected your insertion and I was selected to investigate."

I mulled over her statements. As if time travel itself wasn't complicated enough, now I evidently had some interoffice politics or something to contend with.

"Tell me more about this other agent," Hope said.

I sighed. "Her name is Lauri, at least that's what she told Martin. She's close to my height, has white hair and a great tan." Hope raised a speculative eyebrow, but I pressed on. "Kim, my system, detected the insertion but couldn't pinpoint it. I have no idea why. Anyway, she sent me here to figure out what was going on. I think Martin has something to do with it because Lauri was getting cozy with him in the club where I got arrested."

Hope stared off into space for a few seconds, then her eyes refocused on me. "All right. We're looking into it. Anything else you can tell me?"

I shook my head. "Not that I can think of. Can I see my equipment?"

"I'm sorry, but no. I have the devices in lockdown. Until the Keepers can determine what your system is up to, they don't want it having access to you or your things. I still can't figure out why your system didn't just install aural and corneal implants."

"What?"

"Implants. To interface directly with the system." She pointed to her head. "I can hear and see information from the management system through implants in my ear and eye."

I shuddered. Though, I had to admit, an implant would have made Lauri's initial theft impossible. My eyes narrowed as another thought occurred to me. "Are you human?"

She seemed surprised. "Of course. What else would I be?"

"I thought I was the only one."

"With the Keepers you mean? You were the first, but others have joined since. I've been an agent for about two years."

"How is that possible? I was only recruited two or three weeks ago."

Hope chuckled and shook her head. "Dare, you have to stop thinking of time as this immutable, static thing. It behaves differently when you're outside what we consider the 'normal' universe."

"So, you're saying time moves faster when you're not in a thread?"

"It can. It can also go slower. Or not move at all. I don't understand the tech, I just go where they tell me and fix what needs fixing."

My head swam, trying to make sense of it all. I decided to focus on something I thought was a little more straightforward. "How old are you?"

"By my frame of reference, I'm about twenty-four. But, I'm from what you probably consider the future. I was recruited in 2085."

My thought train derailed, leaving twisted wreckage across my mind. 2085? Had I lost over seventy years? According to Hope, it didn't really matter. But what had happened on Earth during that timespan?

"I have to go," Hope announced. "The system's got a line on Mr. Nussbaum and what your friend Lauri is trying to change."

I stood up. "I'll go with you."

"No. I need you to stay here. Dare, you're untrained and not plugged into the system. Your enthusiasm is admirable, but look at how your first assignment turned out. Besides, I'm sure you didn't get much sleep sitting in jail. Use the bed and get some rest. I shouldn't be too long."

"But—"

"Dare, I mean it. Promise me you'll stay here."

A sly smile crept across my face. "You're not very big. I could make you take me along."

Hope laughed. "You could try. I have other implants besides those in my head."

Despite her laugh, I could tell she was completely serious. My smile vanished and I held up three fingers in mock boy scout salute. "I promise I won't leave the premises."

"Thank you. I'll be back soon," she said, snatching her briefcase and leaving the room with a purposeful stride.

After the door clicked shut, I flopped on the bed and stared at the ceiling. Hope's "Thank you" had sent an embarrassing thrill through me. I'd spent less than an hour with the woman and she already had me under her thumb. My initial reaction had been right: I had simply switched jails. Though, admittedly, the new jail was much more comfortable.

I realized I'd also been right about something else. Martin was the key. Now he had both Lauri and Hope on his tail. A lot of guys might consider that a good thing— garnering the interest of two attractive women— but I had an inkling of what those women were capable of and Martin's wellbeing was probably not their highest priority.

And it was my fault. At least in part.

Hope hadn't known about Lauri or Martin until I'd mentioned them.

Yet, Hope was an agent of the Keepers. She would protect Martin from whatever Lauri wanted to do to him, right? Maybe. If protecting him was in the interest of preserving the time thread, she would. But, what if his safety wasn't important? Something in my gut told me this whole scenario wasn't going to end well for Martin. I needed to find out more about him.

Hope had inadvertently thrown me a lifeline in that regard. She had told me his last name. All I needed now was Internet access.

I sat up and looked around the room. Tastefully and expensively decorated, it felt like the sitting room in my grandparents home— the room children were banned from entering. After standing up, I successfully fought an urge to straighten the bedspread. Although the hotel room was well appointed, it conspicuously lacked in technology. The telephone beside the bed and a large console television, hidden away in a cherry wood cabinet, were the only things that even remotely resembled a computer.

Thinking they must have computers somewhere, I picked up the telephone and dialed 0.

An overly pleasant male voice answered before the second ring. "Front desk, how may I help you?"

"Hi. I need to get on the Internet."

"Of course, sir. We have several computers with Internet access available in our Business Center, just off the atrium."

"Cool, thanks."

"Anything else I can help you with, sir?"

Suddenly I remembered leaving the room was problematic. "Um, yeah. I seem to have lost my key. Any way I could get another?"

"Certainly, sir. Room 619? I'll have an attendant run one up. Will that be everything?"

"Yeah. I think so. Thanks."

"Thank you, sir. Enjoy your stay at the Brown Palace."

I hung up the phone and did my best to wait patiently for the key to arrive. My stomach rumbled, announcing that my tasty prison breakfast was only a fond memory. I thought about ordering room service, but didn't want to waste any more time. Grabbing the remote for the TV, I sat back on the bed and flipped through a frustratingly small number of channels.

A few minutes later, I heard a knock at the door. I opened it to find a well-groomed man, probably just a few years older than me, dressed in a tight-fitting, brown double-breasted jacket with gold buttons and trim. His broad smile diminished slightly once he saw me.

"Your extra key, sir," he said, dangling it in front of me.

"Awesome, thanks!" I took it and awkwardly stepped around him into the hallway, closing the door behind me.

"Is there anything else I can do for you, sir?"

It dawned on me then that it was probably customary to give the guy a tip. "Look, I'm sorry, dude, but my, um, girlfriend kinda left me high and dry, if you know what I mean." I chuckled.

He gave me a slight smile and said, "Of course, sir."

"I'd appreciate it though if you could point me in the direction of the Business Center. I need to use the Internet."

He nodded. "Right this way, sir."

We boarded an elevator and rode to the ground floor. He led me past the front desk and to a room with a handful of small alcoves, each with a desktop computer. Two of the stations were occupied by older men dressed in expensive looking suits. My helper steered me to one of the empty seats.

"If you have AOL or Compuserve, I can show you how to

dial into those."

"What? No. I just need to Google someone."

"Google?"

No Google in 1997? This might prove tougher than I thought. "How do I search for something?" I asked him.

He pushed a few buttons and the computer made some odd beeps and hissing noises. A browser window finally opened showing something called "Netscape". He pointed to the screen. "Type what you want to search for here."

Now on more familiar ground, I typed in "Martin Nussbaum, Denver". After several seconds, some results appeared. Scanning the list, I saw several references to an attorney with a similar name, but nothing that looked like my Martin.

"Pardon me, sir," the attendant said. "But is this someone local that you're looking for?"

I sighed. "Yeah. He's a friend of mine I'm trying to get a hold of."

"Have you tried the phone book?"

I'm sure the blank look I gave him spoke volumes.

"There's a local directory in each room. You might try looking him up there, or calling information," he said.

"Thanks," I said and stood up. "Any idea where I can get a cheeseburger?"

11

Back in the room with the TV blaring, I sat on the bed and savored a juicy bite of the enormous burger one of the hotel's restaurants prepared for me— charged to Hope's account, of course. If she had the resources to acquire the room, I figured she could spring for a meal or two.

I found the gigantic books inside the nightstand that held the phone. Starting with the white residential one, I thumbed through the thin pages as I ate, doing my best not to leave burger stains.

Don't get me wrong, I knew what a phone book was, I just hadn't used one very often. Like twice. Well, three times if having a stack of them stand in for a step stool to reach the kitchen counter when I was little counts as "using".

Reaching the end of the Ns, I discovered quite a list of Nussbaums. After licking my finger clean, I ran it down the lines of small type. To my surprise, there was a Martin Nussbaum listed. I muted the television and picked up the phone. With the receiver cradled against my cheek, I pecked out the numbers and waited as it rang several times.

A machine answered. "Hey, it's Martin! There's beeps and stuff. You know what to do."

I waited for the aforementioned beeps. "Martin. Hi, it's

Dare. Listen, I wanted to thank you for offering to help me out and I hope everything's okay with you. I'm at the Brown Palace hotel, room 619, if you still want to talk. Oh, and the woman you met at the police station might be contacting you again. Just… be careful. Bye."

I hung up and realized I'd left one of the worst messages ever. Why had I warned him about Hope and said nothing about Lauri? I thought about calling back and trying to clear things up, but the sound of a key jiggling in the lock on the door interrupted me. I hurriedly closed the phone book and shoved it back in the nightstand.

Hope entered and slammed her room key on the desk. "I really hate these things." She set her briefcase down and looked over at me. "I see you made yourself at home. What are you eating?"

I popped the last, delicious bite in my mouth and said, "Cheeseburger."

She wrinkled her nose. "As in animal carcass? Don't you know what's in that?"

"Yes, I do. Cow. Moooooo."

Hope rolled her eyes and shook her head as she turned to the bathroom. "I'm going to freshen up."

"Did you find Martin?"

"No. I had just missed him evidently. The system is recalculating this thread and its neighbors based on the changes thus far. It should just take a few minutes." She stepped into the bathroom and closed the door.

I let out a breath. If Hope hadn't been able to track him down, maybe Lauri was having the same difficulty. I tried not to think about the possibility that she already had.

Hope's briefcase caught my eye and a combination of nosiness and curiosity drew me to it. After glancing at the bathroom door, I crouched down and examined the case and its latch. It looked like a very ordinary, hard leather briefcase.

"Don't bother trying to open it," Hope called from the bathroom and I nearly jumped out of my shoes. "The system created it and won't let you in."

Talk about having eyes in the back of your head. Hope even had them outside her head. I grumbled and then heard the shower turn on. Any fantasies I'd conjured up where she asked me to step in and help her operate the primitive washing equipment and, oh, why don't you join me, quickly evaporated.

Hey, it could have happened.

I plodded back to the bed in defeat and pushed the mute button on the remote again, filling the room with the sounds of a cartoon show I'd landed on earlier in a moment of nostalgic weakness.

Weak perfectly described my abilities as an operative as well. The only thing I'd accomplished had been to justify M'sang's lack of confidence in me. I'd botched the mission so bad the Keepers had to risk another insertion to fix the mess I'd made. Though, admittedly, from what Hope had said in our first conversation, the Keepers didn't even know I was on a mission. The thought struck me as odd. How could Hope and her system not know what I'd been doing, or anything about Martin and Lauri? Hadn't they observed the thread before entering it? Something was definitely out of place, but I was as lost as a blind person who'd been asked to describe the concept of color.

Hope stepped out of the bathroom dressed in a fluffy white robe, drying her hair with a plush towel. The robe and towel, along with her milky skin, provided a sharp contrast to her dark brown eyes as they centered on me. "Would you turn that thing off? I can't hear myself think."

Irritated with both myself and her, I found the remote and stabbed the red power button. The sound and light from the cartoon abruptly ceased, not unlike my childhood.

"Thank you," Hope said as she removed the towel from her hair. The still wet strands dropped to her shoulders, framing her bright face perfectly. Recognition suddenly sparked in my mind.

Hope was the girl I'd glimpsed at my birthday party.

Thankfully, she turned away and closed herself in the bathroom again before I could blurt out, "It was you!" or something equally inane.

With her hair pulled back and overdone makeup, I hadn't made the connection before, but seeing her fresh out of the shower it was clear as day. Relief flowed through me. I'd never been attracted to the uptight business type of woman before, so my feelings for her had bothered me to say the least. Apprehension, however, soon took hold. If it had been her observing the party, as M'sang and I were, why was she there? And why had she been so spooked when I'd noticed her?

The bathroom door opened again. "Dare? I hate to ask, but could you give me a hand?"

A rush of emotions contradicted the uncertainty I'd felt only heartbeats earlier. "Sure." My voice caught and I cleared my throat. "What is it?"

Hope came out in her navy slacks and white blouse. "Would

you zip me up?" she asked as she turned around, showing me the open back of her shirt. "I can't seem to reach."

Heart racing, I moved closer to her. She pulled her hair aside and I noticed a circular, puffy scar marring the smooth curve of her shoulder. Hesitantly, I touched a finger to it. "What's this?"

She shifted, breaking the contact. "It's a reminder of a past I'd just as soon forget."

Looking down, I found the zipper and pulled it up. "Why don't you have your management system remove it then? Seems like that's something it could easily do."

Hope let go of her hair and turned around. "Because, it's a reminder of a past I'd just as soon forget."

Her fresh, clean scent filled my nose as I struggled to compose a response.

The phone rang.

She glanced past me to the nightstand, then met my eyes again and a slight scowl formed on her face. Brushing me aside, Hope stalked over and picked up the receiver. "Hello?" She looked back at me and her scowl deepened. "No, he's not here right now. Can I give him a message? Is this Mr. Nussbaum?"

I stepped toward her, but Hope held up her hand. "He hung up," she said and replaced the receiver. "Dare. Why would Mr. Nussbaum be looking for you? And, more importantly, how did he know you were here?"

"He must be quite the detective?"

Her eyes narrowed and she poked a stiff finger in my chest. "You tried to contact him! Why? Haven't you been trained at all?"

"I didn't— I mean, I just thought he should know—"

"Know? Know what? That two time travelers are looking for him? What the hell is he supposed to make of that? Dare, the guy's a computer programmer who's writing software for a probe to Mars that will launch in 1998. The probe will malfunction and crash upon arriving at Mars in 1999, due to an error in the program that Mr. Nussbaum is creating."

"I don't understand. What is Lauri's interest in him then?"

"My system and the Keepers think she wants to prevent the loss of the probe."

"But, why? What effect could that possibly have? We sent lots of probes to Mars."

"I don't know. What I do know is this Lauri is trying to alter the thread. And our job is to prevent that. Your actions so far are only aiding her objective, which, in conjunction with your management system going dark, only lead to suspicion regarding your motives."

I had to admit, I hadn't cast myself in a very good light in Hope's eyes, assuming she was telling the truth. I wanted to ask her about my fifth birthday and her part in it, but until I could be sure whose side she was on— or even how many sides there were— I decided it was best to keep as much information to myself as possible. By all appearances, Hope was working for the Keepers, just as Kim and M'sang appeared to be. Yet, somehow, they weren't all seeing eye to eye.

I sighed and said, "I just get the feeling that Martin is in trouble. Something's not right."

Hope let out a laugh. "Of course it's not right! You, me, and Lauri are making it not right. Every little thing we do puts stress on the thread. Stress it enough…" She made a breaking motion with her hands.

"Yeah, I know. What happens to Martin after all this stuff with the Mars probe?"

"I don't know. It's not important."

"I'm pretty sure it's important to him."

"That's not the point. Dare, I admire your compassion, but you're going to have to learn to set it aside to get the job done. Martin's life has already run its course, for good or bad."

"Right, except there's people like us who can go back and change it."

Hope held up her finger. "No. People like me are here to preserve it. People like Lauri are here to change it. So, what are you? A preserver, or a changer?"

I thought back over my life. If I could go back and change things, correct mistakes, would I? And, if I did, how would that change the person I was? My formerly fond memories of the toy spaceship haunted me. According to what I'd seen, those memories were the result of an outside influence. Would my life be different if I hadn't played with that toy? The possibility seemed ridiculous, yet, what would be the purpose of placing it in my path if not to influence me somehow? "Honestly, right now I'm just confused," I said finally.

Hope searched my face, presumably trying to decipher my allegiances. "I'm going out again. If I can find Mr. Nussbaum, hopefully Lauri will be nearby and I can put an end to this." She walked past me toward the bathroom.

"I don't suppose you'll let me come with you."

She pulled a lipstick case from her pocket and shook her head. "You're too much of a wildcard, Dare."

Too late, I realized it wasn't lipstick, but a stunner, much like the one Kim had fashioned for me. I only had time to open my mouth in protest before she depressed the activator.

12

A loud, regular ringing awakened me and, for a few seconds, I couldn't figure out where I was.

Then I remembered Hope's face, frowning with disappointment as she knocked me out with her stun gun.

Whoever was on the other end of the telephone gave up, but my ears played back echoes for a while longer. Stretched out, face down, on the hotel's king size bed, I licked my dry lips and tried to shake off the effects of the stunner. Numbness ruled my limbs, especially my arms, making movement awkward. Attempting to sit up, I discovered another difficulty.

My hands were tied behind my back.

I finally managed to lever myself up to a sitting position and spent the next few minutes flexing my shoulders and neck, trying to work some blood back into my lifeless appendages. Hope had done a thorough job of making sure I wouldn't cause any more disruptions.

I remembered watching a show, when I was little, about some guy who could escape being bound by contorting his body in several amazing ways. After seeing it, I spent the whole afternoon with my hands clasped behind me, trying to imitate the strange, double-jointed person's maneuvers. Fortunately, my grip broke every time before I managed to do serious bodily harm to myself.

After making a couple of feeble attempts to slide my hips in between my lashed arms, I confirmed what I'd discovered as a boy. I was no contortionist.

The phone rang again and a mad giggle passed my lips before I regained control. I moved to kneel before the nightstand and studied the phone briefly before trying to take the receiver in my mouth. The hard plastic slipped from my teeth, so I resorted to knocking it off the cradle with my nose.

"Hello?" I said, then leaned my ear as close as I could.

"Dare, is that you?" The voice sounded tinny and far away.

"Yeah, it's me," I spoke loudly toward the mouthpiece. "Martin?"

I heard his faint response. "Yeah. I got your message. Where have you been?"

"Sorry, I was out for a while. Are you okay?"

"Yep, I'm fine. Are you really a prince?"

"What? I can't hear you very well."

"Sorry, I'm on my cell phone. I said, 'Are you really a prince?'"

"What are you talking about?"

"I'm at a bar and I saw it on the early evening news."

"Saw what?"

"They said a Prince of Luxembourg was accidentally arrested at the club we met at last night. I figured it had to be you."

Luxembourg? I realized I'd never asked Hope just what story she'd concocted to get me out of jail. "No. I'm not. Listen, Martin, have you seen Lauri or the woman from the police station?"

"No, but I've been out driving around a lot since I went home and heard your message. What's going on?"

I relaxed a little. While I understood Hope's point of view, I still didn't want to see Martin get hurt. "I'd like to talk, but not over the phone," I said.

"Okay, let's meet somewhere."

"I would but I'm tied up at the moment."

"Well, maybe later then?"

"No. I mean I'm really tied up. Hope, the woman at the station, knocked me out and tied me up here at the hotel."

"Seriously? Are you guys like government agents or something?"

"Can you just come to the hotel? And bring some wire cutters or something."

Martin laughed. "This is too cool! Yeah. I'll be there in a few minutes. Room 619, right?"

"Yeah. Please hurry, but be careful."

"Got it!"

He hung up and I listened to the phone make its obnoxious off-the-hook noise while I stood with my back to the nightstand and fumbled to replace the handset on its cradle. I succeeded on the fourth attempt. After pacing around the room a few times, looking for something that might help in my situation, I saw the TV remote sitting on the edge of the bed. I studied the buttons, memorizing their positions, then sat on the bed and operated the remote by feel. Soon, I had the hang of it and was flipping through the channels.

I remembered the "Prince of Luxembourg" thing Martin had mentioned seeing on the news, so I found one of the local stations to see if I could learn more. I sat through the end of the weather report, then some sports stories, before the anchorman came back on. "Lastly, in the wake of Princess Diana's funeral of a week ago, we have reports of a royal visitor to Denver."

The camera panned to the right and an image of a sophisticated-looking young man appeared next to the anchorman, who continued, "Prince Guillaume of Luxembourg was reportedly arrested last night at a downtown Denver nightclub."

The kid looked younger than me, fifteen or sixteen, with darker hair and a sharper nose. Though, in the dimly lit club, I could see how someone might mistake the two of us. If that was indeed the cover story Hope had used, somebody at the police station must have thought it would be worth some money and leaked it to the press.

"Why the young prince was here in Denver and what he might have been doing at the club remain a mystery. We hope to have more details in our ten o'clock newscast."

I switched off the television and stood. Even with movement, keeping the feeling in my fingers remained difficult. I rolled my shoulders a few times, then resumed pacing the room.

With reporters snooping around, it probably wouldn't be long before my mug shots surfaced and people would plainly see that I was not the Prince of Luxembourg. In fact, the police probably knew that already if they had done any subsequent checking with the government people. In that case, both Hope and I were probably wanted for questioning, at the very least.

I heard a knock at the door. "Dare? It's Martin."

I backed up to the door and worked on the handle until it opened. Martin hurried in and closed the door.

He saw my condition and laughed. "Man, you weren't kidding." He held up a small pair of needle-nose pliers. "These were all I had in the car."

I moved farther into the room where there was more light and turned my back to him. "Thanks. Give it a shot."

I felt him work the pliers in between my wrists and apply pressure to the cord that bound me. He grunted, sighed, and grunted again. "Geez, what's this made of?" Martin tried one more time, then removed the tool. "Holy shit. Look at this."

I turned to face him as he held the pliers close to my face. The wire cutting portion near the handles had an eighth-inch oval indentation. My bindings had bent the edges of the tool. Whatever Hope had used, it was evidently something she'd brought with her.

I sighed. "All right. Thanks for trying. We'll have to figure out something else."

"Wait," Martin said. "First you tell me what the hell is going on."

I looked him in the eye, trying to gauge how much I should say. "Okay, but let's get out of here. Hope might be back any time."

Martin returned my look, probably trying to decide if I was lying, then he nodded. "Yeah. Okay. Where do you want to go?"

"I don't know. Just out for now." I moved toward the door.

"Hey, don't forget your key."

My jeans were loose, but I could feel the key I'd acquired earlier still in my pocket. Puzzled, I turned back to Martin and saw him pointing at the desk where Hope's time distorter sat, presumably still doing its job. Next to it was a room key—Hope's room key. She must have forgotten it when she left after knocking me out. "Take it," I said, turning around and wiggling my bound hands. "I can't exactly use it in my current condition."

Martin chuckled. "Right."

We exited and shut the door. I turned right, heading deeper into the hotel rather than going to the elevators. Martin walked silently beside me. I had to admire his patience, I doubted I would have been as calm in the face of the weirdness he'd seen.

"You're a programmer, right?" I asked. "And you're working on something for a Mars probe?"

He stopped in the hallway, which was empty except for the two of us. "How do you know that? Look, I've passed all my security checks. Is this some sort of test, or sick joke, trying to see if I'm a security risk?"

I turned to him and shook my head. "No. I'm just trying to verify some things Hope told me earlier. That's the woman you met at the police station."

"So, how does she know what I do? Are you guys spies? You seem kinda young."

I cocked an eyebrow, but let the comment pass and continued walking down the hall. "No, we're not spies exactly. We're not working for any government. But, it is our job to protect things."

Martin fell in step with me again. "That's pretty vague. How does Lauri fit into this?"

"Honestly, I'm not sure. She's the reason I'm here, and you seem to be the reason she's here, but beyond that it gets fuzzy. Are you a good programmer?"

"What the hell kind of question is that? Yes! I'm good. Do you think Lockheed-Martin just hires any hack off the street to write guidance software for a billion dollar spacecraft?"

I tried to hold up a hand, then remembered my predicament. "Okay, okay. Sorry. But, what would happen— hypothetically, mind you— if you made a mistake in your program?"

He paused and I could tell he was at least seriously considering my question. "Well, I suppose it depends on the mistake. It might not affect the system at all, or it could cause catastrophic failure. But, you don't understand. There's a whole team of engineers that go over every line of code. It's not just me. And we run hundreds of simulations. There are no mistakes."

If what he said was true, then how had the crash happened?

We turned a corner and walked past a man in brown overalls, carrying a pipe wrench. He smiled and nodded to us. Poor guy was probably headed off to unclog someone's toilet or something equally unpleasant, yet he still had a smile to spare for two strangers.

Martin took my arm and turned me to him once the maintenance man was out of earshot. "Dare, what are you not telling me?"

I looked at him and suddenly the solution to my problem dawned on me. "Maintenance!" I said.

"What?"

"A hotel this size must have a good maintenance shop with lots of tools. They probably have a bolt cutter or something."

Martin sighed. "It's always about you isn't it? C'mon. It's probably on the ground floor."

13

We went downstairs and found a service hallway that led to laundry, one of the many kitchens, and maintenance. Unfortunately, the area was quite busy, it being dinnertime for many folks.

"Why don't we just ask someone?" Martin whispered.

"Because there's one too many people involved in this already," I replied, pointedly looking at him.

He made a rude noise. "I still don't understand all the secrecy. What do you do?"

I looked around the bustling lobby and atrium and spotted a small, unoccupied table. "C'mon," I said, motioning with my head. Martin sighed, but followed me.

My arms were growing increasingly uncomfortable. I sat in one of the chairs and tried to ignore the pain and focus my thoughts. Martin plopped down next to me and leaned an elbow on the table.

"If you had known it would lead to all this trouble, would you still have talked to Lauri, or gone down to visit me in jail?"

He shrugged. "I don't know. Maybe. It hasn't been that much trouble. Kind of exciting actually," Martin said with a chuckle. "I don't get out much."

"Okay, but what if it led to something worse? Like losing

your job, or getting arrested."

"Yeah, I suppose I would have walked away then."

"So, knowing the outcome of your actions ahead of time might affect your decisions?"

"Well, yeah. Of course it would. I mean, that's how we make decisions. We look at the possible outcomes and weigh the risk versus the reward," he said.

"Right. So, what if I told you I know what's going to happen to the probe once it reaches Mars?"

Martin chuckled. "I'd probably figure you're either crazy or trying to sell me something."

I looked directly at him. "I'm not trying to sell you anything."

He met my gaze, then looked away nervously. "So, what? You're just flat out telling me you're crazy?"

"What if there was a third alternative?"

"Like what?"

"Do you read any science fiction?"

He paused, confusion evident on his face, but nodded. "Yeah, some. Why?"

"What about time travel stories?" I knew I was breaking all sorts of rules by this point, but I sensed Martin could handle it and it was the right thing to do.

He looked at me incredulously. "Are you trying to tell me you're some sort of time traveler? Come on. Seriously? Do you think I'm an idiot?"

Then again, maybe my senses were out of whack. "No, I don't think you're an idiot and yes, that's what I'm telling you."

"That's the best story you can come up with? I suppose Lauri and this Hope woman are time travelers too."

I nodded. "Lauri came here looking for you, and I was sent to find out what she intended to do. Hope came after I had my… difficulties."

Martin gave me a skeptical look. "So, prove it. Tell me something you shouldn't be able to know."

"More than I already have?"

"Yeah, okay. I'll admit, knowing about my work was a little creepy, but it's not that secret. You could have learned that much without too much effort. Tell me something else."

I sighed and looked away. "I can't. Hope has all my equipment. Well, except for the earpiece Lauri stole when I arrived."

Long, mocha legs entered my vision. "I'd have let you keep it if I'd known you would do my job for me," a familiar female voice said.

I followed the legs up past a hotel waitress uniform and found Lauri's bright blue eyes. She'd bound up her white hair and largely hidden it under a lacy brown hairnet.

"Can I get you boys something to drink?" she asked with a smirk on her face.

"What are you doing here?" I asked.

"Tracking the two of you. At least when I'm not avoiding that little brunette vixen of yours. Where did you find her?"

I chuckled. "She found me."

Martin's mouth hung slightly open. He shook off his surprise and said, "Wait. Was Dare telling the truth?"

Lauri pulled another chair close to Martin and sat on its edge. She leaned in and touched his wrist, much like I'd seen the night before at the club, though her current expression held much more seriousness. "Martin, your team is using English units of measurement, right? Well, the people over at Jet Propulsion Labs are using metric units, and the conflict is going to cause the probe to crash."

Martin's eyes grew wide. "Dammit!" he said, much louder than I would have liked. I looked around the atrium, but his outburst hadn't garnered much in the way of attention. "I asked my boss about that a couple weeks ago. He told me not to worry about it."

Lauri and I exchanged a quick glance. It appeared our exploits hadn't amounted to much after all. Martin had already been aware of a possible problem.

"I see," Lauri said with a sigh. "I guess our research was incomplete. And I'm out of time."

I shifted in my seat and grimaced as a jolt of pain traveled down my arm.

Lauri noticed my discomfort. "Are you all right?"

I shook my head. "Hope, my 'little brunette vixen' as you called her, knocked me out and bound my wrists before she went looking for the two of you. We tried to cut the wire, but it's too strong."

"Hm. I have something that might help," she said. "But, let's go somewhere a little more private."

We left the crowded atrium and went up to the second floor where Lauri led us to one of the smaller, unoccupied meeting rooms. It had the feel of a library when I was a kid, when anything spoken above a whisper seemed loud and inappropriate. Dark wood, and wallpaper flecked with gold, adorned the walls surrounding an oval mahogany table, perhaps fifteen feet long.

Lauri closed the double doors and turned to me with a small cylindrical object in her hand. I backed away, trying to put one of the plush leather chairs between us.

She let out a light laugh. "I'm not going to hurt you. It's a cutting laser. Hopefully it's got enough juice left. I use it on locks and stuff."

After deciding I had little to lose, I walked over and turned my back.

Lauri crouched down. "Make the gap as wide as you can and hold very still. This will probably get a little warm."

I strained against the binding and heard a high pitched whine as she applied the tool. Her description of "a little warm" had been a gross understatement. The intense energy of the laser quickly heated the material wrapped around my wrists. I ground my teeth against the pain and soon smelled burning hair.

Something snapped and my arms flew apart. Reflexively, I tried unsuccessfully to grab both my wrists.

"Martin! Water. On the table," Lauri instructed.

He saw the iced decanter she'd indicated and grabbed it. I gratefully held out my injured hands, but Lauri took the pitcher and dumped its contents on the floor behind me. I looked at her in disbelief.

"What? The carpet was on fire," she said. "Did you really want to add arson to our list of problems?"

Peering down, I saw indeed the rug was charred where the super-heated bindings had landed. I sighed and rubbed my wrists. "You could have warned me."

Lauri gave me a half smile and set the empty container on the table. "I did. Here, let me see."

Reluctantly, I showed her my wrists and she winced in sympathy. "I'll be fine," I said, trying to recover at least a small portion of my machismo.

"Well," a voice said from the doorway. "Isn't this cozy?"

Our heads snapped up and I saw Hope standing confidently at the room's entrance, her stunner aimed at Lauri and me.

14

Hope nodded slightly in Martin's direction. "Nice to see you again Mr. Nussbaum. I apologize for all the trouble we've caused you."

"It wasn't any trouble," Martin said quietly.

Hope turned her attention back to me. "I have to say, I'm impressed, Dare. You almost had me fooled."

I shook my head. "I wasn't trying to fool you. This isn't what you think," I said lamely, like some cheating husband caught in the act on a reality TV show.

Hope ignored my comment and focused on Lauri. "You're good. Very slippery. I was heading back here to regroup when the system notified me Dare was on the move."

Inwardly, I groaned. Of course, Hope's management system would be able to keep tabs on the materials it had created, just like Kim had tracked her earpiece. The stuff Hope had used to tie me up led her straight to us.

"So, what now?" Lauri asked. "Shoot us with your ray gun and take us to time jail?"

Hope took a couple of steps toward us. "First, I have to repair the damage you've done."

"There hasn't been any damage," I said. "Martin already talked to his superiors about the problem before we even got here and they brushed him off. The probe will still crash."

Hope's eyebrows raised. "Really? And how do you know that, Dare? Have you followed the thread forward to see? What if Mr. Nussbaum goes back to his superiors and presents his case again? Don't you understand? The knowledge he's gained here will alter the thread. It's inevitable."

"I… I won't say anything. I promise," Martin said.

I wasn't sure what Hope had in mind, but I didn't like the direction the conversation was taking. "Inevitable? How can anything in this universe be inevitable? I don't care what your management system says, it can't predict everything. I'm pretty sure you didn't intend for your Prince of Luxembourg story to hit the news, but it did."

A hint of uncertainty flashed across Hope's features. "What?"

I chuckled. "Yep, all the local stations ran a story about the Prince of Luxembourg who was mistakenly arrested at a club last night."

"But, I met with the officer privately. The papers were all perfect."

"I'm sure they were. But all it takes is one overheard, off-handed comment to get something started," I said. "It was a pretty outrageous story."

She glared at me. "Well it wouldn't have been necessary if someone hadn't gotten themselves arrested."

I nodded. "Touché. Anyway, my point is—"

"Federal agents! Put your hands where we can see them!"

Two men dressed in dark suits slipped into the room behind Hope, pointing guns with arms extended. I heard more movement behind me from another entrance. Hope slowly turned around to face the two who'd first arrived. I felt Lauri step close to me.

"Nice and easy now," the first agent said. "We just want to ask you some questions and determine who you are."

"I'm Hope Bulova, with the State Department, and these people—"

"No," the man interrupted. "That one's not going to fly here Miss Bulova, or whatever your name is. We've already checked with the State Department and they've never heard of you."

"Look," Hope pleaded. "I'm sure we can work something out."

A high pitched beeping sounded somewhere near me. Guns that had slowly begun to drop, snapped up, focusing on Lauri and me.

"What is that? Shut it off!" the agent demanded.

Lauri slowly held up her right arm. The beeping emanated from a flat band on her wrist I hadn't noticed before since it was nearly the color of her skin and fit snugly. "It's just my watch," Lauri said as she entwined her left hand in my right and the beeping became more frequent. "I have an appointment."

I glanced at Lauri questioningly, but her attention was fixed on the agent. I saw Hope turn to look at us and her eyes became big. Sounds in the room seemed to fade away while I watched Hope's mouth slowly form the word "No".

White blurred my vision and everything vanished.

15

Lights flickered while I dropped to my knees and violently emptied the contents of my stomach. What was left of the cheeseburger didn't look very appetizing the second time around. Next to me, Lauri doubled over and added to my mess.

"Freeze! Don't move!"

I wiped my mouth on my sleeve and tried to coax my stomach back down where it belonged. "Relax, Agent," I croaked. "I can assure you I'm not going anywhere."

Lauri coughed. "It's okay. He's with me. Just give us a second, Karl."

Karl? The lighting dimmed, almost to black, then brightened without wavering. It was then I realized the floor underneath me was no longer the lush carpeting of the hotel, but smooth, white ceramic tiles. I looked up and saw a tall, thin man in a white lab coat, pointing what I presumed was a weapon at me with an unsteady hand. Hope, Martin, and the Federal agents were nowhere to be found.

"Where are we?" I asked.

"Home," Lauri said. "Well, my home at least." She looked at me and smiled with a drop of saliva running down her chin.

I pointed. "You've got a..."

Her face flushed and she turned away to wipe off the drool.

"Sorry," she said.

"Forget it. I'm sure I'm not any better. What happened to Martin and Hope?"

Karl cleared his throat. "Lauri, would you care to introduce your friend?"

She apologized again and we helped each other to our feet. "Dare, this is Dr. Karl Lansing. Karl, Dare…"

"Heisenberg," I filled in. Dr. Lansing's eyebrows rose and I nodded. "Yes, that Heisenberg. He was my great uncle, but I was adopted," I said in explanation. I ceased being upset about people disbelieving my lineage years ago.

"I see," Dr. Lansing said with a small frown, then shifted his attention to Lauri. "And why did he come back with you?"

She wrinkled her nose. "Can we go someplace where's there's less vomit on the floor? And maybe freshen up? I'd like to get out of these goofy clothes."

Karl looked her over. "That is a different look for you. Fine. Meet me in the Situation Room in fifteen minutes."

Lauri nodded. "Yes, sir." She stepped around him and I lost sight of her down a narrow hallway.

Dr. Lansing turned to me. "Dare, if you'll follow me."

He led me out of the chamber, which looked about twenty feet across and hemispherical in shape. The whole place was made of metal, with the exception of the circular patch of white tiling about eight feet across in the center of the room where Lauri and I had arrived. Passing through, I noticed the door was one of those submarine types with the wheel lock mechanism in the center. "Are we underwater?" I asked.

Ignoring my question, Dr. Lansing opened a similar door

a short distance down the tight corridor and pointed inside. "Disrobe in here and step into the cubical on the opposite wall. Clearly state, 'Cleanse, maximum,' and the mechanism will take care of the rest."

I studied his face for any hints of malice or subterfuge and found none. His dark brown hair had grayed at the temples, but his stoic face lacked the lines I would associate with an older man. I made a mental note not to play poker with Dr. Lansing and stepped into the tiny room. He closed the door behind me and I removed my clothing.

My thoughts returned to Martin, Hope, and the government men Lauri and I had left behind in Denver. I assumed we had returned to Lauri's base of operations, probably somewhere outside time, like the facility where I'd trained with Kim and M'sang. Although, Lauri's technology wasn't quite up to Kim's standards, it seemed to serve its purpose well enough. I sincerely hoped Martin hadn't been adversely affected by our involvement in his life. And though I found myself still worried about Hope, even if she'd treated me like a prisoner, I was pretty sure her management system would remove her from the thread before she met any harm.

Chilly in my birthday suit, I stepped into the little alcove and said, "Cleanse, maximum," as I was instructed. Expecting a warm, invigorating stream of water, I was surprised by a low hum and an unpleasant prickling sensation all over my body.

"What the hell is this? Quit! Stop! End!"

The humming ceased and the prickles subsided, although I felt like I had just been vigorously scrubbed all over with a wire brush.

I heard a muffled voice through the metal door. "Are you all right in there, Mr. Heisenberg?"

I rubbed my arms. "Yeah. Just not what I was expecting."

"My apologies. I have a change of clothes for you if you'd like. I believe they will fit."

I glanced at the rumpled pile I'd removed. Something clean to wear probably wasn't a bad thing. "Sure, sounds good."

The wheel on the door turned and Dr. Lansing opened it enough to admit his arm and the folded garments he held, including a sturdy pair of boots. I took them and murmured my thanks. He shut the door, allowing me my privacy. The undergarments were comfortable and fit well, but I groaned at the beige jumpsuit. Didn't any of these time traveling people have a sense of style? At least it wasn't gray.

I turned the wheel and gratefully saw the door unlatch. Apparently the little room wasn't going to also be my prison cell— at least not yet. Dr. Lansing stood in the cramped hallway, waiting patiently. "What should I do with my other clothes?" I asked.

"You can just leave them for now. We'll take care of them later. This way," he said, holding out his arm.

I nodded and he showed me to another chamber just two more doors farther along the corridor. The facility, wherever it was, was not long on diversity or decor. The room held a round table, about six feet across, with five chairs tucked in around it. The far wall was filled with computer monitors, mounted above a built-in desk with two more chairs facing it. Dr. Lansing pointed to one of the seats at the table, so I slid around and filled it. The furniture left little room to maneuver in the tight space. He remained standing until Lauri entered a few seconds later.

She was freshly dressed in a jumpsuit similar to mine, though hers had been tailored closer to her feminine curves. She'd pulled her hair back in a sensible pony tail, tied with a bright red cloth in sharp contrast to the white locks it contained. Flashing me a quick smile, she sat in the chair next to mine.

Dr. Lansing shut the door and secured it before taking a seat across from us. "Okay, so what happened?" he asked Lauri.

She expelled a pent up breath before answering. "Martin Nussbaum was not the source of the error which caused the malfunction. Or, at least, he wasn't in control of the final implementation of the program. I'm assuming the situation here is unchanged?"

The doctor nodded. "As far as I can detect. I haven't checked the history to see if the orbiter crashed or not, but regardless, our guests are still here."

"Excuse me," I interrupted, holding up my hand. "But, can someone clue me in on what's happening? Why was that probe so important?"

Lansing glanced briefly at me before refocusing on Lauri. "What have you told him?"

"Nothing really."

"Yet, you brought him here? Why?"

"I just had a feeling he could help us," Lauri said. "He's a time traveler too."

"Working for whom?"

Lauri looked at me and I realized I would be involved in the conversation after all. "Uh. Well, the Keepers I guess,"

I stammered. "But, I'm not sure, to be perfectly honest, since Hope said she worked for them too and we didn't really see eye to eye."

Dr. Lansing's eyes narrowed. "Who's Hope?"

"Hope is another time traveler. One that came to bail me out of jail after Lauri got me arrested," I said, giving her a dirty look. She merely smiled and shrugged in response.

The doctor ignored our byplay and continued, "So, who are the Keepers?"

Surprised, I said, "You don't know? I figured you knew more about them than I do. Lauri seemed to know I was there to stop her before I figured out she was the person I was looking for. And you still haven't said why you're so interested in a crashed probe that I'd never heard of before."

The two of them exchanged a look and Lansing gave the woman a slight nod, after which she turned to me. "We don't know for sure that preventing the orbiter from failing would have changed anything, but we decided it had the best chance for success. It was designed to monitor the Martian climate and look for signs of water. It might have detected the aquifer that made it possible to establish a colony on Mars, many years before it actually happened."

"I don't get it. What's an aquifer?"

Dr. Lansing answered. "Basically, it's an underground reservoir of water, or water-saturated rock."

"The presence of a large amount of water made colonizing Mars feasible, since it wouldn't have to be transported from Earth," Lauri added.

"Cool, so there's a base on Mars in the future? Why did you

want to make it happen sooner?"

The doctor sighed. "It was our hope that giving it a few extra years to develop would make it stronger. Capable of defending itself."

"Defending itself against what?" I asked.

"Invasion," Lauri said.

I shifted in my chair and tried to let that sink in.

Lansing continued. "They started by knocking out the handful of satellites used for communication. That was a little over four days ago. Since then, they've been surveying the planet. The colony sent a party out to make contact with one of the alien survey crews three days ago. They never returned."

"I don't understand. Why would aliens go to Mars? Wouldn't it make more sense to go to Earth?"

Dr. Lansing sighed. "Our current theory is that Earth was their original destination, but when they got close enough and discovered how populated it was, they diverted to Mars." He rose and squeezed past our chairs to the bank of monitors. "Computer, show the latest images of the alien craft."

One of the larger screens flashed and a dark, fuzzy picture appeared. "This was taken from a ground telescope," Lansing said. "We've confirmed at least three of these massive craft we estimate to be nearly a thousand meters across, as well as over a dozen much smaller ships they use to ferry their survey teams around. A formidable force, but not enough to take on a population numbering in the billions, especially if their desire is to establish a colony. They may have the means to wipe out everyone on Earth, but any method of doing that effectively would likely render the planet inhospitable to them as well for a very long time."

I stood and moved closer to the monitor, trying to make out details from the grainy image. The hull of the vessel looked smooth, at least from that distance, and the overall shape was like a rounded pie wedge.

I staggered back, suddenly light headed. Lauri jumped up and supported me. "Dare, what's wrong?"

The ship in the picture perfectly matched the toy I'd received at my fifth birthday party.

16

I leaned on Lauri a moment longer, then sat in one of the other chairs. "I'm okay. I just need a second."

What did it mean? All I had were fond memories of that toy. I'd spent hours playing with it, creating swashbuckling fantasies of heroes in outer space. Of course, it was possible the whole thing was just a coincidence, but I'd lost a good deal of my belief in coincidences over the past few weeks. Had someone placed that toy in my young hands to create a subconscious sympathy for aliens who wanted to take over my planet? The notion sounded ridiculous even as I thought it. What possible purpose would it serve? And why me?

I rubbed my eyes and asked, "What is NASA, or whoever runs the space program in your time, doing? Are they sending ships or something?"

"We don't know," Lauri said.

"How come? Something like this must be all over the news. I'm sure you don't lose contact with your Martian colony every day."

Lauri glanced at Dr. Lansing, then knelt in front of me. "Dare, I don't think you understand. We don't know what Earth is doing because we're not there. We're on Mars."

I blinked. "This isn't a station located outside the timeline?"

Lauri chuckled and shook her head. "No. We're on the Red Planet, or under it rather. This facility is underground, away from the colony itself."

"You were right when you said I don't understand. So, you're not part of some other universal, time altering organization in opposition to the Keepers? You're just a couple of Earthlings who built a time machine?"

"Well, Dr. Lansing built it," Lauri said. "And technically, I'm a Martian, since I was born here, but in essence, yes, you've got it right."

"Why do I get the feeling you're getting ready to talk about a flux capacitor and show me a DeLorean?"

The blank look on Lauri's face told me my wit did not transcend time. How could a time traveler not get a *Back to the Future* reference?

Dr. Lansing leaned in. "Are you saying the beings you work for actually exist extra-dimensionally?"

"What? I don't know. I guess so."

"I can't even fathom the energy required! To exist outside the normal flow of time… amazing! It took weeks to store enough to send Lauri back for less than a twenty hour stay."

"Karl," Lauri said. "I think we're losing focus here."

He shook his head. "Of course. My apologies. I'm a scientist, not a warrior or adventurer."

"No worries, Doc," I said. "I'm having a hard time wrapping my head around most of this myself."

Lauri stood and leaned on the table. "What are we going to do? We can't assume the aliens are going to be happy just gathering information for much longer."

"Who are they?" I asked. "Have you tried talking to them?"

Lansing frowned. "Besides the party that went to meet their survey team? Yes. The colony leaders have been broadcasting greetings on every frequency with no response."

"But, if they're hostile, why haven't they just destroyed the colony already?"

"Why destroy something you can use?" Dr. Lansing said. "There are less than a thousand colonists, but structures and excavation began nearly thirty years ago. A lot of work has been done. I suspect Mars is as inhospitable for these aliens as it is for us, so it would make much more sense to use what has already been built, rather than blowing it up and starting from scratch."

Everything the doc had said made sense, but something still just wasn't clicking for me. "What do you know about them? Do you have any pictures?"

"Very little." He turned to the monitors. "Computer, display the alien surveillance photos, please." Several grainy images popped up on multiple screens. "These were taken from several kilometers away before the team was sent in to make contact. We know they are bipedal, like us, and of similar size. They wore suits, so we can infer that the thin Mars atmosphere is incompatible with their biology. Although, it's possible they are just being cautious. Past that, your guess is as good as anyone's."

I studied the pictures and quickly reached the same conclusions. "I need to go see them."

Lansing turned to me in surprise. "Why?"

I stood, feeling the need to pace, but the cramped room had no space for it. "Honestly, I don't know. What I do know is the past several weeks I've been used and manipulated on levels

I didn't realize was possible and I'm tired of it. It's time to make my own decisions. Do something."

The doctor looked at me skeptically, and I guess I couldn't blame him. I was just a punk nineteen-year-old in his eyes. What could I do? In all honesty, his attitude was probably justified.

Lauri, however, came to my defense. "I think he's right. I'll go with him."

I'm not sure which of us was more surprised, but Dr. Lansing spoke first. "No. I can't allow it. Look what happened to the others who tried to contact them."

"But, Karl," Lauri pleaded. "That's part of the problem. We don't actually know what happened to them. Communication was lost and they didn't return. We're just assuming the worst."

"With good reason I think," Lansing said. "Regardless, I'm sure the colony director won't approve."

Lauri rolled her eyes. "I don't care. They're all just a bunch of geologists, engineers, and miners. What do any of them know about contacting alien species?"

"That's enough," Dr. Lansing said. "I need to update Director Ruschick on our results, or lack thereof. I'll get his thoughts on sending another greeting party and let you know. In the meantime, why don't you show Dare around the rest of the Hub?"

Lauri looked ready to protest, but instead sighed and said, "Yes, sir." She took my hand and I felt a tumbled mix of emotions: anger, helplessness, fear, and even affection, poured over me in the space of a heartbeat. "C'mon, Dare. Let's give you the grand tour." We left the Situation Room, as Lansing had called it, and Lauri shut the door behind us.

"What was that?" I asked.

"What?"

"When you touched me… I don't know, I can't explain it," I said, shaking my head.

Lauri's face flushed. "I'm sorry, Dare. Karl gets me upset sometimes, the way he bows and scrapes to Ruschick… I lost control for a second."

"Lost control of what?"

She let go of my hand and we started walking. "I'm empathic. I can read emotions in others. I can also project them sometimes, though I'm less practiced at that," she said with a shy smile.

"Wow, that's amazing! How did that happen? Did your parents have special abilities too?"

"No. Not that I know of at least. I was a product of genetic manipulation, born here, in the Hub."

Her words sobered me. They were filled with sadness and loss. "You don't know who your parents were, do you?"

She shook her head. "Technically, I don't really have any. I was conceived in a test tube and my genetic code was manipulated to such an extent I doubt I remotely resemble either person who supplied the sperm or egg that created me."

I stopped and reached for her hand, wanting her to feel the sincerity of what I said. "I'm sorry. I've never known who my birth parents were either. But, whoever they were, all they did was start the biological ball rolling. Who I am is a result of my thoughts and my experiences over the course of nineteen years or so. It may not be much, but it's me. You are you, in just the same way. Where we start doesn't matter, it's how we finish that counts."

Sage advice. I really should listen to myself more often.

Lauri gave me a small smile. "Thanks. I'll try to remember that."

Awkward silence followed. I blushed and released her hand. "So, what is this 'Hub'? It almost sounded like you're not part of the colony."

"We're not really," she said and began walking again. "Construction here started just a few years after the colony was established. We're about seventy kilometers from the colony site, in a vast system of underground caverns and ancient lava tubes."

As we walked, I felt calling the facility a "Hub" did a poor job describing the system of winding corridors, stairways, and random chambers that composed the strange place. Psychotic spider web seemed more appropriate, if not as concise. "So, what do you do here? Besides build time machines."

She laughed— a pleasing sound I wanted to hear again, soon. "There's only the one time machine. What we do is a good question, and you'd get a different answer depending on who you asked. Lots of things, really. And it changes all the time."

"Okay, now I'm intrigued. Things like what exactly?"

"Well, the Hub was built to house scientists and their experiments. But, not just any experiments. These experiments were ones that the world governments considered either too dangerous, or too controversial to be performed on Earth. You name it, it's probably been done, or at least attempted here. Antimatter creation and storage, cloning and genetic engineering, inter-dimensional travel— and those are just some of the successful projects. The list of failures is much longer."

"Couldn't have been anything too catastrophic," I said with

a grin. "You're still here."

"The Hub is highly compartmentalized for a reason. There are sections under permanent seal from accidents of one type or another."

My grin faded when I realized she was serious. "I'm surprised the colony is so close then. Why didn't they put you guys on the other side of the planet if you're so dangerous?"

"We provide energy for the colony. They don't know what really goes on here, except for Director Ruschick."

I sensed her level of agitation rising again and decided to change the subject. "What year is it anyway?"

"It's 2087. What year do you come from?"

"Uh, 2012 actually," I answered, suddenly feeling like Rip Van Winkle.

"Oh, that explains it then."

"Explains what?"

"Why you don't know anything," Lauri said with a mischievous smile. "You hungry? I'm starved, let's eat."

She led me to a door like all the rest and ushered me through. Inside, the room was walled with cabinets and two long tables, with bench seating, occupied the middle. After pointing me to one of the tables, Lauri browsed through several cabinets and returned with an armload of plastic packets and two bottles of water.

"When you said you were starving, you weren't kidding."

"Most of these are for later, so we don't have to come back. Here." She handed me one of the pouches and a water bottle. "Open the packet here and pour a little water in. Then reseal it and pinch the red spot until you feel it pop."

I watched as she performed the operation, then did my own. The pouch heated considerably and I set it on the table while it percolated. "You said genetic engineering was one of the things done here, but I would have thought that'd be pretty commonplace by 2087."

Lauri shook her head. "All modifications to the human genome were banned by a worldwide treaty in 2051, I think. Only specific changes related to a specific list of genetic disorders and diseases were allowed after that, and even then it was frowned upon. Work still continued, of course, but in secret."

"Why did they ban it?"

She chuckled derisively. "The geneticists were getting too good." She plucked two sporks from a tray on the table and handed one to me. "The average human lifespan had jumped by almost thirty years since the turn of the century. Overpopulation became an even more serious issue, causing some countries to perform secret mass sterilizations by putting additives in selected water supplies. Entire cities stopped having babies. That led to riots and rebellions. The geneticists became the scapegoats and they were hunted like witches during the fifties, after the ban."

I thought back to a comment Kim had made, while I was lying in the exam room for the first time, and wondered if she'd spoken from knowledge or supposition at the time.

Lauri continued, after opening her pouch, allowing the steam an escape. "A handful, who'd been captured in the late fifties and early sixties, were given the opportunity to go to Mars and the newly created Hub to continue their work in exile. A few accepted, including the man who engineered me, Dr. Hans Kritchkopf."

I mimicked her with my own meal. "Wow. So, what happened to him? Is he still here?"

She looked away, then took a bite from the contents of her packet. "He died in 2079, when I was seven."

"I'm sorry. Did he mean a lot to you then?"

Lauri glanced at me, then studied her food. "He was a lecherous, sadistic man and I'm glad he's dead. One of his experiments killed him and his section is one of those under permanent seal. Can we talk about something else?"

"I, uh, sure. Yes, of course," I stammered. The coldness emanating from her hit me like a punch in the gut. "Wait. You said it's 2087 now, and you were seven in 2079?"

"Yes," she said around another bite. "I turned fifteen a couple of months ago. He designed me to mature at an accelerated rate."

17

Lauri's statement threw me for another loop. I'd guessed her age to be near my own, probably slightly older, but certainly not almost five years younger.

"What's wrong?"

I shook my head and attacked my meal. "Nothing."

She reached over and covered my hand with her own. "Dare, please don't lie to me. I like you, and want to trust you, but I can't do that if you won't be honest with me."

I looked up from my food and found her warm, blue eyes. Lauri was such a jumble of contradictions— even her eyes. How could they be warm and blue at the same time? "You just… keep surprising me."

"Well, I was genetically engineered as a sex toy, then raised by scientists. I suppose I'm bound to be a little different than most girls," she said with a smile.

I coughed. "A sex toy? That's what he made you for?" I shook my head. "I'm sorry, you didn't want to talk about it."

"No, it's all right. I want you to trust me as well. Yes, that's what he designed me to be, but not for himself. His interests were… different."

"Who then?" I asked, fearing she would say Dr. Lansing.

"Victor Ruschick," Lauri answered with a scowl.

Now her animosity toward the Martian colony director made more sense.

She continued. "I found out one day when I was snooping through Dr. Kritchkopf's computer. After he died, Karl— Dr. Lansing— took me in and raised me like a daughter as best he could. He's been very kind to me."

I nodded in understanding and turned back to my meal. She removed her hand and we ate in silence. The stuff was filling, and chewable, which made it more satisfying than Kim's nutrient pouches, but it hardly delighted my taste buds. I wondered how long it would be before I'd be able to wrap my hands around a cheeseburger again.

"Is there any way we can find out what happened to Martin?" I asked after downing the last of the packet.

Lauri took our trash and deposited it in what I assumed was a recycler. "We can try, but our historical records aren't that extensive. Unless he became someone famous, I doubt he'd show up anywhere. Karl might be able to track down what happened to him, but he'll be busy running tests on the equipment for a while I imagine."

Frowning in disappointment, I helped her gather up the extra packages she'd dumped on the table earlier. Martin had been an innocent pawn in our misguided attempts to either alter or preserve the timeline. Once again I hoped our presence hadn't pushed his thread down an undesirable path.

We left the mess hall and wandered more seemingly aimless hallways. "Where is everyone?" I asked her after several minutes.

"The other scientists pretty much keep to themselves. They're all completely focused on their own work, whatever it might be." She let out a short laugh. "Some of them probably don't even know about our alien visitors yet."

She stopped at a small storeroom and selected several items from various shelves after taking two large satchels off a hook and handing one to me. We stowed the food packets and other things in the bags and I slung mine over one shoulder. "What's all this for?"

"I told you, for later. Now, let's find a terminal and see if there's any information about Martin."

Lauri stopped at a computer station in another corridor and pecked out some instructions on a pad she slid out from the wall. A few seconds later, she sighed. "Martin's not listed in the historical records we have. But, at least that means nothing really drastic happened to him, right?"

"I don't understand though. How did you know to go looking for him if he's not in the records?"

Lauri frowned. "Karl told me about him, and to watch out for you, though I didn't know it was you at the time. He's probably got more extensive records in his own system. This is just a general knowledge base," she said, then entered more commands.

It made sense that someone who wanted to travel through time would have access to more a complete historical record, but that still didn't explain how Dr. Lansing had known to warn Lauri about other time travelers.

"All right," she said with a grin, turning away from the terminal. "Let's continue with our tour, shall we?"

So far, the tour had consisted of the mess hall and a random storage closet, filled in between with ladders, stairs, and seemingly endless tight hallways divided by the submarine-like pressure doors every thirty or forty feet. With no real points of reference that I'd noted, I had no idea how to get back to Dr. Lansing's area. It could have been right around the corner for all I knew.

Eventually, she opened the door to a room filled with bulky suits and other equipment. Lauri selected one she thought would fit me and showed me how to put it on.

"Why are we doing this?"

"I want to show you the garage and it's not pressurized."

We finished suiting up and checked each other's seals for leaks before entering the airlock. It cycled through whatever safety protocols were required in a few seconds and gave us a green light to exit. The garage, as she'd called it, was really just a converted cavern. Weak sunlight filtered in from the cave mouth, maybe a hundred yards away, augmented by artificial light from several banks of floodlights. Five vehicles of varying size and shape sat, lined neatly in a row, along the cavern wall. The only noise I heard, coming from the respirator units on my thighs, vaguely reminded me of Darth Vader.

Lauri motioned for me to follow and headed toward one of the smaller rovers. A sturdy looking roll cage supported a small enclosed cabin with generous windows. It held two seats, with a modest cargo area in the back, and sported six wheels with bulbous, thickly treaded tires, presumably made for traversing the sandy Martian surface. She quickly checked over several external instrument panels before opening a side hatch and climbing inside. She beckoned me again. I sighed and crawled in next to her.

"What are we," I said before remembering to push the

communications button on my wrist she'd shown me as we suited up. "What are we doing?"

She scowled and shook her head inside her helmet. Lauri strapped herself in, then flipped a line of switches on the dashboard in front of her. I felt the vehicle powering up beneath my seat. Deciding to trust her, I found my own harness and buckled myself in securely. Lights changed from red to green on her display and soon we were moving toward the sunlit entrance.

As we passed from the shaded cavern into the Martian day, I felt myself growing lighter in my seat. A small wave of nausea passed through me as my stomach adjusted to the lower gravity. Lauri held the steering wheel with her knees and removed her helmet. I took the hint and unlocked my own.

"Sorry," she said. "I don't get outside much and forgot to warn you about the gravity change. A side benefit from Karl's extra dimensional research was developing artificial gravity. It takes a huge amount of power, but that's one thing we have in ample supply. Gravity inside the Hub is about twice Martian normal, which is still only about eighty percent of Earth's but it's close enough you probably don't notice the difference."

"That's great, but Lauri, where are we going?"

"To visit the aliens," she said, flashing perfect teeth in a bright smile.

"Didn't Lansing nix that idea?"

Lauri rolled her eyes at me while I suppressed an urge to tell her to watch where she was going. We were moving along the bumpy Martian terrain at a good clip. "He and Ruschick were never going to let us go, Dare. To them, we're just a couple of kids. But, you were right. It's time to do something."

I couldn't disagree with her, it had been my idea after all, so I tried to relax and enjoy the scenery. I soon understood how Mars had come by its nickname, the Red Planet. Everything, as far as my eyes could see, had a reddish hue. Dirt, rocks, even the sky was tinged red due to the dust flying around in the planet's ultra thin air. "Do you know where you're going?" I asked.

She nodded. "The computer projected the alien's next survey site based on the pattern of their previous landings. It's about one hundred and twenty kilometers from here. We should be there in a little over two hours, barring excessive detours."

"Why didn't you tell me what you were planning earlier?"

"Because I was afraid you might try to talk me out of it. Plus, it was fun to see the look on your face."

I laughed, thinking I'd likely have done the same thing. "You know, for a base dealing in such secret and dangerous stuff, it must have a lousy security system."

"Why do you say that?" she asked.

"Well, we walked out, stole a car, and hightailed away without any sort of alarm going off."

"The security is actually very good, which is why I deactivated it," Lauri said with a smirk.

"I see. So, how long before they notice—"

A red light accompanied by a persistent buzz interrupted me.

Lauri sighed and punched a button on her console. "This is Hub Rover Four, come in?"

Dr. Lansing's face appeared on a six-inch screen in the center of the dashboard. "Lauri, what are you doing?"

"At the moment, I'm driving."

I smiled in spite of my best efforts to keep a straight face.

Lansing wasn't as amused. "Yes, I see that. The question is: why are you driving and where are you going?"

"I'm driving because Dare isn't familiar with the—"

"Dammit, Lauri! This isn't a game! Turn the rover around and get back here."

She hesitated before saying anything else and I knew, her flippant attitude notwithstanding, she had a hard time disobeying Dr. Lansing.

"I'm sorry, but I won't do that. This is important, Karl."

"It's more important that you come back. I just spoke with Director Ruschick and he's planning to—"

The image on the screen flickered wildly, then turned to static along with the audio.

I chuckled. "Did you just—"

"No. Communication's being jammed, but I can't tell from where," Lauri said, worry evident on her face. She reduced speed and turned to me. "What do you think? Should we go back?"

For Lauri's sake, I wished I felt uncertain about our course of action. I didn't want to damage her relationship with the only person that had ever been fatherly to her, but every instinct I had shouted at me to move forward. "I know you're scared. I'm scared too. But something's telling me it's vital that I contact these aliens. I don't know why."

She studied my face for a few seconds, even as we jounced along. Fortunately, the sandy basin we traveled through was relatively clear of large rocks. Finally, she nodded and we accelerated. "Okay. Let's do this."

18

Because of my anxiety, the ride seemed interminably long. Lauri and I spoke little, each wrapped in our own thoughts.

Her faith in what amounted to simply my intuition caused me to question it even more. What if I was wrong? The aliens might just shoot us on sight. Then what would my prized gut feelings be worth? Looking at where those feelings had led me so far over the course of roughly the last three weeks— at least by my reckoning— being killed by aliens might be seen as a justified end.

"I'm sorry," Lauri said into our prolonged silence.

Startled out of my morose musings, I turned to her. "For what?"

She kept her eyes forward, concentrating to avoid the bigger rocks in our path. "For getting you arrested in Denver. For stealing your earpiece. For all the trouble I've caused you."

I let out a laugh and her face spun toward me with a hurtful glare. "No. I'm laughing at both of us. I was just thinking about how many problems I've made for you."

Her expression softened. "Oh." She returned her attention to driving and swerved sharply to avoid colliding with a beachball-sized boulder. Once back on course, and all six wheels, we shared some relieved laughter.

An indicator flashed on her panel. Lauri abruptly shut power and we rolled to a stop.

"What's going on?"

"Sensors picked up a big chunk of metal, probably their lander. Range is five hundred meters. Hopefully the rover is small enough they haven't noticed us yet."

"Okay."

She reached between our seats into the storage area behind us and pulled out a few pieces of equipment, handing one to me that looked like binoculars. "Power switch is here," Lauri said, pointing at a red button. "Range finder and other information will show in the display. The unit will automatically record any time it's on and focused at something."

I nodded and placed the unit in a pouch on my chest.

"We don't have any weapons," she said with a hint of nervousness. "But, I suppose if we need them, we're probably screwed anyway."

"What's that other stuff?"

"Sensors mostly. Things I don't have time to teach you how to use. Remember," she said, picking up her helmet, "no radio communication. They'll be able to pinpoint us in an instant."

"How will we talk to each other?"

"Stay close and use hand signals."

It occurred to me then we really should have worked some of these things out during the drive instead of brooding like we had. I shrugged and donned my helmet. Flying by the seat of my pants had gotten me this far.

Right. The seat of my pants had stranded me on Mars, attempting to contact a wholly unknown, possibly hostile, alien race.

I checked my seals like Lauri had shown me and gave her a thumbs up. She nodded and started the rover's airlock cycle. Within a minute, the two of us were standing on the Martian surface.

Moving and walking in low gravity is a whole different ball game from simply sitting in it.

All of my movements ended up too fast and over exaggerated. I felt like a marionette with an operator prone to seizures. Lauri smoothly motioned for me to follow and I was glad for our radio silence. Contrary to my earlier desires, I didn't want to hear her laughter.

The rover had stopped near the outer edge of an ancient impact crater. We made our way up the modest ridge while I relearned how to walk in something resembling a normal manner. Near the top, Lauri crouched down and crawled the last few feet to peer over the lip, with the sun at our backs. I followed suit and positioned myself next to her, pulling the binoculars from their pouch as I did.

The crater itself looked big to me, never having seen one up close before. I guessed it to be a half mile across, although I'd found my distance estimation flawed during the drive. Mars is quite a bit smaller than Earth, so the horizon was closer than my eyes were accustomed to. In the belly of the crater, a familiar wedge-shaped craft sat passively while several suited figures moved in and around it. I depressed the power switch and brought the binoculars up to my faceplate for a closer look.

Rather than two eyepieces, I looked at a video screen about four inches across. Besides an image of what it was pointed toward, the unit also displayed distance in meters, air temperature, wind speed and direction, as well as a host of other information that left me baffled. Roughly human height, in their suits, the aliens appeared brawnier, like they were all weight lifters. They moved deliberately, as I had discovered necessary, indicating they too were used to much higher gravity.

I counted eight of them on the ground. Their ship seemed big enough to hold all of them and a considerable amount of equipment comfortably. One particular piece of equipment held the attention of three aliens. About eight feet tall and perhaps two in diameter, the apparatus was cylindrical in shape, supported by five jointed struts, each ending in a foot-wide disk settled firmly in the Martian sand. Any ideas I had as to its purpose were only wild guesses.

A few odd whistles and clicks came to my ears. I glanced at Lauri beside me to see if she'd heard them, but her attention was wholly focused on her instruments. I had set my suit's communication unit to "open receive", which had produced a steady hiss of static I'd quickly tuned out. More strange sounds issued from the speakers in my helmet.

I tapped Lauri on the shoulder. She turned and I clearly saw her questioning look through her faceplate. I pointed to her, then to my ear. Her brow crinkled and she shook her head. Frustrated, I grabbed her right wrist, which held her communication controls, and switched hers to "open receive", like my own.

Her angered expression at my rough treatment changed to one of confusion as she listened to the unusual noises.

My own puzzlement turned to shock as I began hearing words.

"... iron, silicates... high percentage... insufficient..." and other seemingly random words interspersed with increasing frequency between the chirps, pops, and other sounds which made no sense.

A shadow blocked the sunlight between us. Startled, we both rolled on our backs to see three bulky, alien environment suits standing over us, pointing what were quite obviously weapons. Through my speakers, with a different voice than before, I heard, "... slowly... appendages visible..."

The center alien of the trio shifted slightly and its helmet completely blocked the sun from my eyes, allowing me my first real look at their faces.

My mouth fell open as I saw the furry, hamster-like features. The aliens weren't alien to me at all. But for some coloration differences, any one of them could have been my instructor, M'sang.

19

One of the trio stepped forward menacingly. I spread my arms wide and carefully set the binoculars in the sand. Beside me, Lauri mimicked my actions. The random chatter inside my helmet increased and became progressively hard to follow with additional voices. My own internal questions only added to the confusion. More and more of the events of the past few weeks had to be connected, but the hows and whys of those connections continued to elude me.

After several motionless seconds, while the aliens argued over the radio, the three coaxed us to our feet with their weapons and marched us into the crater toward their ship. I moved to adjust my communication unit to transmit, but a sharp prod in my back discouraged that course of action.

A circular platform, about ten feet in diameter, lowered from the belly of the light gray craft and the five of us stepped onto it. I caught a quick look at Lauri's face, which held a mixture of fear and wonder, as we shuffled into position. I did my best to project calm confidence even though my emotions were just as charged.

We rose smoothly into a dimly lit compartment. A door slid open a few feet away, but when I took a step toward it, one of our captors raised his weapon, indicating Lauri and I should stay put. I held up my hands and stood still while our abductors awkwardly backed through the door, which closed after them.

Lauri brought up her wrist and manipulated some controls. I reached over to stop her, but she shrugged me off. "Dare," I heard from my helmet's speakers. "If they wanted to kill us they certainly could have done it already. Besides, I'm pretty sure their technology is sophisticated enough to figure out I'm not doing anything threatening. I turned on communications and I'm sampling the air. They are pressurizing this room."

I chuckled with nervousness and activated my transmitter. "Yeah, I guess you're right. Were you able to hear any words before?"

She looked up from her readouts. "Words? No. It was just a bunch of noise. You heard words?"

I nodded. "Just, like random things. But, that's not the weirdest part. I recognize these guys. My instructor is one of them."

"I don't understand. If they know you, why did they act like we were dangerous?"

I shook my head. "No, I mean he is one of this species. He was plucked away from his thread just like I was from mine. At least I think so." Suddenly, I had doubts about M'sang, just as I'd had about Kim when Hope had explained a bit of her story.

"That seems like quite a coincidence."

I had to agree. "You don't know the half of it."

Lauri turned her attention back to her wrist display. "The atmosphere's stabilized. It's slightly thicker, and oxygen heavy from Earth normal, but definitely breathable. We should take advantage of their hospitality and conserve our suits. We might need them later." She reached up and cracked her seals.

I did the same, eager to be free of the confining helmet. My ears popped, adjusting to the different pressure, but the air was pleasant to breathe. I looked around and noted the room was empty, save for us, and not much bigger than the ten foot disk we'd ridden up that now composed part of the floor. The lighting remained low, but perhaps it was normal for M'sang's people. The few times I'd been able to peek in his room I hadn't seen much because he kept it rather dark.

To the left, an additional low light appeared, revealing a four foot window. Outside, from what looked like a control room of some sort, several dark, furry faces looked back with interest at Lauri and me. They varied in height, and I began to get the impression that M'sang was one of the more impressive physical representatives of his species. A good thing considering he routinely kicked my butt during our sparring sessions.

One of them leaned forward slightly and spoke, but the sound came from somewhere above us. "Greetings. Welcome aboard the scout vessel *Rhusharr*."

I raised my hand. "Hi. I'm Dare, and this is Lauri," I said.

Lauri tapped my arm. "What's going on?"

"What do you mean? He seems friendly enough."

She gave me a perplexed look. "Are you saying you understood that?"

"Well, the ship's name didn't make any sense, but that's hardly a surprise."

"Dare, all I heard was more of the odd noises we picked up outside."

Suddenly, I remembered something Kim had told me shortly after we'd first met. She had done something to my brain that allowed me to understand her and M'sang.

"Do you hail from the third planet in this system?"

I nodded. "Yes, but we have a colony on this world. What are your intentions in coming here?"

The speaker turned to his colleagues but the microphone remained on. "It gives the indication of comprehension."

"If that's the case, why can't we understand it's communications?" one of the others said.

Oh boy.

Lauri moved to stand in front of me. "Dare, what's going on?" Her eyes held more than a hint of fear.

"The Keepers made it so I can understand other languages, even alien ones, but it only works one way. I can understand them, but they can't understand us."

She turned thoughtful. "So, we need to build that understanding. Find some commonality."

"I guess, but how do we do that?"

Lauri removed the glove on her right hand and walked up to the window. Inside, some of the aliens backed away. I watched as she began drawing circles with her finger.

"What is it doing?" I heard one of our observers ask.

She pointed to each circle in turn. "Sun. Mercury. Venus. Earth. Mars." On saying the last, Lauri made a wide gesture with her arms.

I stepped closer, trying to judge the alien reactions. M'sang's facial expressions had been very different and perplexing to me, but I'd been able to figure out some of them during our training.

The original speaker moved up to the window, studying the

barely visible trails left by the oil on Lauri's fingertip. "It's a map of this star system."

I nodded vigorously and pointed to the alien who'd spoken. "Yes, that's it."

"They understand?" Lauri asked.

"That one does. Hopefully he can convince the rest," I said. Then, I pointed to myself. "Dare."

The giant rodent pointed to himself. "Ru'am Koh."

I widened my eyes and sucked in my cheeks, doing my best imitation of M'sang on the rare occasions when he was pleased with my work. I pointed back to the alien. "Ru'am Koh."

"I think it's clear they wish to communicate," Ru'am said.

"Why then did the first group attack us without provocation?" another asked.

"Fear, lack of understanding, who knows? Maybe they are politically opposed, or even a different species! Heaven knows these two look quite different from each other," Ru'am argued.

Uncertain silence followed. Ru'am continued. "Regardless, this pair seems willing to make peaceful contact. We'll keep them confined, of course, but let's take the opportunity to learn what we can."

Growls and grumbles of reluctant assent followed. It appeared to be enough for Ru'am. He pointed at one of his companions. "Get some equipment in there with them so we can hopefully speed up the communication process. How much longer does the survey team need?"

"They should be finished shortly," another alien said.

Ru'am's tiny ears perked. "Good. Prepare the ship for departure."

I took Lauri's arm and guided her away from the window as the aliens dispersed. "Looks like we'll be staying a while. What do you know about the first group that came to meet with these guys?"

"Just what we told you before, why?"

"One of our hosts said they were attacked. Do the colonists have weapons?"

Lauri shrugged. "I don't know. Probably. It doesn't mean they came out here guns blazing though."

"Yeah," I sighed. "I might have been tempted to shoot first, ask questions later, too when we got caught— if I'd had something to shoot." I sat down with my back to a wall. "Might try to get some rest. I have a feeling we're going to be plenty busy soon."

It wasn't long before Lauri and I felt the pressure of acceleration as the craft lifted from the surface. Luckily, the flight was smooth, as we had nowhere to sit but the floor and nothing to hold on to. A few minutes later, a door opened revealing a very small chamber with some electronic devices placed on a wheeled cart. I rolled the cart over to the window, where Ru'am had reappeared. The door closed behind me.

One of the devices was a hand held video screen. I removed my gloves and picked it up. Looking it over, I saw only one moving part: a button, which I pushed and activated the unit. A glance at Ru'am showed me his pleasure and he pointed at the screen. It flashed the picture of a stone and heard the word, "rock," coming from a speaker somewhere in the unit. I said, "Rock," and the picture changed to that of a small container. "Cup," it intoned, and I dutifully repeated.

I looked up at Ru'am and asked, "I don't suppose there's any way we can make this go faster?" I rolled my hand in a circular motion.

"What's the purpose of this anyway?" Lauri asked.

"Well, I guess they can learn the English equivalent of each word and picture the computer displays and build up a vocabulary."

"But they won't learn any syntax or grammar. And how can you relay higher concepts that can't be conveyed by a picture?"

"How the hell should I know? I've never done this before!" I said, my frustration boiling over.

Lauri placed a hand on my arm and I immediately felt calmer. "We need to convey to them somehow that you can understand them perfectly already," she said.

I laughed. "Well I'm all ears if you have any suggestions."

"Let me try something," she said and walked to the window. Ru'am had watched our exchange with interest, but remained quiet. Lauri put her hand flat on the pane and pointed to Ru'am.

I stepped closer, curious about what Lauri intended to do. Ru'am hesitated, then slowly lifted his arm and placed his paw-hand on the window, opposite hers. Lauri's eyes closed and her thin, white eyebrows crowded together in concentration.

Shifting my attention to Ru'am, I saw him bare his sharp teeth in surprise and he nearly pulled away. Apprehension soon gave way to curiosity, however, and he seemed to focus in on Lauri. Several seconds later, the gaze of his small, black eyes found mine and I could almost feel a spark of understanding between us.

Suddenly, Lauri groaned and fell away from the window.

I dove to the floor and managed to catch her head before it hit. Her eyes fluttered momentarily, then she regained control and smiled.

"What did you do?" I asked.

"I tried to get across the idea that you understand their language. It was a difficult concept to describe with only emotions. I'm not sure I succeeded, but it was an interesting experience. Speech, beliefs, and patterns of thought are different in everyone, but I think emotions are universal." She sighed and sat up with only a little assistance from me.

I chuckled. "How did you get so smart?"

Lauri smiled. "I told you, I've spent my entire life surrounded by scientists. I didn't have a choice."

20

"Is… is she all right?"

I looked back at the window and Ru'am, noting that Lauri had evidently portrayed the idea of gender successfully. "Yes, but we could use some water," I said, then shook my head, remembering that Ru'am still couldn't comprehend my speech.

After squeezing Lauri's shoulder, I rose and stood at the window once more. I formed my hands into a cup and tried pantomiming the act of drinking.

Ru'am quickly caught on, despite my assuredly poor acting skills. "There is a container on the second shelf of the cart. We placed several items in it from your ground vehicle."

I found the box he indicated and discovered a handful of meal packets, along with two bottles of water. I opened a bottle and handed it to Lauri, which she accepted gratefully. Taking the other bottle for myself, I turned back to Ru'am.

"You really can understand me, can't you?" he said.

I nodded. "Yes."

"Remarkable. I believe I can make some changes to the language program that should greatly increase its speed in learning. I'll return as soon as possible."

I smiled, remembering not to show my teeth. "Thank you."

He turned away and exited the observation room. I sat

down next to Lauri and sipped my water.

"So, what's going on?" she asked. "Did it work?"

"It seems so. Ru'am is going to adjust the computer somehow so it can learn English faster."

Lauri nodded. "Good. I'd hate to think I caused myself a huge headache for nothing."

"Are you okay?"

"I'll be fine. It's no worse than others I've had before when I've tried something extreme like that. I am hungry though."

I reached over and pulled the box from the cart, handing to her. "Ask and ye shall receive."

Her eyes grew wide and she selected one of the pouches and quickly got it cooking. I decided food sounded good as well and chose one for myself.

"I wonder what they did with the rest of our stuff," Lauri said.

I shrugged. "He didn't say, but it wouldn't surprise me if they brought everything on board, including the rover. The ship seemed plenty big enough. Did the colony send out any search parties when the first group didn't come back?"

"I don't know. I was too busy learning everything I could about 1997 before my jump."

"What will Dr. Lansing do when we don't return? How long will he wait for us?"

She shook her head and winced. "I'm not sure. The range of the rover is five hundred kilometers and it has about eight hours of air, plus the couple of hours in the suits. But, he'll have guessed where we went from the same projections of the alien's movements I used." Her packet finished heating and she ate as rapidly as the hot food would allow.

I chewed my food deliberately, while I sorted through the myriad thoughts hopping around in my head. According to the last transmission from Dr. Lansing, the colony director was getting ready to take action. We just didn't know what sort of action. The aliens didn't seem openly hostile, but, to be fair, we had interacted with very few of them. Their intentions for Mars and beyond were still unclear. And, past my immediate concerns, I still wasn't sure what to think of Kim, M'sang, and even Hope. Who were the Keepers really? It seemed to me that far more manipulation of the threads of time had been going on than I was originally led to believe. The truth remained shrouded and elusive.

Lauri moved over next to me while I picked over the last of my meal. "Karl will assume the worst, and rightfully so, once that ten hours of air we left with is up. We need to get these guys to let us contact him. Let him know we're okay."

"I know. But we can't do that until we can communicate in more than one direction. We still don't really have any idea what these people plan to do. They could be getting ready for an attack on the colony right now for all we know."

"I didn't get that impression from Ru'am while I was in contact with him. He wants to find a peaceful solution."

"I get that feeling, too," I said. "But he's only one of what could be thousands of people on those big ships. They may not be as understanding or patient as Ru'am."

"We're ready," the speakers in the chamber announced, startling me and Lauri. We stood up to see Ru'am back in the observation room. "The portable interface you used earlier will speak words and phrases. Just repeat them back in your own tongue and our computers should be able to begin building a lexicon to translate from."

I nodded and picked up the tablet I'd used before. It began by stating simple words, occasionally accompanied by a picture for clarification, then moved into short sentences. I repeated each one as I heard it, keeping the bottle of water close at hand.

After what felt like many hours, but was probably closer to two, I pushed the single button on the screen, hoping it would turn off, or at least pause its ceaseless litany. It worked and I sat back, reveling in the symphony of silence.

That silence was broken a few seconds later by Ru'am's voice over the speakers. "Are you all right?"

"I'm fine!" I croaked in irritation. My throat felt like it was coated in a thick layer of sand. "I just need a break. And more water."

After a pause, Ru'am said, "It's working! Water is on the way."

Silently thanking any deity who might be paying the slightest bit of attention, I slumped to the hard floor. The enforced rest, courtesy of Hope's stunner, I'd had at the Brown Palace in Denver seemed like a long time ago.

Lauri came over and placed a comforting hand on my shoulder. "And here I thought you'd never tire of the sound of your own voice."

"Ha. Ha."

"Just rest, you've earned it."

I sighed. "Unfortunately, I can't. We have to get these two peoples talking before one or the other does something stupid."

She nodded. "There's a lot of anxiety and frustration on

this ship. I believe there are about twenty crew total, but it's hard to tell for sure."

Lauri had been quiet while I'd been helping the computer learn English, but she evidently hadn't been idle. "Remember, they can likely understand a good portion of what we say in here now," I cautioned.

"Right. I don't suppose you know another language?"

I laughed. "I got kicked out of Spanish class, on the second day in ninth grade, for using a few words one of my grandparents' gardeners had taught me."

"Oh?"

"Yeah. They were rather frowned upon in polite society. The words I mean, not the gardeners."

Lauri giggled. "I see."

The airlock door opposite the observation window slid open. Lauri kindly got up to retrieve the items left for us. She brought back an open container with half a dozen bottles inside. I plucked one out and puzzled over how to open it.

"Squeeze it into your mouth," Ru'am said, startling me again.

"We really need a bell for him," I mumbled. I pointed what appeared to be the business end of the bottle toward my open mouth and squeezed. A pleasantly cool stream of fresh water hit the back of my throat. I downed the rest, noting the bottle kept constant pressure until it was empty and wondered how Ru'am's people managed that little trick. I rose and stood before the window again.

"Okay, time for the question and answer portion of the game," I said, then paused to let Ru'am's computer work through the translation.

He tilted his head down and slightly to the left, which I remembered from working with M'sang was a gesture of assent. I mentally scolded myself for not thinking to use the gesture earlier instead of nodding. I really needed more practice at this alien ambassador thing.

"Tell me about your people. Why did you come here and what do you plan to do?"

Ru'am listened to the translation, then spent a few moments in thought. I hoped he wasn't trying to come up with a plausible lie. "We come from a star system roughly forty light years from here. We've been aboard ship for over a hundred years, though the actual journey has taken somewhat longer than that."

His statement confused me until I remembered Einstein's relativity and how he said that time would slow down for someone traveling very fast with respect to those he'd left behind.

"I am fourth generation ship-born," Ru'am said. "My people have known, for seven hundred years or more, that our world was doomed. Another planet in our system had a wildly eccentric orbit. An orbit which would eventually cause it to collide with our home." He paused, collecting his thoughts. "That discovery, by a group of early astronomers, galvanized my people who, until that time, had ceaselessly squabbled and fought among themselves. It sparked an unprecedented scientific revolution that eventually led to spaceflight and our colony projects. Three fleets of three ships each set out for three different worlds that were identified as habitable."

"And Earth was one of those I'm guessing."

He tilted his head again. "Yes. We didn't know the third planet, Earth, was inhabited until we began our deceleration several years ago. After much deliberation, our ship leaders decided to divert to the fourth planet to see if it would be possible to colonize here."

I glanced over at Lauri and saw an anxious look on her face. "What's wrong?"

She let out a breath. "I'm dying to know what he's saying, but I didn't want to interrupt."

"I'm sorry," I said. "It's too easy to forget you can't hear them like I can." I quickly relayed the basics of Ru'am's story.

Lauri walked over and laid her hand on the window. "Ru'am, I'm so sorry. Your people are very brave."

He bowed slightly and folded his arms, indicating thanks, which I conveyed to her. Then he asked, "Are the two of you typical of your species?"

I glanced at Lauri's fine features and bright eyes before answering. "No. We're rather atypical I suppose."

"I suspected as much," Ru'am said. "We saw no indication of your abilities when we encountered the first group."

"What happened with that?" I asked him.

His black eyes narrowed. "It was a terrible situation. One that will be difficult to overcome for fostering relations, I'm afraid. They came with a force of twelve. At first, we thought the messages of greeting we'd been broadcasting since our arrival had finally been interpreted, but the hostile intent of your people soon became obvious. They opened fire with projectile weapons, forcing us to retaliate. We employed a broadband sonic nullifier from the ship, which is designed to be non-lethal. Due to the thin atmosphere of this planet, however, the operator used the maximum setting to insure effectiveness. When our team went to secure your unconscious people, they discovered the environment suits of three had been compromised from our weapon. The three were dead by the time we got them back to our ship."

"But the rest are still alive?"

"Yes. They are being held aboard one of our colony ships."

I translated for Lauri, yet she still seemed confused.

"If they came peacefully, why did they destroy our satellites?" she asked.

Ru'am's computer demonstrated its ability to interpret the differences in Lauri's voice from mine. He answered her question directly. "That was an unfortunate result of the method our ships use to decelerate upon entering the planetary system. It creates a gravimetric and electromagnetic disruption which your satellites were inadequately shielded to withstand."

"Wouldn't the colony on Mars have been affected too?" I asked him.

"Possibly, but I believe it was on the far side of the planet at the time of our arrival. So, the planet itself would have protected it."

After relaying Ru'am's information to her, Lauri posed an interesting question. "What about satellites that were also on the far side of Mars at the time? Wouldn't they have been protected too?"

Ru'am inclined his head to the affirmative. "That is correct. We show two satellites as still operational. However, they have both gone silent since our arrival."

"I don't get it," I said to Lauri after restating Ru'am's words. "Didn't Dr. Lansing say that all the satellites were destroyed?"

"As far as I knew, they were," she replied.

"Seems like we haven't been getting the whole story."

"I've known Karl nearly all my life," Lauri said. "He wouldn't have any reason to lie to me."

"Which leaves the colony director."

"Ruschick," she said with venom.

"But what would he have to gain from attacking Ru'am's people and lying to Dr. Lansing?"

Lauri shook her head. "I don't know."

I turned back to our host— it felt like a better term than jailor or captor and I'd had too many of both lately. "Ru'am, we really need to get a message to Dr. Lansing. Let him know we're okay and that Director Ruschick is withholding information from him."

"That may be difficult. My superiors have been increasingly pessimistic about a peaceful resolution to our situation."

"What do you mean?" I asked him.

"Our fleet's resources were designed to last for a specific amount of time. Your colony's water source, and other assets, are vital to our survival since we diverted from our original destination. Sentiment is growing for plans to take what we need by force."

That didn't sound good at all. "Is there anyone we can talk to? Convince them we humans aren't all bloodthirsty war mongers?"

"The last bit didn't translate, but I think I understand. I will see what I can do. The survey team will be finishing up soon. I must make preparations for departure."

"Just out of curiosity, what exactly are you looking for in your survey?" I asked.

"Gathering general information about the planet, of course, but mostly we are trying to determine if it's possible to stimulate activity in the planet's core. Some time in the distant past, the interior of this world fell dormant. Geologic activity ceased and the planet's magnetic field grew too weak to protect the atmosphere from your star's solar wind. If we can reactivate the core, it's possible the planet could eventually become habitable again."

Astounded, I said, "You can do that?"

Ru'am chuffed in amusement. "That's what we want to find out. I'll return as soon as I can."

21

Alone once again, Lauri and I discussed our situation after I shared Ru'am's last tidbits.

"How much longer before Dr. Lansing would assume our air supply was gone?"

Lauri checked a display on the forearm of her suit. "About five hours. Maybe less."

"And we don't know what Ruschick was up to, though, if he had sent out another party to attack the surveyors, you'd think Ru'am would have told us."

"Makes sense," Lauri agreed. "Whatever he's planning, though, I'm sure it won't be good."

"What's his deal?" I asked her. "I mean, it's hard to believe everyone hates him like you do or else how would he be in charge of the colony?"

"You have to understand, Dare, those who've been sent to Mars weren't necessarily the best and brightest. It's a hard life and the ones that agreed to come often had no alternatives. Many of the colonists are simple laborers who couldn't find work and refused to submit themselves to a labor camp back on Earth."

"Labor camp?"

"They're called 'Infrastructure Initiatives' by Earth's various governments, but 'labor camp' is a better description. People who get themselves too far in debt, and don't have any other useful skills, are given the opportunity to work in an Initiative to get back on their feet. Very few, however, ever manage to work their way out once they've joined."

"Sounds like slavery," I said.

Lauri nodded. "It's the same in many ways, but the governments are always quick to point out that it is a choice, and widely publicize the handful of success stories— people who rejoined regular society— to deflect that label. Mars is offered as a last alternative to the truly desperate."

"So, what's Ruschick's story? Was he one of these downtrodden folks who climbed above it all?"

She shook her head. "He came about twenty years ago to be the facility's administrator. Everyone assumes he must have gotten in some sort of trouble on Earth to get himself shipped out here, but it's all just rumor and speculation."

I thought about this and tried to make some connections. Obviously, the guy was more than a bit off if he'd asked a scientist to genetically engineer him a living blow-up doll. But what benefit could he derive by provoking the aliens to attack the colony? He must have realized they possessed superior technology. And why hadn't he been using the working satellites to scream to Earth that Mars was under attack if he thought the aliens were hostile? I couldn't just chalk it all up to the guy being a few cards short of a a full deck. So, what was the angle? "Is he in charge of the Hub, too then?"

"I'm not sure, honestly," Lauri said. "Karl checks in with Ruschick often, but I don't think the other scientists have much to do with him. They always talk privately. I think Karl wants to protect me from him."

I felt like I was trying to put together a picture with pieces from about ten different puzzles. Nothing fit. "When he told you to show me around, Dr. Lansing said he needed to update Ruschick on his progress. Ruschick knows Lansing built a time machine?"

Lauri nodded. "Karl told him our plan to keep Ruschick from sending an armed force to retaliate against the aliens when the first group didn't return. We thought the original party was supposed to try to make peaceful contact. Obviously, Ruschick lied about that as well as the satellites."

"Do you think the first group might have acted on their own? Gotten scared, or trigger happy?"

She shrugged. "Could be I suppose. But there's still the satellites."

I sighed in frustration. Someone was hiding the truth and I didn't believe it was Ru'am. Had that belief grown from the seeds of my relationship with M'sang and a toy I received for my fifth birthday? Why was I willing to trust an alien above someone of my own species?

Because I understood what humans were capable of.

I tried a different tack. "Do you think Ruschick knows what the other scientists were working on in the Hub?"

"Probably, yeah. He knew enough to ask Dr. Kritchkopf to create me."

"Right. So, are there any projects going on that might be valuable in some way?"

Lauri laughed. "You mean like a time machine?"

"Okay, yeah. But I'm assuming for a minute that Ruschick didn't know about that before. Is there anything else? You said the Hub sends energy to the colony. How is it made?"

"Dare, there are twenty or thirty scientists— maybe more— in the Hub, working on things thought to be too dangerous to be carried out on Earth. If any one of them were successful, the results would be priceless. As far as energy goes, you name it, we've probably got it. Nuclear, both fission and fusion, geothermal, microscopic antimatter detonations, and I think there was even one person working on direct matter to energy transformation. I see the connection you're trying to make, but how would Ruschick ever hope to profit from any of it? He's stuck on Mars."

"Not if he gets control of something that can transport him through time and space."

Lauri's eyes grew wide. "Oh! But wait, he can't use it. It'll be weeks before Karl can store enough energy to activate it again."

"Is Ruschick aware of that?"

"I don't know."

The line of thought felt plausible, even right, but we were still stuck inside a spaceship, at the mercy of an alien race.

Movement in the window caught my eye. Ru'am had returned. "I've been given permission to show you around the ship. I'll meet you at the airlock," he said, pointing to the doors where we'd previously received supplies.

I smiled. "That's great! Thank you."

Eager for some exercise and new scenery, Lauri and I impatiently waited for the door to open. It finally slid aside and Ru'am was there to greet us. Slightly shorter than the two of us, his black eyes looked up and searched our faces while his nose appeared to be working overtime. I noted he bore a faint, musty odor, similar, but weaker than M'sang's had been.

Ru'am chuffed and shook his head. "Fascinating. Your odors are so different. Not entirely unpleasant," he said and then handed Lauri a small, odd looking device. "I apologize if the fit is poor. Your ears are so large and located down on the sides of your heads, it was difficult to create something that would work."

"Work for what?" I asked him.

"Translation. The unit is connected to our computer. It should offer Lauri at least rudimentary understanding."

I explained to her what Ru'am intended and helped her fit the piece around her ear. It hung awkwardly, but looked like it would stay put. "Okay," I said. "Let's see if it works."

"Greetings, Lauri," Ru'am said. "Welcome aboard the *Rhusharr*."

Lauri smiled. "I understand. The voice is a little rough, but it's good."

"Excellent!" our furry ambassador said, puffing his cheeks. "All of us on board wear a communication device in our ear and I've programmed the ship's computer to automatically translate to us when you speak."

I grinned, glad to be relieved of my translation duties for Lauri. "So, let's have a look at this ship of yours."

There wasn't much to see, in all honesty, one bulkhead looked just the same as another, but it was very nice to be able to stretch our legs. Our tour ended on the ship's bridge: a space somewhat smaller than the cargo hold we'd previously called home, but filled with many video screens and other equipment. Four of the hamster-folk sat at consoles, busy with whatever tasks were required to operate a spaceship. They could have been playing video games for all I knew.

"Ru'am, I've been meaning to ask you, what do you call yourselves?"

"Generally, we refer to ourselves as 'pahsahni', which is an ancient word that simply means 'the people'. Does the word 'human' have some other meaning for you?"

"I'm not sure. Earth has so many languages, it's hard to say."

"It comes from Latin," Lauri offered. "Humanus, meant 'man', or 'of man'."

I chuckled. "Well, Ru'am, there you go. Thank you, Professor," I said to Lauri. She responded by jabbing me in the ribs with her elbow.

Nonplussed by our antics, Ru'am said, "If you'll take a seat back here, we will be leaving shortly." He motioned to a bank of four empty chairs against the back wall of the bridge.

Lauri and I sat as instructed and buckled ourselves into the simple harnesses attached to the functional, if not overly comfortable, seats. Ru'am took a station to our left and busied himself at its controls. The view out the front window showed a Martian twilight, the sun having set just a few minutes earlier. The ship rose smoothly and I felt my body pressing firmly into the unforgiving cushion. Soon, the acceleration leveled off and the added pressure relented.

Ru'am rejoined us as Lauri and I released our restraints. "Our surveys are complete. Now we must go over the data we gathered and find out if there is any hope of making this planet habitable again."

One of the other pahsahni came back to address Ru'am. "Academician, we received a transmission intended for the human's land vehicle, right before take off. The content is rather… puzzling."

Ru'am cocked his head in confusion. "Transfer it to this screen, please."

The three of us moved over to the viewer Ru'am had indicated. Seconds later, a static-filled image of Dr. Lansing appeared. "How's the weather out there my little Pixie?" I felt Lauri bristle next to me and Lansing continued, "I wish you hadn't gone out alone, but your friends are here waiting for you. Oh, and remember that the front door is locked when you get back. Take care." The image faded and I had to agree with Ru'am's assessment of the message.

"What the hell was that?" I asked.

"Karl's in trouble. I think Ruschick put together a force and took over the Hub."

"What?"

Lauri sighed. "The message was all code because Karl evidently thought it might be intercepted. He and I always say that Ruschick is like the weather: everyone talks about him but no one does anything about him. You know, like that Mark Twain quote. He threw the pixie thing in there just to get my attention. Dr. Kritchkopf used to call me that and I hated it. Anyway, Karl knew you were with me and I wasn't alone, plus I don't have any friends to wait for me. His comment about the front door being locked is probably a warning that the security system's been reactivated and Ruschick will be watching for us."

"This 'Ruschick' is the leader of your outpost?" Ru'am asked.

I pursed my lips. "He's the leader of the colony, yes, and the more I find out about him, the less I like him. The Hub is a place away from the colony where a lot of scientific experiments are taking place. Lauri believes Ruschick has taken it over. I think he might be looking for a way to get off Mars."

"Or maybe a weapon to use against you," Lauri added.

Ru'am made a gesture of understanding. "We noted a number of unusual energy readings coming from what I assume is the place you describe."

"We need to stop him before he does something stupid and dangerous. Well, more so than he's already done," I said. "Will you help us?"

Ru'am appeared conflicted and paused several seconds before answering. "I cannot. The ships' leaders met a short time ago and have decided to proceed with a plan to appropriate your colony. I've been ordered to keep you under observation."

I groaned and Lauri asked, "What does that mean?"

"They're going to attack," I answered.

"No! What about all the people?"

Ru'am said, "The plan is to use every non-lethal means at our disposal, but the source of water and food production facilities were simply too tempting for the leaders to pass up."

I asked, "What if the colonists mount a resistance?"

Ru'am hung his head, a gesture that needed no translating.

"Dammit, there must be something we can do," I said. "When is this happening?"

"The teams are being assembled as we speak. They will depart within the hour."

22

"An hour?!" The whole situation was getting worse by the second. "Ru'am, you have to let us go in with you."

He puffed his cheeks. "Dare, I don't see how that will be possible. The leadership was reluctant to allow me to show you around this vessel. I'm sure they won't approve of you accompanying a military mission against your people."

A wave of dizziness swept over me and the whole world felt fuzzy. I found myself sitting on the floor with my back to the wall and Lauri knelt at my side.

"Dare!" She reached for my face. "Are you all right?"

I caught her hand with my own and felt a rush of worry and fright. Those feelings mixed uneasily with a sense of dread growing in the pit of my stomach. "I… I think so. But, something just happened. Changed, maybe. I don't know."

"Might just be everything catching up with you. We've been running mostly on adrenaline for a while now," she said.

I shook my head. "I don't think that's it. What were we talking about?"

"You asked Ru'am to let us go with them to the colony. He said it wasn't going to happen and then you got all jelly-legged."

"Yeah. I remember now." I looked up at our host. "Wait, we're on our way back to your base ships?"

"Yes," Ru'am answered. "Are you sure you don't require medical attention?"

"I'll be okay. My head's clearing now. But we have to turn around."

"Why?"

"I just have a feeling…"

I looked out through the main viewport, seeing the deep black of space, filled with thousands of brilliant pinpricks of light. Suddenly, a blinding flash filled the window, causing all of us to flinch away. Seconds later, the ship shuddered and alarms sounded throughout the bridge.

Lauri's sea blue eyes met mine and I knew she'd picked up on the despair I felt building within my gut.

Ru'am shouted orders and the rest of the pahsahni frantically moved to obey. The ship ceased trembling just as two more intense flashes burst forth outside, rocking our craft unsteadily once more. The waves passed and slowly the sounds of alarm quieted.

Without warning, Ru'am shoved Lauri aside and pinned my shoulders painfully against the hull. "What did you do?! How did you know!" he shouted, sharp teeth flashing.

I struggled against his weight, but the scientist was surprisingly strong. The dark orbs of Ru'am's eyes bulged with rage. "What was that?" I asked, fearing his response.

"Our ships— our homes— have been destroyed! Over fifteen thousand people— possibly the last of my people— gone! But you knew!"

"Ru'am, I swear to you I didn't know. I felt something, but I had no idea what it was. This is wrong and wasn't supposed to happen."

My statement confused him, giving momentary pause to his anger. "What do you mean?"

I had an idea, but I knew he wouldn't be easy to convince. "What if I told you there might be a way to make this right? To fix the damage that's been done."

"Impossible! How?"

I glanced at Lauri, who had backed away from the two of us. Her eyes were filled with tears and I knew she was feeling the effects from the raw emotion pouring off of Ru'am and the other pahsahni on the bridge. Turning back to him, I said, "There's a device within the complex outside the colony that can help us. Something capable of undoing this."

Ru'am's black nose wrinkled in disbelief. "Preposterous! You're making up nonsense in an effort to save your miserable life. I should throw you out the nearest airlock! Let space suck the air from your treacherous lungs!"

Panic rose in me. "Ru'am, please! I'm not lying to you." I decided to take a chance and appeal to his baser instincts. "Besides, wouldn't you rather kill me yourself, with your own hands?" I recalled a proverb of his people M'sang had said to me during one of our training sessions. "Claws and teeth sharpened from an enemy's bones shine brighter."

I read an expression of shock on his face. "Where did you hear that?"

"A recent teacher of mine, one of your species, M'sang Tah, told it to me."

"M'sang Tah? Your teacher? That's not possible. He was one of our most revered astronauts, but an experimental craft he flew was lost over two hundred years ago! You must have heard his name from someone on the ship," Ru'am said in dismissal, but his grip on me lessened slightly.

An astronaut? Interesting. At least I knew when M'sang had been recruited by the Keepers, for all the good that knowledge would do me. "How? We've only talked with you since we've been on board. Besides, where would I have heard the proverb? We don't have claws and humans rarely fight with our teeth."

Lauri collected herself and moved closer to the angered scientist. "Dare is telling the truth, Ru'am. We may be able to fix this, if you'll let us."

Ru'am hesitated. He was clearly conflicted, but some of his murderous rage had ebbed away.

I pressed him. "What do you have to lose? If we succeed, your people could be saved. If not, you can take your revenge on me any way you like."

"All right," Ru'am finally said, sitting back. "I'm listening. What do you propose?"

Turning to Lauri, I asked, "Can you deactivate the Hub's security system again?"

She thought briefly, then shook her head. "They would detect us before I could get close enough to work with the computer."

"Hm. Ru'am, do you have anything on board that might shield us from their sensors?"

"I don't know. Possibly. I would need to know the exact technology they operated with—"

"Oh! Wait," Lauri said. "The conduit tunnel!"

"What's that?" I asked, getting caught up in her excitement.

"In order to move the energy generated in the Hub to the

colony, the engineers constructed an underground line between the two. Basically, it's a huge, encased wire, but the point is they built a tight tunnel around it, with access points every couple of kilometers for maintenance purposes. We'll have to walk a long way, but it should get us in undetected."

"What about the colony? Don't they have sensors too?"

She nodded. "Yes, but they're not as sophisticated. The range on the Hub's is about twenty kilometers. As long as we enter the tunnel beyond that, we should be okay."

Twenty kilometers would certainly be a long walk, but it sounded doable. "What do you think, Ru'am?"

"What is the plan after we get in?"

"We'll need to find Dr. Lansing— he's the one from the message you received. After that, I'm not sure," I said. "We'll have to play the rest by ear."

"How will playing with our ears help?"

I laughed. "Sorry, just an expression. It means doing things without a plan. Without knowing the situation inside, it's hard to predict what we'll need to do."

"I see," Ru'am responded pensively. "I will present the idea to the rest of the crew. Although what you offer is only faint hope, it is hope. In the meantime, I think it would be best for the two of you to return to the hold."

I indicated my understanding and Ru'am escorted us back to our makeshift cell. After he left and the door slid closed, I said to Lauri, "If they don't kill us in the next hour or so I think we'll be fine."

"That's comforting," she said. "What was that, Dare? Did you know the ships would explode?"

"No. I'm not sure what happened, but I think someone altered the time thread. Those ships were not supposed to blow up, but something changed."

"How do you know that?"

"I don't. But it feels right. I can't explain it. We have to get to Lansing's machine and see if we can fix this."

Lauri took my arm and gave me a friendly pat. "I hope we get the chance."

"Me too."

Ru'am's people were resilient and at least somewhat forgiving; less than an hour later, he came to the observation window and told us to suit up. We felt the ship land, then Ru'am ushered us outside to board an eight-seated vehicle hovering placidly a foot or so over the Martian sand. Lauri and I sat together in the middle of three burly hamster-folk who wore armored environment suits. One seat, in the back, was filled with equipment and Ru'am climbed in after us, taking the last unoccupied chair next to the driver up front.

Wide windows flanked the sides of the transport, offering a clear view of the lifeless terrain. Night had descended, filling the sky with a bounty of stars, shining brightly through the planet's thin atmosphere. I tried to forget the blinding light I'd seen earlier during my last look into space. The craft lifted slightly higher, then moved forward at an impressive rate of speed. After a minute or two, the pahsahni removed their helmets. Lauri and I followed their lead. The scent of the furry aliens was much more pungent in the closeness of the vehicle.

Ru'am turned in his seat and my eyes met his. I didn't need Lauri's abilities to see the pain there. "The consensus was not total, but we have decided to give your plan a try. As you said, what have we to lose? We are headed to a place midway between the colony and this Hub of yours. From there, Lauri, you can guide us to one of the access points you spoke of."

Lauri nodded. "The tunnel is small and unpressurized. We'll have to travel single file and remain fully suited. Radio silence will also be necessary."

Ru'am gestured assent. "Understood. This transport is equipped with technology that should confuse or disrupt any sensory devices your people may employ. For now, attempt to rest. We will have a long trek ahead of us."

I wanted to say something to ease his loss, but no words came. Any apology I might make seemed hollow in the wake of the suffering Ru'am and his crew were going through. If our plan didn't succeed, I had no doubt he would collect on my offer. Any pain I felt, however, would end quickly compared to the burden of emptiness he and his people would carry for the rest of their lives.

23

Ru'am's voice startled me awake. "We're here. The power conduit is beneath us. Which way should we go, Lauri?"

I rubbed my eyes, surprised that I'd fallen asleep, but I did feel a little more energetic.

"How far are we from the Hub?" she asked.

Ru'am checked some of the instruments in front of him. "A little over twenty-eight kilometers."

"Okay, head south, towards the Hub. We should find a maintenance door before we enter their sensor range," she said.

Our craft turned and began running perpendicular to our previous course. Night still ruled the barren landscape, starlight rendering the normally reddish rocks and sand in blacks and grays. My suppositions about the pahsahni's eyesight proved true as the driver appeared to have no difficulty navigating around the larger rocks littering the ground. The ride would have been far bumpier if I'd been at the controls.

After a few minutes, Lauri leaned forward and pointed. "There."

The driver cocked his head in acknowledgement. "I see it."

Lauri's night vision must have been better than mine as well, for it wasn't until several seconds later that I realized what I'd thought was a boulder was actually a manhole protruding from the ground. Of course, I told my bruised ego, it must have helped to know what to look for. Unfortunately, my ego didn't buy it.

We slowed to a smooth stop and Lauri spoke again. "Ru'am, how much air supply do your suits carry?"

"They each have enough for about six hours, depending on exertion."

Lauri closed her eyes briefly. "That will be cutting it close. There are refilling stations every five hundred meters in the tunnel, but I doubt your connections will match."

Ru'am said, "Pergru Rin will carry an extra unit we can share if it becomes necessary."

"Okay," she said, then turned to me. "Dare, you and I will need to refill our supplies a couple of times along the way. Everyone remember it's radio silence after your suits are sealed. The Hub is pressurized so we can unsuit once we're inside. The tunnel is tight, but pretty smooth. Still, be careful not to snag your suit on anything. Any questions?"

The pahsahni sitting next to me leaned forward. "No tricks, human. We will avenge our people… by any means necessary."

Lauri bravely reached over and clasped the big alien's hand. "If we succeed, no avenging will be required. Dare and I want this to work just as much as you."

He tensed at her touch and broke contact after she spoke, but his demeanor softened slightly. "We'll see," he said.

"All right," Ru'am announced. "Equip your headgear and check your seals."

I gave Lauri's gloved hand a squeeze and went about the business of making sure I didn't die after the transport's hatch opened.

A short time later, we stood outside in the hostile Martian night while Lauri bent over the control panel for the tunnel access door. After keying in a few commands, she twisted the wheel and pulled open the circular portal, revealing a ladder leading underground. She descended, followed by Ru'am and one of the other pahsahni. My turn came next, then the last two members of our escort trailed me, closing the door behind them.

The space was indeed cramped as Lauri had described. Lights, mounted on the ceiling every twenty yards or so, created a dizzying infinity effect as I peered down the tunnel—like looking at a mirror image of yourself from another mirror. On my left, a huge number of dark, metallic pipes ran as far I could see in both directions. The pipes varied in size from a couple of inches to almost two feet in diameter. I had no idea how anyone would know which was which, or how to repair them if they broke. The walkway where we stood was less than three feet wide and only marginally taller than me. It took a conscious effort not to hunch over for fear of hitting my head on the ceiling.

Lauri set a brisk pace, made easier by the light gravity of the planet. I did my best to settle into the rhythm of the hike and not think about the tight space or seemingly endless tunnel we traversed.

An indicator flashed on my wrist readout, telling me I had less than thirty minutes of air. We stopped for a quick rest at the next oxygen supply station. I sucked some water from the tube inside my helmet, then watched a comical bout of hand waving between Lauri and Ru'am. My amusement ended when Ru'am and the pahsahni immediately in front of me crouched down and Lauri waved for me to come forward. Realizing she needed to help me fill up my tank, I climbed awkwardly over the two aliens to stand by her side. Ru'am stood up and I tried to wordlessly convey my apologies if I'd accidentally stepped on anything tender. I couldn't read his expression through his faceplate. It might have been apathy, or disgust, or something else completely alien to me. Lauri topped off my air supply and we were off again, with me at her back.

I focused on the fabric of Lauri's suit, watching the shadows under the folds flex and move, becoming more distinct as we passed under one of the tunnel's lamps before fading in the dimmer light between. The pattern continued monotonously until we stopped for air once more.

Sweat ran from every pore in my skin, causing the clothing I wore under the environment suit to cling uncomfortably. If not for the weak Martian gravity and Kim's biological adjustments to my body, I probably would have collapsed before our first oxygen refill.

I pressed my faceplate to hers. "How much farther?"

"Five or six kilometers I think. We're making good time."

If she had said a thousand miles, I doubt my body would have reacted differently. I forced myself to simply nod, however, and Lauri disconnected my suit's hoses after the indicators turned green. She looked past me to Ru'am, making sure they were ready before turning and walking again through the claustrophobic nightmare.

Some time later, the pattern of shadows on Lauri's back changed and I nearly stumbled into her when she stopped.

Startled by the transition, I felt like I'd just woken from

an unexpected nap, so focused— or maybe unfocused— my mind had been. The tunnel had widened by a foot or so to accommodate an imposing metal door and an instrument panel. Lauri set to work on the controls while the rest of us leaned heavily against the wall or the pipes for support.

After a minute or less at the panel, Lauri grasped the wheel in the center of the door, turned it to the left, and pulled. Dust puffed away from the outer edges as air escaped from inside. I helped her swing the heavy metal portal open, and the seven of us bustled into the tiny room beyond, standing shoulder to shoulder. Once the outer door had been resealed, Lauri worked her magic on the controls beside the inner hatchway. After many hours in the suit, I was eager to breathe something other than my own stench.

A light above the door turned from red to green and Lauri checked the readings on her wrist display before unsealing her headgear. The rest of us did likewise, but the air wasn't quite as fresh as I'd imagined in the close quarters. I couldn't recall M'sang ever being as malodorous as these pahsahni. They were clearly tired; some had their mouths hanging open, almost panting like dogs. Then, the thought occurred to me that maybe M'sang had never exerted himself enough while training me to cause his body to produce unpleasant smells.

Or, Kim had manipulated him so he wouldn't stink. Yes, that sounded much more plausible to my already suffering self confidence.

Lauri addressed us in a quiet voice. "Okay. I think I've deactivated any alarms that would alert someone about the airlock being cycled. I've also turned off all the cameras and motion sensors in the Hub. Beyond the door is a long hallway that leads into the Hub itself. You'll start to feel the gravity increase as we go."

"Are you capable of determining the number of enemies we face?" Ru'am asked.

"Not exactly," Lauri answered with a frown. "The residents of the Hub all have a locater chip embedded in their skin. Once we get to one of the Hub's computer terminals inside, I can find their locations within the base, but I don't know if members of the colony have something similar, or what frequency to look for if they do."

"Very well. Some information is better than none," Ru'am said. "Sah'ano Dem, from this point forward, this is a military mission and I defer to your leadership."

"Thank you, Learned One. I will work to reward your trust," said the pahsahni who had spoken to Lauri in the transport. "Human female, do you know the location of the device we seek?"

I bristled at his tone and saw Lauri do the same before she answered, "Yes. I know every inch of this place."

"Good. Then please open the portal and get down in case we have opposition beyond."

I exchanged a glance with her before helping with the door. We pushed it open and crouched out of the way. Our caution proved unwarranted as the long, straight hall was well lit and empty.

We spilled into the corridor, gratefully exiting the confines of the airlock. The pahsahni immediately went to work unpacking equipment and weapons, while Lauri closed and resealed the door.

"I reactivated the airlock alarms," she told me when she'd finished. "Now we just need to get to a regular terminal so I can locate Karl."

"Do you think it's possible that he and Directer Ruschick are working together?" I asked her.

She answered without hesitation. "No. Karl would never do anything that would lead to loss of life. Not willingly anyway. If Ruschick did somehow use the time machine to blow up those ships, he did it without Karl's help."

"Okay. I'm just trying to look at this from every angle. We've had too many surprises up to this point. I'd like to avoid any more if we can," I said.

She nodded, then focused her attention over my shoulder.

"Human female," Sah'ano said behind me. "Can you provide us with a map of this facility?"

Lauri's eyes narrowed. "Yes, once we reach one of the regular computer stations. There is one a few meters beyond the end of this hallway."

I turned and faced the burly pahsahni. "Why won't you use her name?"

His nose twitched. "Neither of you has earned a name. The esteemed Ru'am Koh has been polite with you in the interest of fostering relations. I have no such interest. I have a task to perform."

"Yeah, you do," I said. "A task that requires our help, so a little politeness on your part might make things go a bit smoother."

"Maybe. But the task would not be necessary if not for the heinous actions of your people, so I choose to hold politeness in reserve."

"We don't know for sure that it was our people who destroyed your ships," I pointed out.

Sah'ano cocked his head to the right and puffed his cheeks. "Who else could it be, Human? I see no one else here."

I wanted to tell him that the universe was a much bigger place than he imagined, but I knew arguing was pointless. Besides, who was I to try to explain a broader view of life? My universe had consisted of finding my next meal and catching a movie when I had the chance only a few weeks before. "Fine. Let's both do our jobs and see if we can fix this mess."

"Agreed. The next objective is finding her a computer so we can develop a plan of attack." Sah'ano gestured and barked orders to his comrades.

Two of the pahsahni carried impressive looking weapons and took the lead. Sah'ano walked directly behind them with a smaller weapon in one hand and some sort of sensory device in the other. Ru'am trailed him, right in front of Lauri and me. Behind us, the last pahsahni guarded our rear, and probably kept an eye on us two suspicious humans as well.

I felt heavier and more tired the farther we went, then I remembered the gravity. After hours of walking in less than half of Earth normal, my body protested at being subjected to the stronger force.

The long hall ended in another metallic portal. It opened easily, revealing a corridor perpendicular to the one we exited. Lauri hustled to the terminal and began entering commands. Soon, she had a schematic of the Hub up on the screen. The place was only slightly less confusing viewed as a whole than it had been wandering around inside with her previously. She tapped the pad several more times and a number of small red dots appeared within the map, nearly all of which were crowded in one location.

"These represent all the people who live and work in the Hub," she said to me and the pahsahni peering over her shoulders.

"Looks like there's a party going on," I said.

She nodded. "That's the mess hall we ate in before. It looks like Ruschick has all the other scientists, except Karl, gathered there. Karl is here, in his lab." Lauri pointed at a room some distance away from the main group of lights.

"Who is this?" Ru'am asked, indicating a single dot at the far edge of the map.

"Crap," Lauri said. "That's me! I didn't think about my own tracker."

"And there's no way to determine the number or distribution of the enemy?" Sah'ano said.

"I could turn the Hub's cameras and motion sensors back on for a minute and see what we get, but the more I monkey with the system, the more likely it is someone will notice," Lauri responded. "Just the presence of my tracking chip may have tipped them off already," she lamented.

I put a hand on her shoulder. "It's all right. We couldn't have gotten here without you."

"Still, I should have thought of it."

Ru'am interrupted. "What's done is done." I smiled privately at the irony of that statement, considering what we were attempting to do. He continued, "Knowing this Ruschick, can you make a guess at how many people he may have brought with him?"

Lauri sighed. "I don't know. I can't imagine too many. There were, what, a dozen men in the group that first attacked you, right? There's about a thousand colonists, but many are scientists, engineers, and the like. There can't be too many that have any sort of military training. Plus, he knew he was just rounding up a bunch of researchers here that wouldn't put up much, if any, resistance."

Sah'ano grumbled. "We must assume we are outnumbered. Still, if he is holding prisoners here," he said, pointing to the cluster of dots, "they are probably guarded by at least some of his force."

"Are you suggesting we free the captives?" Ru'am asked.

"No. I'm only making the assertion that our opposition is likely split up and we know where some of them probably are."

"Where we need to go is here," I said, stabbing my finger at Dr. Lansing's position.

Ru'am had another question. "What are these dimmed areas?"

"Those are under permanent seal," Lauri said. "Places where an experiment went wrong or became too dangerous to—"

A loud bang reverberated down the corridor, followed by shots from a variety of weapons.

"Get down!" Sah'ano shouted, aiming his own gun toward the disturbance.

I pulled Lauri from the computer screen and we landed in a heap next to Ru'am on the hard floor. The pahsahni continued to fire at their attackers.

Lauri brushed aside some white locks of hair that had fallen in her face. "Dare, we have to put doors between us. Block them off."

I nodded understanding and nudged Ru'am's arm. "Tell them to fall back. Get to the next hatchway," I said, pointing down the hall away from the fighting. I began crawling in the direction I'd indicated, while keeping an eye on Lauri next to me. The door in question was only about twenty feet away, but it felt like a mile.

Behind me I heard, "Sah'ano Dem! Retreat to the next doorway." More gunfire obscured the response.

As we crawled, I asked Lauri, "Is there any way to lock the doors?"

"Not directly," she answered. "But there might be a way to slow them down."

We reached the hatch and crawled through. Our rearguard pahsahni was already there, crouched next to the opening and firing in short bursts down the hall. Ru'am followed us through seconds later.

The bulkhead of the door offered some cover on either side. I stood and tried to make myself as skinny as possible against the wall. Lauri did the same on the opposite side while fishing through her pockets. Another pahsahni came through under cover fire from his comrade. Sah'ano backed in next, dragging the body of the last pahsahni.

"Close it!" he ordered.

The metal door clanged shut under the weight of two of our alien friends, who then twisted the wheel, sliding a metal bar to the latched position.

"Don't let go!" Lauri shouted as she found the object she'd been searching for: the cutting tool she'd used in Denver to break my bindings. She stepped forward and applied it to the latching mechanism. "Dammit! I'm out of power. Are your weapons energy based?" she asked.

Sah'ano stood. "I understand. Move aside."

Lauri backed away and the imposing pahsahni made an adjustment on his weapon before discharging it at the edge of the door. Sparks flew and an acrid smell stung my nose. He then motioned for the two holding the wheel to move and fired several bursts. Metal melted and re-solidified into a contorted mess. Tendrils of smoke drifted from the ruined wheel.

Something banged twice on the other side of the door and I heard a muffled shout. "That ought to hold them for a little while at least," I said.

"Long enough to find a better defensive position I hope," Sah'ano confirmed, then addressed Ru'am, who knelt beside the fallen pahsahni. "Please activate the splint function in Birin Seb's suit so Pergru Rin and I can carry him easier."

Ru'am looked up. "Birin Seb is journeying down the long tunnel. He's gone."

Sah'ano and the rest of the pahsahni lowered their heads. I looked down at Birin Seb. The right side of his suit was soaked with dark, red blood, some of which pooled on the floor. I hadn't known his name until after he'd died.

After bending over and running his hand over the wound, Sah'ano stepped in front of me. "This blood," he said, wiping it across my chest, "is yours. As is all of those who died in orbit around this miserable rock. I will see you to this machine you say can make things right. But when your lies are exposed, I will collect all the blood you've stolen."

Solemnly, I inclined my head. "I understand."

Sah'ano looked back at his brethren. "Gather Birin Seb's communicator and other equipment. And give the human his weapon." The imposing pahsahni commander then focused on me. "He can't harm us any more than he already has."

24

After quick instructions from Pergru Rin on the operation of the cumbersome rifle, we headed into the Hub, following Lauri's lead.

"How long will it take them to find a way around?" Sah'ano asked.

"Several minutes," Lauri replied. "Even if they are familiar with the place, which I'm pretty sure they aren't."

We climbed up a ladder, hidden in a shadowy alcove, to another level. "Where are we going anyway?" I asked her.

"There's a secondary access to the mess hall, but it's rarely used because it runs by one of the sections under seal. I'm betting they won't have it guarded."

"How will we get to Dr. Lansing?"

"One thing at a time, Dare. One thing at a time."

Lauri led us through so many corridors, rooms, ladders, and stairways, I expected to see a giant block of cheese appear before us as a reward for running the maze. The weapon the pahsahni had given me wasn't particularly heavy, but it was awkward, especially climbing ladders and maneuvering through tight staircases. I hoped Ru'am's people built things tough. As often as I'd banged the rifle against walls and railings, I'd consider myself lucky if it didn't blow up in my face the first time I fired it.

After passing a darkened, connecting hallway, Lauri hesitated, then continued on through another portal.

"Something wrong?" I asked her quietly.

She shook her head. "I'm fine."

"Down!" Sah'ano ordered from behind us.

A blast of hot energy crackled over my head, impacting a wall several feet ahead. Shouts from human voices reached my ears a second later, followed by the blasts of returned gunfire.

I pulled the rifle from my shoulder and pointed it down the corridor, cringing slightly as I depressed the trigger. A barely visible wave of energy, like heat coming off a road in summertime, filled the hallway, momentarily blocking the sound coming from ahead of me.

"Narrow the beam," Sah'ano instructed as he fired his own weapon again.

Struggling to remember what Pergru had showed me, I found a dial on the side and twisted it. Taking aim again, I pulled the trigger. A tightly confined ray of force erupted from the muzzle and the rifle's kick knocked me off balance.

"Dare, be careful!" Lauri admonished. "We are underground, but if you blow a big enough hole down here, we'll all be dead."

I looked down the hallway and stared in shock at what I'd done. A corner of the next intersection had melted away almost two feet.

Sah'ano grumbled. "Dial it back a setting or two, Human."

A shout rose up from our attackers, who'd been startled to silence by my unintentional barrage of destruction, and they began firing in earnest again.

Ru'am called from behind. "This way!"

I crept backward at Sah'ano's side after adjusting my gun and firing another shot, powerful, but somewhat less devastating than the previous.

"No! That's a dead end!" Lauri shouted.

I turned just in time to see Ru'am duck into the darkened corridor we'd seen moments before. The other two pahsahni were already out of sight.

Something hot fizzed past my ear and Sah'ano fired several bursts. "Go!" he ordered.

I took one more shot, then grabbed Lauri by the arm and hustled us after Ru'am. In the darkness, I barely made out another portal and saw a furry body slide through. I felt Lauri tense but held tight as we moved into the shadows. Sah'ano came at our backs, covering our retreat with blasts of deadly energy.

The three of us bustled through the door and the pahsahni commander melted its mechanism after we pulled it shut. The darkness became total and afterimages of the muzzle flash from Sah'ano's weapon flickered across my eyes. I became acutely aware of the sweat running down my face in the chill of the room we'd entered.

"This isn't right," Lauri said. "How did you get through the door?"

"By turning the latch, like all the others," I heard Pergru respond.

Still holding her arm, I felt Lauri tremble. "What's wrong?" I asked.

"This is the genetics section," she said in hushed tones. "Dr. Kritchkopf's labs, where I was born."

"But you told me that was sealed off."

"It has been. For the last eight years."

Ru'am powered up a small lantern and a soft, low light mingled with the cold gloom. We stood in a small room, perhaps ten feet square, with cabinets and storage lockers, most of which hung open, along the two walls without doors. A portal, situated directly across from where we'd entered, sat slightly ajar, but Ru'am's lantern didn't penetrate to the space beyond. The six of us, two humans and four pahsahni, crowded the room, our combined breath creating an eerie fog in the low light.

Next to me, Lauri gasped. "Dare, you're bleeding. Are you all right?"

"What? I'm fine." I said, turning to her. Reaching up, I felt my ear and winced in pain. My hand came away bloody. "I guess that ricochet was closer than I thought."

Lauri reached into one of her pockets and pulled out a small first aid kit. "Hold still," she instructed.

Sah'ano shouldered his way past me and peered through the next doorway. "Where does this lead?"

"Living quarters and laboratories, for the most part," Lauri answered as she pressed a piece of fabric against my head.

"Is there another way out?" Ru'am inquired.

"Yes. Two. Whether we can use them or not remains to be seen," she said, taking my hand and placing it over the bandage. "Dare, hold this and keep pressure on it for a second."

"What do you mean?" Sah'ano asked her.

Lauri picked a tube, with a spray nozzle on one end, out of the kit. She pulled my hand away, still holding the bandage, and sprayed my ear. The substance felt even colder than the room and soon the area numbed, to my relief. She then took the fabric from me and tried to wipe off the excess blood from my cheek and neck as she replied. "I mean that I don't know if opening this door caused the others to become unsealed as well. I know the Hub's computer system inside and out, but even I don't know all the protocols for an emergency closure like this section experienced. And I certainly don't know how to reverse it— I didn't even think it was possible until now." She finished with my ear and stowed the kit back in her pocket. "Even with all that, we have a bigger problem."

Sah'ano made a sound of disgust that needed no translation. "And what's that?"

Lauri sighed. "There's no way Ruschick's men could have cut us off unless they saw where we were going. He must know about the Hub resident tracking devices and used mine to find us."

"Is there no way to turn it off, or remove it?" I asked.

"Not that I know of, short of major surgery. It's implanted at the base of my skull."

The room remained silent for some time, each of us contemplating our ever worsening situation. Thirsty, I reached inside my suit for a water pouch and opened it. The water felt good going down my throat, then I remembered I only had one more packet left. I took another sip, then resealed the pouch. A thought struck me. "What about the motion sensors, or the cameras? Ruschick could have tracked us that way if he had turned them back on."

She shrugged. "It's possible, but I can't check from here. There's no power. That's why it's so cold and dark."

Ru'am's head perked up. "But, if that's so, then those sensors would be inoperative here."

Lauri nodded. "True. You guys, at least, can move around within this dead section undetected."

"Then we can determine if the other exits can be used," Ru'am said. "Can you make us a simple map of just this area?"

"Yeah, sure. It's not very big."

Sah'ano straightened and looked at Lauri. "There's something I still don't understand. Why was this place cut off from the rest of the facility?"

Lauri paused before answering. "Dr. Kritchkopf, the scientist who worked here, was killed by one of his genetic experiments."

"But why seal off the whole area?" Sah'ano pressed. "Couldn't they just have destroyed the experiment and started over?"

She shook her head and tears welled in her eyes. "No. Once I explained what had happened, and what Dr. Kritchkopf had created, permanent seal was the only solution."

"Why?" I asked.

"Because, no one could figure out how to kill the thing he'd made."

25

"What!" I said in surprise. "Then it could still be running around in here?"

"Dare, it's been eight years," Lauri reminded me. "It's been isolated with no source of food or water."

"What was this scientist trying to create?" Ru'am asked.

"He wanted to make a life form that could survive on Mars without the help of technology. Something that would also begin the process of transforming the planet into a place humans could eventually live."

"Ambitious," Ru'am remarked.

Lauri nodded. "He was brilliant. He was also cruel and sadistic."

"Did your people try to destroy it?" Sah'ano wondered.

"Yes, but I don't know, or remember, all of what they did. I was only seven at the time. I'm sure they tried chlorine gas and radiation, at least, but neither had any effect."

"How did they know if the place was closed off?" I asked.

"Because the motion sensors and a few cameras were still working," she answered. "Eventually they gave up and shut off all power to the section."

"All right," Sah'ano said. "We'll assume the thing died of starvation, or old age, and proceed. Please map this area and we'll split into two groups, one to cover each potential exit. You will remain close by here in case your theory about the tracking device is correct."

Lauri sighed. "Okay. Who's got something to write with?"

A few minutes later, I found myself paired with Sah'ano, exploring the dark corridors of the abandoned section. As Lauri had mentioned, the layout was pretty simple. Two spacious, circular rooms, connected by a small airlock, occupied the center, while a curved hallway hugged the resultant oval. Flanking the hall on the outside were several storage rooms, a lavatory, and living quarters. The three entrances to the section formed a Y-shape, as Lauri had drawn the map, and we had initially entered at the bottom. Sah'ano and I had gone left, while Ru'am and Pergru had ventured right. Lauri had stayed behind with the remaining pahsahni.

While Sah'ano seemed comfortable in the darkness, I needed light. Lauri had pulled a pen light from one of the pockets of my suit and handed it to me. She took charge of Ru'am's lamp and wished us luck.

We wasted no time making our way to our potential escape route and discovered the inner door hanging open. Cautiously, Sah'ano stepped through and I followed at his heels. The intervening space was empty, lined with cabinets and shelves along the walls to our sides, just like the first room we'd encountered.

Sah'ano crept to the outer door and pressed his head against it. After a moment, he turned to me. "How is your hearing, Human?"

I shrugged. "I don't know how it compares to yours, but I'll give a listen." I cupped my uninjured ear to the cold metal. Hearing nothing, I shook my head.

Sah'ano grasped the wheel and slowly turned the lock. The

latch moved aside with a squeak that caused me to wince, but no further noise came. He pushed the portal open just enough to admit a small amount of light coming from the hall beyond, then pulled it shut and latched it once more without a sound.

He then drew a device from one of his pockets and wedged one end of it in the door jamb. Once satisfied it would stay put, he explained, "A warning system. If the door is opened, contact with the metal will be lost and the unit will sound an alarm."

"How do you turn it off?"

"Depress the two prongs and keep them closed. Like this." He removed the tiny piece of equipment, then replaced it.

"Got it. At least we know we can get out of here."

"Yes. The question is: when we leave, will we only open a door to another firefight?"

Unfortunately, I didn't have an answer for him.

We turned to head back inside when my thin light passed over a dark spot on the floor. I moved the beam back and found it again: a black circle, less than an inch across.

"Looks like blood," Sah'ano said, noticing my attention.

I let out a breath, which formed clouds in the light, and shivered.

Sah'ano bumped my shoulder, breaking my concentration. He pointed to my head. "Your ear. The wound is probably seeping. Relax, Human."

I nodded, realizing he made perfect sense. Childhood nightmares of the boogeyman had been teasing my thoughts since Lauri had relayed her story.

"Let's go find the others and decide on a plan," the big pahsahni said, with a hint of amusement on his furry face.

We met Ru'am and Pergru in the corridor, midway between the two exits.

"Any trouble?" Sah'ano asked.

"No, Honored One," Pergru said. "The door is unlocked, like the others. We placed the alarm without difficulty."

"Good. Let's make a sweep of the central rooms. Pergru Rin, take point."

We approached a door that led to the circular chamber on the left of Lauri's map. As Pergru moved to open it, my light found another shadowy area on the floor, bigger than the last.

"Wait," I called out in a harsh whisper and motioned to Sah'ano on my right. "Look. More blood, but I'm sure that's not mine."

He bent down to examine my discovery. The dark patch was smeared, as if something had been dragged through the puddle, toward the door. Sah'ano wrinkled his nose, then touched the area with his hand. "It's frozen, which is why it has little scent. Still, it doesn't look like it's been here long. Hours maybe."

My anxiety level rose. "What does that mean?"

Sah'ano stood. "I don't know. Maybe whoever unsealed this area injured themselves somehow."

"Do you think they're still here?" I asked.

"I don't know, but let's find out," he said. "Pergru Rin, turn the latch slowly, then push it open on my signal."

Pergru indicated his understanding and shouldered his weapon. I backed away and held my rifle ready. Sah'ano took a crouched position against the wall opposite the door while Pergru carefully turned the wheel. After it would move no farther, he glanced back at his commander. Sah'ano gave a short grunt and Pergru shoved on the door.

Metal clanged on metal as the door slammed into the side of a storage locker and bounced back a short distance. I flashed my light inside, but nothing moved. Shining the beam down, I found a body, lying prone on the floor near the middle of the room.

At a motion from Sah'ano, Pergru took his weapon in hand and leapt into the chamber. Sah'ano went next, moving his gun purposefully around the space. Ru'am followed, and I entered heartbeats later after stowing my awkward rifle and switching the pen light to my preferred right hand.

The room must have served as Dr. Kritchkopf's main work area. I shined my light over several video screens mounted on the wall to my left, above an expansive desk. Two other long tables held pieces of scientific looking equipment in various states of disarray. Four chairs, tucked under the tables and desk, and two tall storage lockers rounded out the furnishings. Directly across from us was another closed door that led to the corridor near where we'd left Lauri, and past the desk, a sturdier airlock door hung halfway open.

After swinging my tiny light beam around the space, I reluctantly came back to the body. Positioned face down, the man seemed peaceful enough, almost in a sleeping posture. He wore the same style of jumper I had under my environment suit, only light blue instead of beige. The durable cloth was torn in several places, the ragged edges darkened from blood.

I looked up and saw the three pahsahni staring at me. Oh, hell. They were waiting for me to examine the body! I began to protest then resigned myself to the duty. Of course, being the only human in the room, the job fell to me.

I knelt next to him, trying to decide how to proceed. The unfortunate man's ears had turned a light shade of blue, the body having turned cold as the room. Knowing we needed to determine how he died, I steeled myself and rolled him over.

My stomach rolled with him.

Green eyes stared back at me, frozen in shock and anguish. His clothing and skin around his chest were rent open— slashed repeatedly by something sharp and jagged. What caused my guts to clench, however, were the lumps; they covered his body, as if someone had embedded a hundred marbles underneath the man's skin. I stared, unbelieving, trying to swallow the dry knot in my throat.

Then, one of the lumps moved.

I yelled and jumped back, bumping into Ru'am, who had crept in for a closer look. "He's got something— parasites— I don't know, under his skin." I discovered I was holding tightly onto the pahsahni scientist. I let go and stepped away. "Sorry."

Ru'am patted my arm in a very human gesture. "It's all right. I take it from your reaction you haven't seen anything like that before."

I shook my head. "No. Never."

"Move away," Sah'ano said. "Human, hand me your weapon."

Still shaking, I unstrapped the rifle from my shoulder and gave it to him. Pergru moved closer to Ru'am and me. Sah'ano adjusted the weapon's settings and took aim on the body.

"Ssstop," a raspy voice, sounding like rocks being ground together, said from somewhere in the darkness. "Or I will kill all of you."

26

Sah'ano remained still. "Who are you?" he asked, rifle still trained on the body. "Show yourself."

The wheel on the door opposite us turned and the portal swung open, revealing another dim light source and two familiar figures. "We heard a shout. Are you all right?" Lauri said, eyes wide.

"Lauri, stay there," I said. "Don't move."

"Lisssten to him," the harsh voice said.

I shined my light in the direction the sound came, up and to my left. It blended so well with the metal wall, I nearly missed it.

Spider-like, with an abdomen easily two feet wide, the creature shifted slightly in the light, as if it wanted to make sure I saw it. The outside of it appeared metallic, yet my light didn't reflect from it. Rather the opposite, like the creature absorbed it somehow. Six inflexible, spindly legs clung to the wall, while two forelimbs swayed slightly in front, each ending with three manipulative, sharp-looking digits. Compound eyes protruded from an oversized head sporting a frightening set of mandibles.

Overall, it gave me the impression of precise lethality.

"Lower your weaponsss," it ordered. I had to suppress the urge to clear my throat, its voice sounded so dry.

"Why?" Sah'ano wondered. "There are six of us and only one of you."

"I do not underssstand your ssspeach," the monster said, then pointed at me with a claw. "You. What did he sssay?"

"He wants to know why we should do what you ask," I told it.

"While you are no danger to me, my clutch isss vulnerable. I will kill you all, if needed, to protect it."

I looked back at the dead man on the floor and my stomach clenched. The thing was using the body as an incubator. I wanted to scream and grab the gun from Sah'ano's hands— blast away until the monstrosity had ceased to exist, such was my revulsion. Fear for my friends only barely held me in check.

Sah'ano kept steady. "I find it hard to believe my gun presents no threat to it."

"It's true," Lauri said. "Dr. Kritchkopf created it to withstand the harshest conditions. It was designed to survive even inside a volcano."

"How is that possible?" Ru'am asked.

"I don't understand it," Lauri answered. "But from what I remember, he used a combination of carbon-based and silicon-based biochemistry. The data's probably still in the computers if you want to look."

"Not any more," the creature said. "Director Russschick came several hours ago and removed the memory unitsss."

Lauri gasped. "That's why the seal was broken! Ruschick wanted Kritchkopf's work."

"For what purpose? I didn't get the impression he was a scientist," Ru'am said.

"I don't know. Maybe to sell, or use as leverage to get back to Earth," she said.

"Thossse filesss had information about you too, my little Pixie."

Lauri shot a glare at the mutated horror and moved a few steps into the room. "Don't call me that!"

I tensed, anticipating an aggressive response from the creature. What it said surprised me.

"My apologiesss. I have trouble ssseparating my memoriesss at timesss."

I shook my head. "I don't get it. How does this thing know so much about what's going on?"

"Kritchkopf knew his creation would need to think independently to overcome unforeseen obstacles in surviving on Mars," Lauri said. "So, he made it intelligent. Problem was, he didn't want to take the time to engineer a highly developed brain for it from scratch."

"He used himself as a model," I guessed.

"Ah, but that'sss not the whole ssstory isss it, *Liebchen*?"

"Enough!" Sah'ano declared. "I am not interested in genetics or human social interactions. We have a mission to complete."

"The fuzzy one ssseemsss very agitated."

"We all are," I said. "We're trapped and running out of time."

"Perhapsss we can help each other?"

I shuddered at the thought of teaming up with the monster and wondered when Sah'ano's patience would run out and he would try shooting it.

"Tell it I'm listening," the pahsahni commander said, much to my surprise.

I relayed the message. "Why are you here?" the creature asked.

Lauri said, "We have to get to Dr. Lansing's section. He has some equipment we need, but Ruschick's men can track our movements."

"Ah, and they chasssed you in here."

"Yes."

"Then, I think I can be of aid to you. But you mussst help me in return."

Sah'ano glanced in Pergru's direction, while still keeping an eye on the creature. "You have Birin Seb's communicator?" Pergru plucked the small piece of equipment from a pocket in response. "Human, tell it to take the device so it can understand me."

Still uncomfortable with the idea of helping something so abhorrent, I reluctantly complied. "This machine will translate their speech." I took the communicator from Pergru and tossed it toward the creature. One forelimb flashed out, neatly snatching the device from the air. After examining it briefly, the creature held the communicator to the side of its head.

"What do you want?" Sah'ano asked.

"Freedom."

"I don't understand," Sah'ano said. "You look like you are fully capable of operating the doors."

"The doorsss, yesss. The airlock to go outsside, no. Plusss, I now have my clutch which I mussst protect."

Sah'ano glanced at Ru'am, then asked, "May we have a few minutes to discuss this?"

The creature nodded. "Of courssse."

"Pergru Rin and Bahsim Nah, keep your weapons trained

on the body to make sure our new friend remains honest," Sah'ano ordered.

The two pahsahni stepped forward and pointed their guns at the dead man, keeping a nervous eye on the creature all the while.

Sah'ano moved to the door Lauri had opened and motioned for Ru'am and me to follow. I offered my light to Pergru, but he waved me away. The four of us, two pahsahni and two humans, went into the corridor, Lauri still holding Ru'am's lamp. Both my ears and the tip of my nose had gone numb from the cold. Sah'ano swung the door almost closed, leaving an inch or two of space.

"What do you think?" he asked in a low voice.

"Are you crazy?" I whispered emphatically. "You're not actually considering trusting that thing."

"I am considering it. If you have nothing to offer besides emotionally charged objections, I'll ask you to remain quiet."

Lauri put a hand on my arm. "Dare, I don't get the feeling it's lying. It's just doing what it was created to do: survive. Its methods are alien to us, even more so than the pahsahni's, but it's only acting from its nature. Its programming."

"But it's using that man's body as a nursery. How can you condone that?"

"I'm not," Lauri whispered. "But the man is dead. We can't undo what's happened by arguing."

I grumbled, knowing she was right. "How did the thing make babies anyway?"

"It was designed to reproduce asexually. Each one is essentially a clone."

"All right," Sah'ano interrupted. "No more biology lessons. Can we use it to accomplish our goal?"

Lauri nodded. "I think so. I'm sure it would give Ruschick's men all they can handle. We've already seen it can be lethal."

"Will it do what it says?"

"As long as it feels we will hold up our end of the bargain, I believe it will," she answered.

Sah'ano turned to Ru'am. "Any other ideas, Learned One?"

"Not from me. It seems to be our best option and Lauri is familiar with the creature. Let's give it a try," he said.

"Very well. Let's see how it wants to proceed," Sah'ano said, opening the door once more.

I touched Lauri's shoulder and held her back while the two pahsahni went in to negotiate with the creature. "I'm sorry I snapped at you," I said.

She gave me a slight smile. "It's okay. I don't blame you. I'm disgusted by it too, but, in some ways, I feel responsible for it."

Surprised, I asked, "Why?"

Lauri dropped her eyes. "Dr. Kritchkopf made it when I was about six. He knew the thing was extremely dangerous, so he kept it sealed in a steel crate in the lab, only occasionally interacting with it to perform experiments. I could feel its anguish, its frustration, its loneliness, even from my room with several walls in between. After a while, I began to reach out to it with my emotions. It frightened me, because its mind was so like Kritchkopf's, but its situation was similar to my own, so I sympathized with it a great deal."

She paused, taking a shuddering breath, then continued, "One night, I snuck into the lab and undid the closure on its cage. It was waiting for Kritchkopf when he entered the lab the next morning. I heard the screams, then I ran to find Karl to tell him Kritchkopf had been attacked."

Lauri met my gaze, tears welling in her eyes. "I was the one who convinced him and the other scientists to seal off the section. The creature saved my life— Kritchkopf tortured me in ways I can't describe— but all I did in return was give it a bigger cage."

The tears broke loose and I hugged her close. "You unleashed one monster to destroy another," I whispered.

"I never told anyone," she sobbed into my shoulder. "I was afraid they'd lock me up too."

"It's okay," I said, stroking her hair, which appeared to glow in the soft light of the lantern. "It's okay."

27

Lauri and I returned to the workroom a minute or two later.

"I am agreeable to that," Sah'ano said. "Let's get moving before they find their courage and come in here looking for us."

"What's the plan?" I asked.

Sah'ano glared at me with contempt. "If you had been here, you would know, Human."

"I'm sorry! We had things to discuss."

"We need something to wrap the body in," Ru'am said.

I looked to Lauri who wiped her cheek and took a clearing breath. "What about a bed sheet?" she said.

"I'll go," I offered, sensing she still needed time to collect herself. "Where can I find one?"

She pointed. "Out that door, turn right, then the second door you see should be one of the living quarters."

"Got it," I said, giving her arm a squeeze. Sah'ano and the other pahsahni busied themselves checking over their weapons and equipment. I left, grateful to be away from the commander's disapproving gaze, even for a few minutes.

Arriving at the second door I found in the lightless corridor, I turned the wheel and entered. The cramped space held little more than a rumpled bed and a chest of drawers. Perched on a shelf next to the bed, I saw a photo of a middle aged man, wearing a lab coat and shaking hands with an elderly gentleman in an expensive looking suit. Clamping the pen light between my teeth, I pulled the bedding off, rolling it up as I went. As I reached the end of the mattress, I noticed a blanket piled in the corner on the floor. Tucked in the folds, a doll's cloth face stared back at me with dark eyes and an innocent smile.

I shivered, realizing this must have been Dr. Kritchkopf's quarters and the doll and blanket had likely belonged to Lauri. I considered retrieving the doll, then decided a physical reminder of the childhood she'd suffered wasn't something Lauri would probably want. I finished bundling up the sheets and hustled back to the workroom.

"Will this work?" I asked, dumping the linens in a pile near the body.

"Yesss," the creature answered in its gravelly voice. It took the sheets and carefully spread them out on the floor, meticulously smoothing out folds and wrinkles. Once satisfied with the bedding, it proceeded to fuss and fawn over the corpse. My stomach roiled and I couldn't watch any longer.

Turning away, I bumped into Lauri, who had moved in behind me, also watching the creature. "It's amazing. From a technical standpoint, I mean."

"It's disgusting," I said, my throat burning from swallowed bile.

Her eyes, still puffy and red, left the scene behind me and focused on mine. "I would imagine the pahsahni find some of our habits and behaviors disgusting."

"That's different."

"Is it? To me, things humans have done to each other throughout history are just as vile and grotesque, more so even, than what this creature has done. Yes, it killed. But people kill each other every day for far worse reasons than wanting to survive."

I figured a good portion of her sympathy for the thing stemmed from the feelings of guilt she'd expressed earlier, but I also knew she had a point. "You know, no one likes someone who's right all the time."

Her eyebrows raised. "I'm not right all the time. I was wrong about you."

"Oh?"

"When I first met you, I thought you were a bad guy. Though, I was right about one thing."

"What's that?"

"You are cute," she said with a wink.

The room seemed to turn a few degrees warmer, then I felt Sah'ano's presence next to me. "If the humans are finished exchanging pheromones, I believe we are ready to move."

"What? I wasn't— I mean, we weren't— oh, never mind," I said with a sigh. Lauri had the audacity to giggle.

Sah'ano handed me the rifle I'd been carrying earlier. "The settings should be adequate for your needs. Don't change them," he said.

I gave him my best boy scout salute as he turned to the others. "Pergru Rin and Bahsim Nah will carry the body." The two pahsahni each hoisted an end of the freshly wrapped corpse in response. "Ru'am Koh, will you please act as our rear guard?"

"Of course," Ru'am replied.

"Which exit is closest to our destination?" Sah'ano asked Lauri.

"That way," she said, pointing in the direction of the one Sah'ano and I had investigated.

"Then we shall start with the other. Once you determine the status of the visual and motion sensing equipment, the human and Ru'am Koh will backtrack to the other exit and proceed with the original plan while the rest of us occupy any opposing force." Then, Sah'ano addressed the creature, "Hans, will you lead the way?"

Puzzled, I leaned close to Lauri and whispered, "Hans?"

"While you were getting the sheets, it asked to be addressed as Hans. It was Dr. Kritchkopf's first name." She shrugged. "It's better than calling it 'creature' all the time."

"Oh, sure," I said. "The giant, murderous bug gets to have a name but we're stuck with 'human'."

Lauri smiled and patted my cheek. "There you are. I wondered where you'd gone."

What the hell was that supposed to mean?

Our increasingly strange party exited the workroom and turned right, toward the exit Ru'am and Pergru had checked out earlier. Sah'ano deftly removed the warning device and spoke softly. "If anyone has indications of company on the other side, please speak up."

Silence served as his response. "Very well," he said and used his free hand to turn the mechanism. He pushed slowly, allowing a small amount of light from the corridor beyond to spill through. The instant the opening was big enough, Hans the Spider skittered out. Sah'ano and the rest of us followed.

The hall came to a T after only twenty feet and warm air teased my numb nose and cheeks. Hans waited patiently near a computer terminal at the intersection. With no danger readily apparent, Lauri jogged forward and began making inquiries to the Hub's system.

Suddenly anxious, understanding Ru'am and I would soon be separated from the rest of the group, I hefted the awkward rifle in preparation and had another thought. "Sah'ano," I whispered. He didn't respond, so I whispered again, louder. "Sah'ano."

He rounded on me with a ferocity I hadn't seen before. "What is it, Human?"

Taken aback by his reaction, I stammered, "I, uh… I was just thinking that, um, it might make more sense for us to trade guns. Seeing as how yours is smaller, I'd be able to move better."

Baring his sharp teeth, he said, "First you insult me, now you want my weapon?"

"Insult you? I don't understand."

"For a species with such prominent hearing organs, your listening skills are atrocious. My name is Sah'ano Dem. When you leave off my maternal, it is as though you are calling me motherless spawn." He leaned in so close I felt his breath. "Is that your intent, Human?"

I thought back in horror to all the times I'd left off "Tah" when talking to M'sang. No wonder he'd seemed pissed at me so often! I mean, besides the fact that I'd been a complete screw up. Why hadn't he said something? "No! I'm sorry. I meant no disrespect." I set the rifle down and executed the bow M'sang Tah had taught me to do before we sparred.

The pahsahni commander puffed his cheeks in surprise. "There may be hope for you yet, Human," he said and handed me his pistol.

I smiled, being careful not to show my teeth. "Thank you, Sah'ano Dem."

He bent down and retrieved the rifle. It looked sleeker and more menacing in his capable hands.

Lauri called back, "All clear."

Knowing that was our signal to move, I looked over at Ru'am and my mind blanked on the rest of his name. "I'm sorry, but I've forgotten your— what did he call it? Maternal?"

"Koh," he told me. "Ru'am Koh."

I made sure to remember it and said, "I'm sorry if I've offended you before."

"It's quite all right, Dare," he said, then added quietly, "I'm sure Sah'ano Dem is especially sensitive right now, having lost his whole family."

His words stung me. "What about you?" I asked. "Didn't you have family aboard the ships too?"

"No. I've never taken a mate and my parents journeyed down the long tunnel a few years ago. I grieve heavily for my people, but my pain is not as raw as the Honored Sah'ano Dem's."

I heard a sound like gravel crunching underfoot and saw Hans leap forward with incredible speed, out of sight. Screams and weapons fire followed.

Lauri caught my eye as she ducked behind the pahsahni who added their guns to the chaos. "Dare, go!"

Ru'am Koh took my arm and we hurried back into the chill darkness of the genetics section. The sounds of fighting muffled upon closing the door and I tried not to think about the danger we had left our friends in.

I flicked my pen light on and we ran through the empty

corridor to the other exit. In my rush, I nearly opened the door without deactivating the alarm we'd set. Hands shaking, I plucked it from the crack, keeping the contacts closed as Sah'ano Dem had showed me. "What do I do now?" I asked, realizing if I let go, the prongs would spring open and the device would go off.

"There should be a clamp. Don't you have it?"

"No."

"Give it to me. I'll hold it."

I gingerly passed him the tiny piece of equipment and opened the door, taking care to make as little sound as possible. A brush of warmer air and light greeted me, nothing more. Letting go of a tense breath, I stepped through, allowing Ru'am Koh to follow before I re-secured the portal.

After putting my pen light away, I drew the gun Sah'ano Dem had given me and saw Ru'am Koh pull out a smaller pistol with his free hand. We crept forward, reaching the end of the short hallway and looked both directions at the intersection, when something deeply troubling occurred to me.

I had no idea where I was going.

28

"Shit!"

"Is something wrong?"

"I forgot to ask Lauri which way to go."

Ru'am Koh pointed. "There's another computer terminal. Can you use it?"

"I don't know. It's worth a shot," I said, angry at my stupidity.

I shoved the gun in my belt, then approached the screen and pulled out the entry pad from a slot underneath as I'd see Lauri do before. It immediately lit up with an image of a conventional keyboard. At least the alphabet hasn't changed in the last seventy years or so, I thought with relief. I typed in "MAP" and tapped a green button I assumed served as "enter".

The word "Specify" appeared on the screen above. I considered for a second, then keyed in "HUB", hoping the computer understood the pet name the inhabitants used for the facility. Half a heartbeat later, the same image Lauri had shown us earlier popped up on the screen, minus the locater dots for the Hub's residents. A small, orange pulse of light served as a "You Are Here" marker.

Ru'am Koh watched over my shoulder as I studied the map. The place remained intensely complicated and I wasn't entirely sure I remembered the location of Dr. Lansing's dot from before.

"I think it's here," I said, touching the screen. The section flashed and two lines of text appeared: Dr. Karl Lansing, Interdimensional Physics. "Well okay then," I said with a grin. "Looks like we're close. Down this way and hang a right."

I pushed the pad back in its slot and drew my gun. We advanced to the next intersection and I peeked around the corner. Seeing nothing, I whispered, "All clear," and we kept moving.

Subtle differences came to my attention as we took the right turn indicated by the map. The metal composing the walls and floor was slightly darker than the hallways we previously traversed and the space felt compressed. It occurred to me Dr. Lansing's section might be older than the parts of the Hub we'd visited recently. Everything had been so new and strange on my first visit, I hadn't noticed the differences in construction as Lauri had given me her tour on our way to the garage.

We turned another corner and I heard a voice coming from an open doorway a few feet away. "Fall back and seal the door."

Another voice, full of panic, sounded through a speaker. "We can't! The thing's too fast. Phillips and McReady are already—" the transmission ended with a scream and static.

"Hinson! Dammit," the first voice said, then I heard the scrape of a chair on the metal floor.

I dropped to a crouch and braced my weapon, aiming for the open door. A blonde-haired man in light blue coveralls stepped through. Before I could squeeze my trigger, light flashed from behind me and the man slumped awkwardly to the floor. Glancing back, I saw Ru'am Koh lower his pistol.

"My weapon is non-lethal," he said. "There's been enough loss of life already."

Nodding, I stood and walked cautiously to the doorway and realized it led to Dr. Lansing's Situation Room, where we'd first met to discuss what had happened on Mars. The bank of computer monitors showed schematics of several sections of the Hub, along with a lot of text I couldn't read from the distance. At least it looked like Lauri's sabotage of the security systems was still in place. I bent down and checked on the fallen man. His eyes were closed, but his breathing was steady. I didn't see any wounds.

"He should remain unconscious for several hours," Ru'am Koh said.

"Okay. Down there is the device we need. Hopefully we'll find Dr. Lansing there as well."

We passed by a few closed doors, arriving at one more at the end of the corridor. Muffled voices reached my ears, but I couldn't make out the conversation.

I looked to my pahsahni partner, who cocked his head to the side, indicating he was ready. I took a breath and spun the latch.

As I yanked the portal open, a male voice said, "Wilson, I told you we didn't—"

Ru'am Koh jumped in ahead of me, brandishing his pistol. I hurried in after him. My mind registered three figures in the room before all hell broke loose.

A wave of barely visible energy struck the pahsahni before he could get a shot off. His body went limp, momentum carrying him to my right, and his grip loosened on the small device he'd held pinched between his fingers.

Sound, like a smoke alarm on steroids, blasted through the room with physical force. Dazed from the concussion, I dropped my gun and managed to clap my hands to my ears before falling to my knees. My only coherent thought was to wonder how such a tiny thing could make such a commotion.

Five seconds later, the screeching ceased, leaving what felt like a permanent ringing in my ears. I blinked a few times, trying to clear my head, then looked up.

The other three people in the room were in similar states of bewilderment. I recognized Dr. Lansing, on the far side of the room, bent over an instrument panel. To my left, a portly, balding man, wearing dark blue pants and a lighter colored dress shirt, struggled to his knees. The third figure crawled to the center of the chamber, where a dull gray sphere, about two and a half feet in diameter, sat in the middle of the white-tiled section of floor. I should have been surprised, seeing who it was, but I wasn't in the least.

Hope.

She looked at me with a mixture of sadness and disbelief, shaking her head before pressing a button on top of the gray ball. White light flashed around her, forcing me to look away. I turned back a second later, with spots in my eyes, but she was gone.

The overweight man, who I assumed was Director Ruschick, looked to the spot where Hope had been and yelled in anguish, his face reddening from the strain. The sound seemed to come from far away, as if I had cotton densely packed in my ears.

I pushed myself up and stumbled over to Dr. Lansing, just as he managed to stand. "Are you all right?" I yelled, barely able to hear my voice.

He winced, but nodded. "What was that?"

I looked with despair over to Ru'am Koh, sprawled unmoving on the floor. Then I saw his chest rise and optimism sparked in me. If Hope had shot him, her stunner would have only put him to sleep, much like he had done to the man in the hallway.

"Dare! Look out!" Dr. Lansing shouted, shoving me down.

A blazing beam of light struck the equipment next to Lansing, sending sparks and bits of metal and plastic flying. The scientist landed next to me in a heap, but he looked up and nodded. Across the room, I saw Ruschick had picked up the gun I'd carelessly left on the floor. "What have you done?!" he screamed. "That girl was my ticket off this rock! Now she's gone!" He aimed at me.

Rocketing through the open door, a blurred form barreled into the colony director, knocking him to the ground and sending his shot wide. The two tumbled across the floor and bumped to a stop against the wall. Hans, the monstrous genetic experiment, loomed over an apoplectic Ruschick. Somehow, the man had kept a hold on the gun during his spill and trained it on the German Shepherd-sized spider. His face full of hatred, Ruschick blasted a piece of the sun directly into the creature.

Hans laughed.

The monster's gunmetal-colored carapace drank in the destructive radiation like lemonade on a summer afternoon. Ruschick's rage soon transformed to fright as he continued to fire the pistol's energy at the horror perched on his chest. Finally, something in the weapon couldn't take the strain any longer and broke with a puff of smoke and a pop audible even to my damaged ears.

Ruschick bellowed in pain and threw the gun away.

Still glowing with unabsorbed heat, Hans grinned wickedly. "Sssomething wrong, Director?" One of the creature's forelimbs deftly frisked the shuddering man and pulled two black objects, each the size of a deck of cards, from a pocket. "Were thessse worth the cossst of admissssion to my lair? I wonder if the men you lossst think ssso." Hans tossed the dark items aside with a casual air.

"It doesn't matter now," Ruschick sputtered. "We'll all be dead soon, even you."

I levered myself up. "No one else has to die, Director."

His head turned in my direction. "No? Hope apparently didn't share your opinion. She activated the last bomb before she disappeared. Once the shielding decays, the antimatter trapped inside will make a kilometers-wide crater of this place."

"What?" I ran to the large ball, still sitting placidly on the white tiles. A red light blinked innocuously on a tiny instrument panel near the top. "How do we shut it off?"

Ruschick laughed, which shook his belly and Hans on top of him. "We don't. She didn't want to risk having the aliens deactivate them." He continued to giggle. "She promised to send me back to Earth. She promised—"

Hans slashed the man's throat with the claws of a forelimb. Blood sprayed a ragged line on the wall.

"Why did you do that?" I asked, cringing.

"He had nothing more usssefull to sssay." Hans climbed off the body and moved close to me, examining the ball with a delicateness sharply contrasting the brutality it had displayed only seconds before.

The quick thuds of running feet mixed with the ringing that had begun to grow in my ears. Lauri entered the room breathless, followed by Sah'ano Dem.

"What happened?" she asked, seeing the bodies on the floor. "Karl!" she cried and ran to Dr. Lansing, who was lying amidst pieces of broken equipment.

I left Hans to puzzle over the bomb and knelt next to Lauri, while Sah'ano Dem bent to check on his compatriot.

Dr. Lansing groaned and I saw fresh blood on his lab coat. With great care, Lauri rolled him on his side, exposing a jagged shard of the blasted console protruding from his ribs.

I gasped. "No! I thought you were okay."

Lansing tried to smile, exposing teeth stained with blood. "My initial assessment appears to have been incorrect."

"Why are you both shouting?" Lauri asked. "Karl, just be quiet and lie still. I'll get a med kit."

"No," Lansing said, grabbing her arm. "Ruschick was right, it doesn't matter."

"What are you talking about?"

I sighed and tried to explain. "That big ball is a bomb, same as what blew up the pahsahni ships. Hope turned it on right before she zapped out."

"Hope? Hope was here?"

"Yeah."

Dr. Lansing coughed, then reached into a pocket of his coat. "Dare, I should have given this to you before, but the name you used made me uncertain." His unsteady hand removed something gray, slightly larger than a tooth. Then, I recognized it.

It was the earbud Lauri had lifted from me in Denver.

She plucked it from his fingers before I could react. "How is this possible?" she asked.

Lansing took my hand and guided it to hers. "Make it right."

My fingers made contact with Lauri's and the elusive, recalcitrant device.

Dr. Lansing smiled as my vision blurred to white.

29

Dry heaves racked my body as I stared into a uniformly gray floor.

"Welcome back, Dare," a gruff, but familiar voice said.

"No," I coughed, closing my eyes in grief. "I can't leave them like that."

A hand— a human hand— grasped mine and I felt a wave of reassurance, tinged with sadness. My eyes popped open in disbelief and I saw perfect, mocha-colored fingers covering my lighter and much abused digits. "You brought Lauri, too?"

"Of course I did," Kim's acerbic voice scolded.

A furry arm offered me a nutrient pouch. "Here, drink this," M'sang Tah said, handing one to Lauri as well.

I tore open the top and guzzled gratefully. Wiping my mouth, I looked up at my instructor's stern face. "M'sang Tah, I need to apologize. I had no idea—"

"Save your apologies for later, Dare," Kim interrupted. "You have work to do. Insertion in forty-five seconds."

Shocked, I stammered, "What? I mean, yes, we need to fix what Hope did, but shouldn't we get some rest first or something?"

"No time," Kim stated. "You must go back before Hope's management system deduces what occurred and takes action, which I estimate will happen in approximately fifty-two seconds."

"I don't understand."

"Of course you don't. Insertion in thirty-five seconds. Ready yourselves."

Bewildered, I stood. "But, aren't we outside time here? Why does it matter how quick we go back?"

"You are currently outside time, we management systems are not. We can manipulate the higher dimensions, but we still exist in the normal universe and obey its laws. I have to reinsert the two of you in the thread, then lock that portion down. Twenty seconds."

"Lock it down? What does that mean?"

"To describe it in terms you can understand, I will essentially be tying a knot in time, preventing any further tampering for the length of the section within the knot. Meaning no more insertions can be made, and I will not be able to contact you for the duration. What you do within the knot cannot be undone. Ten seconds."

Fear gripped me and my heart hammered. I took one of the control rods and pointed for Lauri to hold the other. My free hand found hers and I tried to calm myself, though I found it difficult with Kim's words repeating in my mind. Distantly, I heard M'sang Tah offer us well wishes.

"Three… two… one."

Gray became white, which in turn became black. My insides rebelled and I fell to my knees. So much for my quick meal. "Dammit," I lamented after spewing the limited contents of my stomach. "Why did he give us that just so we could toss it up a minute later?"

"Oh, I don't know," I heard Lauri say beside me, clearing her throat. "I feel like some of it stuck with me. Must have been some stimulants or something in there."

"Where are we anyway? I can't see."

"Probably a storeroom, somewhere in the Hub," Lauri said. "But I won't be able to tell for sure until we open the door."

"Well, at least there is a door. And I can hear again. Kim must have worked some of her magic on my ears." Something in my pants pocket buzzed. I reached in and realized the incredibly sarcastic and powerful computer had dressed me in jeans and a T-shirt once again. I pulled out a communicator like the one I'd had in Denver. The screen lit up and I saw we were indeed in a tight room full of boxes piled on shelves. A green circle appeared on the display along with the words, "Press when you are ready to begin."

Lauri and I exchanged a glance. I shrugged and pushed the button. Text replaced the image and read, "Dare and Lauri: The thread is now bound and immutable from external forces for the next two hours and fifty-six minutes. The information in this message is the last communication you will receive until that time period ends. While nothing new can enter the thread, it is also impossible to extract you, so try not to get yourselves killed."

"She's so helpful," I commented, then continued reading.

"Hope and her management system will be governed by the same restrictions, but it is doubtful she will understand what has happened. Her talents and resources will likely still be considerable, but not unlimited. You must gain control of the situation, and her, before the lock expires or she will be able to simply do it all again once she is reconnected to her management system.

"I have supplied you with a capsule containing nanotechnology— microscopic machines which, when ingested, are programed to seek out and eliminate any foreign mechanical systems within a biological entity. That should sever her link to her system just as I lost contact with you, Dare, when you lost your equipment and clothing."

"My clothing?" I thought back and remembered I'd exchanged my original pair of jeans and other items when Dr. Lansing had given me the Hub coveralls to wear. "Wait a minute."

"What's wrong?" Lauri asked.

"That means Kim was still tracking me the whole time until we arrived here. Damn her! She could have pulled me out at any point in Denver, but she just let me suffer through that entire mess!"

Lauri smiled. "Maybe she thought you were doing just fine."

"Yeah, right. She and M'sang Tah were probably sitting back and laughing their heads off. Whatever."

I turned my attention back to the text. "Regarding foreign mechanical systems, I have removed the signal emitter from Lauri's cranium. In addition, you have a handful of devices stored about your persons which you should find useful. Unfortunately, the unpredictable nature of the situation made it impossible to anticipate your every need. The display on this unit will count down the time you have left until the lockout has ended. It also contains a map of the science facility and basic instructions on each piece of equipment I've supplied you with. I am cautiously optimistic, Dare, with Lauri's help, that you can realize some of the promise the Keepers have seen in you."

I chuckled. "Gee, thanks for the vote of confidence, Kim."

Lauri rubbed the back of her head. "Hard to believe it's gone. Poof! Just like that."

"It's kinda scary the stuff that computer can do. Let's see what toys she gave us. Is there a light in here?"

Lauri stood, then reached over to the wall beside the door and activated a lamp above our heads. I got up as well, realizing with the light just how small the room was Kim had dropped us into. Lauri met my eyes and gave me a nervous smile. Her environment suit was missing, just like mine, but she still wore the tan coveralls, indicative of a Hub resident. At least Kim hadn't dressed her in the racy fishnet outfit.

"Kind of reminds me of our first date," I said with an uncertain chuckle. "Standing face to face with vomit at our feet."

She laughed and I gratefully felt some of our tension slide away. I brought the communicator up and tapped the screen. It remained blank but for a countdown clock in the upper right corner. "Um, explain equipment," I said.

The display changed, showing more text. "Because of the thread lockdown, all the devices have a finite power supply and thus their usage will be limited."

A holographic image appeared above the screen, depicting a necklace with an oval pendant. Below it, new text read, "Each of you is wearing one of these around your neck. The unit bends light and other radiation around the wearer, effectively making them invisible, but only when they remain motionless. Movement decreases the efficacy of the device and observers will notice distortions of vision. Once activated, by firmly depressing both sides simultaneously, it will function for approximately ten minutes with available energy."

I reached up with my other hand and felt a prune-sized lump under my shirt. Lauri did the same, but pulled hers out so it lay exposed on her chest. My face flushed as I realized where my eyes had landed. Clearing my throat, I refocused on the communicator. Predictably, Lauri giggled at my discomfort.

The image shifted to that of the compact, cylindrical stunner I was familiar with. "In your left pant pocket," the text below now said, "you will both find a synaptic neutralizer. Its performance will be inhibited, rendering your target unconscious for only an hour or less, and will be capable of three or four shots, depending on conditions."

I patted my pocket, confirming the presence of the small weapon. Next, something that looked like a vitamin pill appeared in the air above the communicator. I read the new text. "Dare, this is the capsule containing the nanomachines I mentioned in the first message. They are suspended in a saline gel and the capsule is in a sealed packet in your right pant pocket. The machines must be inside Hope's body for them to work."

"That's going to be easier said than done," I scoffed.

The pill vanished, replaced by an oblong tool four or five inches in length. Kim's explanation read, "I've given this device to Lauri since she's already familiar with something similar. It creates a confined beam of energy, which can be used for cutting or welding as needed. The dial on the side controls the length and intensity of the beam." The image faded out and the screen went dark.

"I guess that's it," I said, stating the obvious in an attempt to muster up some courage. The task before us seemed to loom larger every second.

Lauri must have picked up on my growing anxiety. "Dare, we can do this. Look at all we accomplished with the pahsahni."

I shrugged, feeling the weight of failure. "Yeah? What good did it do? They all died."

"Only because Hope cheated and changed the game. Look, maybe things didn't work out like we thought, but we still have a chance to make it right."

Dr. Lansing's last words replayed in my mind, echoing Lauri. Make it right. I took a breath and shook off my funk. "Okay, we have less than three hours to make sure Hope doesn't get to change the game. Where do we start?" I asked.

"We need to find out what time Kim dropped us into."

"Right." I turned back to the communicator. "Current time," I said and was rewarded with the following on the screen: Local Time: 15:24, 18 May, 2087. I showed it to Lauri. "That help?"

She nodded. "We left in the rover around ten this morning."

"So, it's a good bet Hope and Ruschick are already here and have taken over the Hub."

Lauri nodded again.

The sound of a number of boots striking the metal flooring beyond our door grew steadily louder. I stabbed at the light switch and prayed whoever it was hadn't come looking for whatever had been stored in our closet.

A male voice I didn't recognize said, "If I may ask, sir, what are we after?"

"Memory units," another familiar-sounding voice answered, as the group passed by our door. "It shouldn't take long."

The footsteps receded and Lauri grabbed me by the shoulders. "That was Ruschick," she whispered.

I'd heard him only a few minutes before, but he'd been under considerably more stress and my ears hadn't been functioning properly. "That makes sense," I said. "Wait. Memory units?"

"They're on their way to Kritchkopf's lab!" Lauri said, completing my thought.

A vision of the man's body, infested with the creature Hans's offspring, burned inside me. "We have to stop them."

30

After listening closely at the door, we opened it and stepped into the hallway. The loud procession of boots we'd heard made me thankful to be wearing tennis shoes again.

Lauri led the way, stopping briefly at a computer terminal. "I'm shutting off all the internal security— cameras and other sensors— hopefully that will slow them down," she whispered.

"Won't that alert them that something funny is going on like before?"

"Probably, but they don't have my tracking transmitter to zero in on this time. Plus, we have these," she said, holding up her pendant.

"Right, but only for ten minutes," I reminded her.

She finished her computer sabotage and we continued on, moving with soft feet and keeping our ears alert for Ruschick and his men. A handful of turns later, Lauri stopped before an intersection and crouched low. I followed her lead, hearing footsteps and low voices somewhere ahead of us.

Lauri turned to me and pointed to her invisibility device with a questioning look on her face. I hated to use what was probably our biggest advantage so soon— we hadn't even begun to search for Hope— but we weren't going to get any closer to Ruschick without being seen. I nodded and pulled my own necklace from beneath my shirt.

Taking it between my thumb and forefinger, I squeezed. I felt a slight tingle, but nothing else. Looking up, I panicked for an instant, seeing Lauri was gone.

"Pretty cool, huh?" I heard her whisper and felt her hand touch my leg. "I can still sense your presence through your emotions, but otherwise it's like you just vanished."

Her hand left my leg and I saw ripples in the air, like heat rising from a hot road. "Keep your movements slow," I whispered. "Let's go."

I stood and walked with deliberate motions around the corner. I caught shimmers of Lauri a few times, but I trusted her to avoid blundering into me since she had a better idea of where I was than I did of her.

Ahead on my left, I noticed a darkened corridor and headed for it. I peeked around the corner and saw shadows moving through an open doorway. Flashlight beams played across the walls in the room ahead. Ruschick had already unsealed the section and gone inside. Realizing I'd have to rely on their lights to see, I hurried forward. I found the stunner in my pocket and held in front of me as I entered the freezing gloom.

Ruschick's group turned left into the curved hallway encompassing the workroom and laboratory. I counted a total of four figures ahead as I stepped through the threshold.

A touch on my arm nearly made me fire my stunner. I felt Lauri lean in close. "I'm going to the right," she whispered in my ear.

"Be careful," I said as softly as possible. She patted me in response and moved away.

I caught up to Ruschick and his entourage as he opened the door to the workspace. Before stepping inside, he turned to the men and said, "I believe what I need is in here, but you two check the rest of the rooms for computer equipment. If you find something, report back to me. Don't touch anything."

"Yes, sir," the two he'd indicated said together and moved farther down the hall.

Ruschick then went in the workroom, followed by his remaining man. I decided to stay with the colony director, figuring Lauri would meet up with the other two as the corridor looped around. I tiptoed inside, positioning myself against the wall next to the door, opposite the storage cabinet.

The portly director spent a minute examining the room, waving his flashlight all over before going to the desk and crouching down next to the chair with a grunt of effort. He pulled a flat case from his pocket, then held up his light. "Ellis, hold this," he ordered.

The guard who'd remained behind hustled to comply, setting his own light on the desk. His face became clearly visible for an instant as the light moved and I knew him to be Hans's victim.

"Shine it down here so I can see what I'm doing," Ruschick said. Silently, Ellis obeyed while the director selected a thin tool from his case and bent to the computer equipment.

A few minutes passed and I became increasingly nervous, knowing my time to remain hidden was growing short. The memory components Ruschick wanted had given him more trouble to extract than he'd expected, evidenced by his frequent cursing. Something popped and Ruschick exhaled forcefully. "Finally!" He removed the two dark objects I'd seen Hans brandish over the director's prone form not half an hour before. After sliding them into a pocket, Ruschick replaced his tools and levered his heavy body off the floor.

I heard footsteps from the hallway and, shortly afterward, the other two men entered the workspace. "The rest of the rooms are clear, sir," one of the men said.

Ruschick nodded. "All right, good. Let's get out and close this place back up."

Movement caught my eye, behind Ellis, in the direction of the lab door. Without thought, I raised my stunner and pressed the trigger button. In the same instant, Ellis must have heard something, causing the man to turn into my line of fire. The stunner's energy hit him square in the chest and he dropped like a stone.

Limbs extended and mouth open, like something straight out of an H. P. Lovecraft nightmare, the monster known as Hans sailed over the unconscious Ellis, screeching in frustration.

Director Ruschick screamed and scrambled around the desk toward the door and his men. I dove to my right, into the center of the room, trying to put some distance between myself and the others. With impressive speed, one of the men drew a pistol and fired two rounds at the giant spider.

They sparked off the creature's tough carapace and only served to enrage Hans further.

I rolled to my knees and aimed, knowing I only had one shot before someone in the room died. I pushed the button.

Hans's legs folded and the beast fell to the floor.

Kim had called the weapon a synaptic neutralizer. Lauri told us that Kritchkopf had used his own brain as a model for the creature, so I had bet the stunner would work on it where other weapons had proven ineffective. Luckily, my theory had been correct.

"Where the hell did he come from?"

Suddenly, I didn't feel so lucky.

The man who'd shot at Hans trained his gun on me. Evidently the energy in my invisibility necklace had expired at a most inopportune time. The second man at the door also had a pistol drawn and pointed in my direction.

Ruschick recovered some of his composure and straightened. "You must be the young man Karl mentioned. Nice shooting," he said, glancing down at the monstrous, unmoving spider. "Now drop whatever that is and put your hands up."

I considered trying to stun the two guards, knowing Lauri was still outside somewhere, but I doubted I could shoot both of them before one or the other shot me. Unfortunately, their weapons weren't as passivist friendly as mine. I dropped the stunner and watched it roll a few feet away before raising my arms.

"A wise decision," Ruschick said. "Thomas, if you would."

The first man walked over to me. "Get up."

I struggled to my feet, still holding my hands up for him to see. Thomas stood almost a head taller and outweighed me by at least fifty pounds, all of it muscle. He took my right wrist in an iron grip and twisted my arm painfully behind my back. "From here," he said, "two more inches and your shoulder will dislocate. Might break your arm too. If you're quick, you could spin out of it before I could push the rest of the way. Care to test me?"

I shook my head, standing up on my toes in an attempt to relieve some of the pressure on my arm.

Ruschick took a step toward us. "Where's your lady friend?"

The guard still by the door slumped down, revealing Lauri standing in the corridor, holding her stunner.

Ruschick jumped back and I felt the hard metal of Thomas's gun shoved under my jaw. "Drop it! Or I spray your friend's brains all over this room!"

Her eyes wide, Lauri didn't hesitate, tossing the small weapon away.

Thomas cleared his throat. "Director, could you find something to bind them with, please?"

A few minutes later, Lauri and I stood with our hands tied securely behind us with plastic tubing Ruschick discovered in Kritchkopf's lab. Although I was glad to see Ellis still breathing as he slept on the floor, saving the man's life seemed small consolation for getting caught and putting our main mission on the skids.

Thomas roughly patted the two of us down, presumably looking for more weapons, then he moved behind, restraining us with a firm grip on our arms. He had removed my communicator, but failed to discover the capsule in my pocket, which lifted my spirits slightly. Not that I could use it in my current state of affairs, but knowing I still had it gave me a small amount of comfort.

After Thomas handed him my communicator, Ruschick bent over and picked up my stunner from the floor. Shining his flashlight over it, he twirled it around his pudgy fingers. "Interesting device. Should fetch a good price from someone to reverse engineer. How long will they be out?" he asked me, jabbing a thumb toward the unconscious men.

I saw no point in lying. "An hour or so." Then, remembering his reaction to Hope's disappearance in Lansing's lab, I decided to try breeding some distrust. "Hope will never take you with her, Director."

He stopped his examination of the stunner and looked at me, his eyes not quite level with mine. "You know her?"

"We… work for the same people."

Ruschick laughed, which set his belly jiggling. "Rival companies I might believe, but the same people? No. The two of you seem to be at cross purposes."

"She's using you," I pressed. "Once she's got what she wants here, she'll be gone. I've seen this movie before. I know how it ends."

"You've got it all wrong, kid. I'm using her to get off this rock." He turned his attention to Lauri, standing beside me, and I felt her stiffen. "I told Kritchkopf I wanted long legs, but he made you too tall." He reached up and stroked her cheek. "Such beautiful work." Ruschick's hand brushed her neck, then moved down and fondled her breast. Lauri lunged at him, but Thomas held her fast. Ruschick chuckled. "Too feisty, as well." He patted his pocket which held the memory units. "But, I'll make sure the next version is more to my liking."

"Good luck with that," Lauri said. "You better make her blind and deaf, too, if you expect her not to gag in your presence."

Ruschick gave her a smile only fit for a flasher lurking near a school playground. I wanted to punch it from his face. "Oh, but that's all part of the fun, Sweetheart. If she's too compliant, how will I ever punish her for anything?" He looked up at Thomas. "Let's move," he said, then pointed to the sleeping men. "Send Michaels and Henry down to get these two once we're back at Operations."

"Yes, sir. What about that thing?" Thomas asked, referring to Kritchkopf's other creation, lying on the floor.

"Have them lock it back up in the lab until we figure out how to kill it. I can't believe it survived all these years."

Thomas gave us a shove. "You heard the man, move it."

31

Director Ruschick, and his henchman Thomas, marched us back to Dr. Lansing's section. We saw a few more men along the way, all dressed in the same blue jumpsuits as the rest of Ruschick's people. The man I recognized as the one Ru'am Koh had stunned during my last trip down this particular hallway stepped out from Lansing's Situation Room.

"Sir, something's gone wrong with the internal security system. Cameras, sensors, everything's locked up," the man said, frustration and a hint of fear in his voice.

"Where's Dr. Lansing?" Ruschick asked.

"Still in the washroom, sir."

"All right. Put these two in there with him for now," Ruschick instructed Thomas. "I'll have a look at the computer, but I think I have an idea what happened," he said with a smoldering glance in Lauri's direction.

"Yes, sir," Thomas replied and pushed us forward.

He guided us down the narrow corridor to a door with a younger man, who looked as if he might collapse from boredom at any second, standing beside it.

"Open it up," Thomas said.

The guard punched a short code into a locking mechanism placed on the door's wheel, which prevented it from turning.

After removing it, he spun the wheel and opened the door. Dr. Lansing sat in one corner of the tiny room, his lab coat smudged in a few places. He looked up with apprehension plain on his face, which turned to relief when he saw Lauri.

"Get in." Thomas ordered.

We complied before the predictable shove came and the door pulled closed. Lauri leaned into Dr. Lansing and he hugged her tight.

"I'm sorry I yelled at you," Lansing said. I couldn't figure out what he meant, then I remembered his stern communication to the rover soon after we'd left the Hub. It seemed like a long time ago.

"I'm sorry we left without telling you," Lauri said. "Everything's become such a mess."

"I know. I'm just glad you're safe."

Barely bigger than a closet, the washroom offered just enough space to turn around with the three of us inside. My foot bumped into something and I looked down to see my old clothes piled haphazardly in the corner. I chuckled softly.

"What is it, Dare?" Dr. Lansing asked.

Meeting his eyes, I saw marks on his face and his left cheek had swelled. "Oh, nothing. What happened to you?"

He noticed my attention and touched the injured area. "One of the colonist peacekeepers got a little overzealous when they decided to lock me in here a little while ago. I'll be fine."

"Peacekeepers?" I said with a laugh.

Lansing nodded. "The men with Director Ruschick are the colony's police force. I see they tied you up. Let me undo those."

He reached for Lauri's. "Wait," I said. "My shoulder's

killing me, but something tells me we should keep these on for now. If we have to be tied up, I'd much rather it was with this stuff than the super cuffs Hope had me in before."

Lauri looked disappointed, but agreed. It meant a great deal to me that she trusted my hunches. "Why did they stick you in here instead of putting you with the other scientists?" I asked Lansing.

"Victor— Director Ruschick— and his new lady friend wanted my help recalibrating the time machine. I refused, so they sent me in here to, 'think about it.' I'm sure, whatever they're planning, I don't want to be a part of it."

I nodded slowly, glad to have Lauri's faith in Dr. Lansing confirmed.

"Speaking of the time machine," the doctor said, reaching into his pocket. "I think I should have given this to you earlier, Dare, but your name made me hesitate."

I had a flash of deja vu as he revealed, once again, for Lauri and I at least, Kim's earbud I'd lost in Denver.

"You said that before— I mean, what about my name caused a problem?"

"I'd… been told someone else might be coming back with Lauri from her trip, but that person was supposed to be Dare Arthur, not Heisenberg. So, I became cautious."

"Hold on," Lauri said. "Who told you someone would come back with me? And how did you get Dare's earpiece?"

"Martin Nussbaum," Lansing said. "He was my great-grandfather."

Martin! "Um, I think you better start at the beginning," I said in disbelief.

Dr. Lansing chuckled. "Yes, I suppose so. I never actually spoke with Great-grandpa Martin, I was only two when he passed, but he left a lockbox to me in his will. My mother kept it until I turned eighteen, although it wouldn't open for me until almost four years later."

"Did they forget to give you the key or something?" I asked.

"No, nothing like that. It didn't even look like a lockbox. It was just a gray block of hard material about this big." He held his hands about eight inches apart. "Martin's will had described it as a lockbox, probably so my parents wouldn't just throw the thing away. Truthfully, I'd forgotten about the box until I was packing to go to grad school and I stumbled across it. I picked it up and it just popped open in my hands. Inside was a journal and this thing that looked like an old fashioned hearing aid, the same gray color as the box."

Some things started to fall into place and, if my suspicions were correct, Kim was going to have a lot of explaining to do if I made it out of this mess.

Lansing continued. "Martin's journal spun an amazing tale of espionage and time travel, the secrets of which, he promised, were connected to the hearing device that came with the journal. I was, of course, skeptical as to the purportedly factual nature of Great-grandpa's story— especially since I was beginning my masters in physics, and time travel as he described was thought to be pure fantasy. Mostly on a whim, I decided to take the little lump of gray material into the lab and run some tests. What I discovered over the following weeks and months led me to fully believe Martin's words."

My mind raced, thinking about the level of orchestration

involved underlying Dr. Lansing's story. Lauri's concerns were more personal.

"You sent me back already knowing what would happen? Why didn't you tell me?"

"I'm sorry, but Martin expressly forbid it in his notes to me. He said it could affect your decisions and change the course of time."

"What about the reason you gave me? All that stuff about the Martian probe malfunctioning. That was all just a lie?" Lauri asked, clearly upset.

"No. That was all true. The information came from Martin's journal, but I truly hoped it could change things for the better," Lansing said. "The fact that it didn't just proves the immutable nature of time."

I shook my head. "No. It proves that the people who recruited me monkey around with the threads of time way more than I was led to believe. Look, Dr. Lansing, we're here to prevent Director Ruschick and Hope— that's the woman who came with him— from doing something terrible. They plan to destroy the alien ships in orbit, killing thousands in the process. We've met them, and they aren't bad people. Their home planet is gone and they are looking for a new home."

"I don't understand. How can you know all this? You only left a few hours ago."

"There's another version of us still out there. We've probably already been captured and taken aboard their scout ship. By nightfall, the big vessels, which hold thousands of living beings, will be so much dust."

Lansing leaned back against the wall, visibly shaken by

what I'd said. "How? I… I don't… How did you get here?"

I inclined my head toward the earpiece, still in his hand. "Because you already gave me that a little while ago. Right before the Hub was destroyed by the last of Hope's bombs."

Lauri pressed close to him. "It's true, Karl. We have to stop them."

He hugged her and kissed her forehead. "I believe you. What can we do?"

I sighed. "I'm still working on that. But I can tell you what we don't do and that's help them with the time machine."

Metal clanked against metal outside the door and soon the wheel turned, releasing the latch. The door only had room to open part way, but Hope's bright face greeted me.

"Oh, it seems a bit cramped in there," she said with a mock look of concern. "Why don't we go somewhere a little more spacious and have a chat?"

32

Hope, who wore a blue jumper like the colony police, stepped back to make room and pointed down the hall. Ruschick, Thomas, and another peacekeeper stood passively along the wall. The director wore a smirk of superiority. A lack of options made my decision simple; I exited the washroom and walked the short distance to Lansing's lab and time machine. I shrugged my shoulders several times, trying to keep the blood flowing in my arms.

The rest of the group followed me inside. The room was bare but for the instrument panel and the circular patch of white tile on the floor. An absence of gray, spherical bombs lifted my spirits a little. Lauri and Dr. Lansing moved to stand close to me, facing Hope and her cronies near the door. In spite of what Ruschick had said, I knew who pulled the strings in this outfit.

Hope shook her head. "You act completely incompetent, Dare, but I have to say I'm impressed with you and your management system."

"Uh, thanks?" I said, unsure of her meaning.

"We couldn't trace you after you left Denver," she said, then nodded toward Lauri. "Fortunately, this one we found some background on and my system was able to establish her point of origin. But, how you managed to get here too, without leaving an insertion signature? My system is still stumped."

"Maybe you need a new system. What are you doing here, Hope?"

She blinked in surprise, then laughed. "I don't believe it. You really think I'm the bad guy here, don't you? I'm trying to clean up the mess that you and these… pretenders have made," she said, waving her hand at Lauri and Dr. Lansing. "Your system must have you completely brainwashed if you think you're the one who's setting things right."

"I certainly don't see how I could be the one messing with things. Hell, I've been tied up half the time!" I said, flexing my arms against the bindings. "What does your system have to say about that? Oh, I forgot, you can't ask it right now, can you?"

A shadow passed across Hope's face. She turned to Ruschick. "Would you mind checking on the casings? They should be almost finished."

The director scowled, but nodded. I sensed an opportunity and pounced. "You haven't told him, have you? That you've lost communication with your system."

Hope glared at me. "Which is due to more interference from you I'm guessing. Dare, your attempts to divide us won't work. These men all deserve to return to Earth and that's what I'm offering. After this incident with the aliens, a ship would likely be sent to retrieve the colonists in any case. I'm simply speeding up that process." She nodded to Ruschick.

"Shall I leave Thomas and Yannick here with you?" he asked.

"No. I'm perfectly capable of handling these three. See to the casings and let's put an end to all of this."

Ruschick and his men left the room, closing the portal behind them.

"That was quite a performance," I said. "Definitely Oscar worthy."

"What?" Hope asked.

"Oh, come on," I said in shock. "Don't tell me they don't have the Oscars any more in your time. Man, all my best lines have been wasted on you people."

"No more games," she said, waving her hand as if she were swatting a fly. "Dr. Lansing, have you reconsidered assisting me with your device?"

"No," he said.

"Expected, but unfortunate," Hope replied. "I understand you have an affection for this girl? I don't want to harm anyone, but I will if it becomes necessary."

Dr. Lansing stiffened and I took a step toward Hope. "Can't you see this is wrong?" I asked her. "You're changing the thread, not protecting it."

She drew her stunner. "Stop right there. Yes, I'm changing it. It's the only option because the thread's been altered in so many places it's become impossible to repair. These aliens aren't supposed to be here, Dare."

Her statement had a ring of truth to it I couldn't ignore. "And you think that's somehow my fault?"

"You or your system. I saw you observing your own birthday party. We detected the insertion of the toy and investigated. It was an exact replica of the ships orbiting Mars right now."

"I know."

"That can't be a coincidence, Dare."

"You're right. It can't. But we were just as surprised to detect the insertion and see the toy as you were."

"So you say. And it may be true for you, but can you be certain about your management system?"

I had to admit I couldn't be. "No. But I can ask the same question of you. Regardless of where you think the thread should go, is genocide really the answer here? Thousands of lives are about to be snuffed out because you, or your system, want to play God and set the universe straight."

"They were supposed to die already!"

"How do you know that? Because your system told you so?"

The ivory skin of Hope's face became blotched with red. She took a breath before answering. "I'm not going to argue with you any more. I've been an agent of the Keepers for two years. I know what I'm doing." She shifted her attention to my companions. "Dr. Lansing, I need your help to program your machine. As long as you comply, the girl will remain safe. If you refuse..."

"Karl, don't," Lauri said.

Lansing shook his head. "I can't let them hurt you." He looked at Hope. "I'll help. Just leave her alone."

"Thank you," Hope said. "You can begin by completing the energy alignment sequence I started before my communication was cut off." She finished with a glare in my direction.

"All right, but none of this will do any good. There's not enough power stored up yet to make a jump," Dr. Lansing said.

"What's there will be sufficient," Hope replied. "The trips will be very short." She pointed her stunner at Lauri and me. "You two, come with me. Dr. Lansing, I'll be back in a minute."

Hope opened the door and waved us through. She took us back to the washroom and I heard her engage the locking mechanism outside once the latch was secure.

I sighed. "That could have gone better."

"Yeah." Lauri leaned against the wall and expelled a long breath.

"I'm sorry. I really thought I could show her how wrong this was if she didn't have her supercomputer constantly spewing nonsense into her brain."

"I understand," she said. "Hope is conflicted. I could feel it. But you're not going to reverse two years of training in one conversation."

Spelled out that way, I felt like an idiot. "You're right. It was stupid. That may have been our only chance to get control of her, three against one."

Lauri shook her head. "It wasn't stupid. It was noble. And it's the difference between who you are and who she is."

I blushed. "Thanks. But I doubt my nobility is going to get us out of here before our time is up."

"Maybe not," Lauri admitted. "But that's why you have me around."

"What do you mean?"

"I still have the laser cutter Kim gave me," she said with a smile.

"What? Where?" I asked, trying to keep my voice down.

"I tucked it in my bra when we snuck into Kritchkopf's section. My arm kept bumping it when I walked so I took it out of my pocket. I was afraid Ruschick would find it when he was having his fun, which is why I went at him. Otherwise, I wouldn't have given the bastard the satisfaction of a reaction."

Elated, I wanted to hug her, then the reality of our

predicament hit home again. "We're still both tied up, what good will it do?"

"Well, I can't reach it, but you can," she said with a wink.

33

Soon, Lauri sat on the floor, with her legs straight out in front of her, while I crouched over her, facing away and feeling blindly with my bound hands.

"Come on, Dare. If I didn't know better, I'd think you were taking your time on purpose."

I felt my face flush. "This is more than a little awkward, you know."

"If you think it's a picnic back here, I've got news for you."

Finally, I found the top of her zipper and managed to pull it down a few inches. Feeling inside her jumper, my numb fingers bumped into the end of the hard tool. After two attempts, I got a firm grip on it and stood up slowly. "Now what?"

Lauri struggled to her feet and stood with her back to mine. "Give it to me."

I felt her take hold of the cutter and I carefully let go. I turned around and watched her practiced fingers manipulate the controls and activate the beam. The plastic tubing immediately gave way and Lauri pulled her hands free, twisting the cutter in the same motion to avoid a nasty burn. I turned back and, seconds later, my hands were free as well.

"Thank you. Now what?" I asked, rubbing my wrists. "The lock is on the other side of the door."

"Right, but the bar that holds the door closed isn't. The only problem is it's going to be painfully obvious to anyone out there that we're cutting our way out. I can't control the sparks and spitting hot metal."

That was certainly problematic. "Can you tell if someone's there?"

She nodded. "The same guy as before. He's bored out of his mind."

"Anyone else?"

Lauri closed her eyes. "There's at least one person in the Situation Room and Karl and Hope are still in the lab. That's all I can feel."

I rubbed my hands in frustration. We had the means to escape, but it looked doubtful we'd get much farther than the washroom door. "Do you think you could, I don't know, put a whammy on the guard outside? I mean, you were able to send emotions to Ru'am Koh through the glass on his ship."

"I don't know. That was different. I was just trying to convey some ideas. I certainly didn't have control of his mind or anything."

"Okay, but could you maybe make him nervous? Or scared? Enough that he would feel the need to get away from here for a minute or two?"

She thought about it. "Maybe. I suppose it's worth a try."

"All right. Show me how to use the cutter."

After I felt comfortable operating the device, I crouched at the edge of the door where she indicated the bar was. If she could get the guard to leave, we had no idea how long the effect might last, so I'd have to act quickly. I nodded to her and she placed both hands against the metal door and closed her eyes.

Several minutes passed and my muscles began to protest. I shifted to a kneeling position and looked up at Lauri for the thousandth time. Tiny beads of sweat crowned her forehead and her brow creased in concentration.

Suddenly, her eyes snapped open and she whispered, "No."

I heard a rumbling outside in the corridor. Pressing my ear to the door, Ruschick's voice sounded tense. "Keep going. All the way to the end of the hall, into the lab."

I sat back and stretched my legs. Lauri sank to the floor next to me. "I'm sorry," she said. "I'm just not strong enough."

Setting the cutter in my lap, I leaned over and hugged her. "It's okay. We'll figure something out."

The rumbling faded and I could barely make out Ruschick, muffled by walls and distance, barking orders from the lab. The bombs had arrived, rolled in by more of his peacekeepers I guessed. "How long did it take Dr. Lansing to prep the time machine to send you to Denver?" I asked.

"A while. I probably sat on the pad for a good half hour before it was ready."

"Good. That means we still have time."

"Time for what? There's even more guards out there now."

Disappointment and despair flooded me, drowning any kernels of optimism I'd been able to foster. The hopelessness of our situation finally hit home. The Keepers, or whoever had chosen me, had been the worst kinds of fools. What had possessed them to think a high school dropout, living on the streets in Colorado, could jump in and fix the problems of the universe? This was a job for a superhero, not some kid who never knew where his next meal was coming from. My adoptive parents had been right to give up on me. Hell, my biological parents had made the best choice: casting me aside immediately so I couldn't infect their lives with my failures.

"Oh, God. No. Dare, stop."

I found myself curled in a tight ball on the unforgiving metal floor, with the business end of the laser cutter in my mouth. Lauri gently pulled my finger away from the actuator, then removed the tool from my grasp.

Warmth and caring, mixed with just a hint of fear, invaded the gloom that had settled in my thoughts. "What happened?"

"I pushed myself too hard with the guard and lost control," Lauri said, stroking my cheek. "I am so sorry."

Slowly, my head cleared. I looked up at her beautiful face, framed by strands of white hair that had escaped her pony tail. Her eyes held nothing but concern. Why did she have to be so young? I forced a smile. "Let's not have any more talk about you not being strong enough, okay?"

She laughed. Her bright smile banished the last bits of darkness from my mind. "Okay," she said.

I pushed myself up to a sitting position and leaned back on the wall. "How long do you think it's been?"

"Since we got here? I don't know, an hour. Maybe more."

"That's about what I was thinking. So, we have less than two hours before the thread unlocks," I said.

"Yes, but probably a lot less before Hope and Karl are ready to send the bombs to the pahsahni ships."

Something nagged at my thoughts, but I couldn't pin it down. I tried working through the events as we knew them.

"All right, it's late afternoon. What do you suppose our other selves are doing right now?"

Lauri sat back and considered my question. "It's hard to say. I guess we might be touring their ship by now after you'd finished with the translator. Why?"

I nodded. "Things have changed. Dr. Lansing sent us that message, remember? It doesn't seem likely he'd do that now."

"Okay, right. But we wanted to change what happened, so what's wrong?"

"The changes are occurring here, but not so much out there. What were the pahsahni doing at that time?"

Her eyes grew big. "Getting ready to invade the colony!"

"Bingo."

"The ships blew up before that though," Lauri pointed out.

"Yes, because the thread altered. I think that's why I got dizzy on the ship before it happened. Hope found out the pahsahni were going to attack, so she sent the bombs back in time—maybe just an hour or two— to prevent it and I felt it somehow."

"Why didn't she just destroy them before they even got to Mars then?"

I shook my head. "I don't know, not enough energy maybe? Or some other piece to this puzzle we don't have yet. The real problem is, the pahsahni will be coming, and probably very soon."

"So, we can just wait for their help," Lauri said.

"No. Remember, they aren't coming down to help. They're coming down to take over. People are going to die. On both sides. Once shots are fired, I don't see either side backing down until only one is left standing."

A bit of light left her eyes. "What do we do?"

I let out a breath and realized I'd been hoping she'd contradict me— find some point to argue. "We still have to stop Hope, but we also need to get a message to the pahsahni. Tell them to hold off."

"And just how are we supposed to do all that, Mr. Heisenberg?"

"Patience, Grasshoppah. Patience," I said with a wink, trying to portray confidence I didn't feel. "Look, the first step to solving a problem is identifying it, right? I thought I was doing pretty good there." I stood up and wished for room to pace. "If only we hadn't used up all the power in the invisibility pendants…"

She got up and said, "Mine still has some."

"What? How?"

"I shut it off when I started tailing the two guys outside Kritchkopf's lab. It was dark and they made enough noise to cover any sounds I made, so I didn't see a need for it."

I wanted to kiss her. "Why didn't you list that among our assets?" I said instead, with a soft English accent.

She looked at me like my hair had sprouted flowers. "What?"

I really needed to stop quoting old movies to these people, but it had just popped out. Hell, we even had Rodents Of Unusual Size running around. "Never mind. How much time do you think it has left?"

"Maybe three minutes."

"Okay," I said, nodding and sifting through ideas in my head. "What do you think of this…"

34

I pressed myself against the back wall of the washroom as Lauri kicked the door while holding a longer piece of the plastic tubing in her hands, clasped behind her to look like they were still tied up.

"Hey! Somebody! This guy just disappeared!" she yelled.

"Cut it out," the guard said, his voice dulled through the door. "What's your problem?"

"I told you. The guy I was with in here is gone. Poof!" She punctuated the last with another kick.

"Just hang on," came the response.

Seconds passed, then I heard footsteps approaching. Lauri showed me two fingers.

"What's going on?" Ruschick asked through the door.

"There was a bright light and Dare's gone," Lauri said. "He left me here."

"Open it," I heard the director say.

Lauri stepped back and I activated her pendant, now around my neck, just as the door began to move. I felt the slight tingle as before and held my breath.

Ruschick peered into the washroom with a furrowed brow. "Dammit," he said, then looked at Lauri. "C'mon. You can tell Hope what you saw."

The three marched down to the lab. I expelled my breath and waited five seconds before following.

"Lauri! Are you all right?" I heard Dr. Lansing ask as I approached the open door. One of the spherical bombs sat on the white tiled area in the center of the chamber, just as I'd seen when I'd arrived with Ru'am Koh previously. Three more waited by the wall near the doorway. Lansing met Lauri and embraced her, while Hope stood impatiently with a hand on her hip, sipping water from a bottle. Ruschick and the peacekeeper moved into the room and I slipped in behind them, moving slowly along the wall, away from the bombs.

"I'm fine," Lauri said after Lansing released her. "But Dare's gone."

Hope perked up at this and set her drink on a shelf by the instrument panel. I focused on the bottle, figuring it was my best shot. "What happened?"

"There was this bright flash of light, then he wasn't there." Lauri paused, then added, "He told me he was going to take me with him."

Hope looked at the taller girl skeptically and I winced. If Hope was suspicious, everything could fall apart quickly. My progress around the room was agonizingly slow, but I couldn't risk being noticed.

The sound of running boots in the corridor distracted everyone. A peacekeeper leaned inside. "Director! You have to see this."

"See what, Wilson?"

"The aliens, sir. They're sending a large number of smaller ships to the surface."

Ruschick's face turned purple. "Contact Thomas. Tell him to have every available man suit up and get to the entrance to prepare for assault."

"Yes, sir!" Wilson said and ran back down the hall.

"How much longer?" Ruschick asked Hope.

"Fifteen or twenty minutes."

"What about all these smaller ships? We don't know how many there are," the director said.

Hope shrugged. "Doesn't matter. We should have enough power to send these things back in time an hour or so as well as placing them in the big ships. It'll be like the smaller ones on the way now never existed."

Ruschick looked confused for a moment, then he smiled. "I like the way you think. Still, we need to prepare for an attack. You," he said, pointing at Lauri. "Come with me. You're going to undo whatever you did to the security system. We're going to need it."

"All right," she said, hanging her head. "I'll help since it looks like I'm stuck here with the rest of you."

Maybe they didn't have the Oscars anymore in 2087, but I was going to make sure that girl got one. Ruschick took her by the arm and led her out. The other peacekeeper followed, securing the door behind them.

I had managed to make it to Hope's drink during the commotion. I dug in my pocket for the capsule of nanomachines, knowing I had precious little invisibility time left.

"Okay," Hope said. "Back to work, Doctor."

Lansing pursed his lips and walked back to the instrument panel as I pulled out the packet which held the capsule. I had to open it by feel since it was enveloped by the invisibility field, just as I was.

"Can you make the adjustments to send the devices back in time as I said?" Hope asked Lansing.

"Yes. But we'll have to recalculate spatial positioning for the ships."

"Of course."

I finally got the packet open and held the capsule over the mouth of the bottle. Hope stood next to Lansing at the controls, less than two feet away. I broke the casing and watched the contents drop, seemingly from thin air, and dissolve in the water.

Hope turned toward me and I froze. She appeared puzzled, then reached for the bottle.

I moved my hands away to avoid a collision and it was Hope's turn to freeze. She'd noticed the ripples my motion had caused and a scowl formed on her face. She backed away from the bottle and slowly reached in her pocket.

Knowing if she drew her stunner the fight was over, invisibility or not, I lunged.

I hit her just as her hand emerged from her pocket. The stunner went flying and the two of us landed in what I'm sure was a strange looking heap.

I found out quickly that Hope hadn't been exaggerating about her other implants.

Her knee came up, just missing my groin, but impacting painfully on my leg. A small fist blasted my ribcage and I rolled away, trying to recapture the breath she'd forced from my lungs.

"Dare, you don't seem to know when to give up," Hope said, crouching near the edge of the tiled section of floor. Dr. Lansing had his back to the wall, startled from the sudden activity.

I stayed quiet and still, watching Hope scan the room. I searched for the stunner, but couldn't see it anywhere. Moving while her eyes were elsewhere, I pulled the laser cutter from my other pocket.

Dr. Lansing gasped and Hope's head snapped in my direction. So much for the invisibility. "Ah, there you are," she said with a smile.

I got to my feet and activated the cutter. "I don't want to hurt you."

She straightened and took a step toward me. "Then you're putting yourself at a disadvantage, because I do want to hurt you."

Hope rocketed forward before I could bring the cutter to bear. She swept my arm aside with a blow from her forearm and planted the heel of her other hand in my sternum with extreme force.

I felt something pop in my chest and I staggered backward. Somehow, I kept a grip on the cutter, but pain lanced through my ribs with every breath.

She came at me again, this time with a roundhouse kick to my head I barely managed to duck. I swung the laser tool, hoping to catch her on her follow through, but she dodged it effortlessly.

"You really should have asked for the upgrades, Dare," Hope said with a laugh. "People always think they can take advantage of a girl my size. Not this girl."

I faked throwing a punch with my left hand, then dove in with the cutter in my right. Hope sidestepped and grabbed my arm. Using a combination of my momentum and her considerable strength, she sent me careening across the room. My back impacted first, then my head, and I wasn't sure if the ringing I heard was from the metal wall or just inside my noggin.

Stars danced in my eyes. I lowered my throbbing head and noticed a bottle of water sitting on a shelf next to me. Thirsty, I grabbed it and took a drink. The slightly salty taste triggered something in my mind and snapped me back to reality.

Hope stood a few feet away, smiling. "After all the trouble you've caused me, I thought this would be more fun. But really, it's just pathetic. What did the Keepers ever see in you?"

"Oh, I don't know. From what I've seen so far, time is just one big mess. I think they were looking for someone with some janitorial skills. You know, wet clean up on Mars in 2087."

"Wha—"

I pointed the bottle at her and squeezed. The water erupted, drenching her face and hair.

Hope sputtered, blinking water from her eyes. "Are you insane?"

Behind her, the door to the lab opened. Director Ruschick's pear-shaped frame filled the entry. "What the hell is going on in here?"

Hope spun around, still dripping. "Victor, it's fine. I have everything under control."

He stepped inside. "Yes, it certainly looks like it. What's he doing here again?" Ruschick said, pointing at me.

"He's just a minor annoyance I was about to…" Hope stumbled and fell. "What's happening?"

Kim had said the nanomachines needed to be ingested

to do their work. Since they were microscopic, I figured any opening would do: mouth, nose, eyes. I hadn't expected the little suckers to work so fast.

Ruschick growled and moved toward me.

"Stop right there, Victor!"

Past the instrument panel to my left, Dr. Lansing stood with Hope's stunner pointed at the colony director.

The heavyset man did stop, then chuckled. "Karl, are you really going to shoot me when my men have Lauri in custody down the hall? The aliens are on their way in force. We'll all be dead shortly if we don't do something."

At my feet, Hope groaned softly, but I kept my eyes on the two men.

Lansing hesitated, lowering the stunner an inch or two.

Realizing he didn't understand what the little weapon would do, I shouted, "Doctor, just shoot him! It'll only put him to sleep."

Ruschick took advantage of the confusion and drew my stunner from his pocket. He dropped down, using the bomb in the center of the room as cover, and fired at Lansing.

The scientist ducked and the shot went wide. I crouched and scrambled to Lansing's side. "Here, give it to me." The doctor happily handed the weapon over and crawled closer to the time machine controls. I spun around trying to locate Ruschick.

I didn't see him at first, the bomb sat between us, then I noticed a chubby hand reaching for the top of one of the deadly spheres by the door.

"No!" I jumped up and fired.

Ruschick's body slumped away from the gray ball, just

before his finger reached the activator.

That's when I noticed red lights flashing on the other two bombs beside it.

35

I tried to take a calming breath, but gasped instead as what felt like hot needles tortured my chest. Hope hadn't been kidding when she'd said she wanted to hurt me.

"Dare, are you all right?" Lansing asked, putting a hand on my shoulder.

"I'll manage. Do those lights mean what I think they mean?"

Dr. Lansing glanced at the bombs. "I don't know, but the one on the pad is doing the same thing."

I looked over at it and groaned. "Why did they make these so easy to turn on?"

Walking over and reaching down, I patted Ruschick's clothes until I found the communicator Kim had given me. The countdown clock showed we had just over an hour left before the thread unlocked. I picked up my stunner from the director's limp hand and pocketed it, along with Hope's. The woman, who'd caused a substantial amount of grief for her size, moaned from a fetal position on the floor. I went and knelt beside her. If anyone knew how to turn off the bombs, she would.

Her head turned toward me, revealing an empty eye socket. I winced at the sight.

"What did you do to me, you bastard!?"

Hope's remaining eye was full of pain and hatred, still I focused on it. "Microscopic robots. Kim, my system, made them to destroy your implants."

She coughed. "Clever. I suppose you didn't know that several of those implants were keeping me alive."

Shocked, I said, "No. I didn't."

"Dare, I was only so much ground up meat when the Keepers found me and saved my life. Don't you see? I owe them everything."

"I don't understand. Why didn't they just reconstruct your body?"

"My management system thought the organic components were inferior. And it was right!" She coughed again.

"Look, I'm sorry, but we have a bigger problem. Ruschick activated three of the bombs. How do we turn them off?"

Hope managed a brief smile before she choked and spit up a bit of blood. "You can't. We couldn't take the chance our visitors would figure out how to do it. The magnetic field holding the antimatter will degrade over the next twenty minutes or so. Nothing can stop it." She grimaced in pain and fell silent.

I looked to Lansing who had come over to quietly listen in. "Any ideas? Can we put another magnetic field around them or something?"

He shook his head. "Guessing at the structure, once the vacuum is breached inside the casing, the antimatter will react with that material. We couldn't create a field strong enough to contain that much energy."

"So what do we do?"

Hope's voice croaked. "Send them to the ships like you're supposed to."

"No. I won't do that." In the previous thread, Hope had transported a bomb onto each of the pahsahni colony ships. What if we put the bombs where the ships weren't? To Lansing, I asked, "What about into empty space? Would that work?"

His face brightened. "It should, yes! I'll reconfigure," he said and jumped up to the controls.

Beside me, Hope's body tensed. "Disaster," she said. "You have no idea what you're doing."

"Maybe not. But I know what I'm not going to do, and that's kill thousands of innocent people." I took a deep breath and flinched at the jolt my ribs sent in protest. "Hope, I'm truly sorry. I didn't mean for this to happen, but we had to stop you. Is there anything I can do to help you?"

"Shoot me."

"What? I can't—"

"Stop being so dense, Dare. With the stunner."

"Oh. Right." I stood up and plucked one of them from my pocket. She closed her functioning eye and I depressed the trigger. Her body relaxed and I prayed it would at least keep her from feeling the pain for a while. I felt confident Kim could patch her up if we made it through the next hour or so.

I looked up in time to see Lauri jog into the chamber. "Is everything okay? I heard shouting."

"Yes and no," I said. "Are you all right? Did you get a message through?"

"I had a little trouble with the peacekeeper in the Situation Room, but now he's locked up in the washroom where we were.

I sent a message using Ru'am Koh's name, asking them to hold off their attack, but I don't know if it was received."

"Okay, that's all we can do for now," I said, speculating for a moment on how she'd handled her "little trouble", then decided I maybe didn't want to know. I moved over to Ruschick's limp form. "Help me move him."

Lauri gave me a sour look, then grabbed his feet. "Why?"

"So we can roll those bombs onto the pad. Ruschick turned them on."

Her eyes grew wide as we slid the colony director to lie next to Hope. I explained our situation and what Dr. Lansing was attempting to do. Lauri and I stood, looking nervously at the large spheres.

Finally, I shrugged. "They rolled them in here from wherever they put them together, so they can't be delicate. Besides, if they blow up, we'll be dead instantly."

She rolled her eyes. "That's comforting."

We put our hands on opposite sides of one and started it rolling. "Wow, they're heavy," Lauri said. After two or three minutes, we had all three situated on the tiles where we felt like they were stable and wouldn't roll off. I would have preferred to ship all four bombs into deep space, but the pad barely had enough room for the three.

"How much longer, Doctor?" I asked Lansing.

"Another five minutes or so. The calculations are quite complex, even for the computer."

Silence filled the room as we waited for the time machine's computer to finish its work. I stared at the stone-like balls, which barely fit together in the white-tiled circle. So much potential destruction sat passively, awaiting release. Time might have stopped but for the three red lights, blinking slightly out of sync.

"*Liebchen*?"

My head whipped around in the direction of the unexpected sound. The spidery Hans stood in the open doorway.

Lauri was just as surprised. "What are you doing here?" she asked in a soft voice.

"I thought I felt you near me earlier. Then I fell asssleep, right before I wasss about to have my firssst meal in a long, long time. Very ssstrange."

Mentally, I urged Lauri to keep the creature talking as I gradually reached into my pocket, not wanting to attract its attention.

"How did you get out of the lab?" she asked it.

"The door wasss closssed, but not locked asss it hasss been for ssso long."

Evidently, the peacekeepers hadn't thought it necessary to do anything more than shut the portals. They probably hadn't understood how dextrous Hans was, or maybe how smart.

Then Lauri asked the question I dreaded the answer to. "Did you find a meal on your way here?"

"No. The men were called away jussst asss I awakened."

I released a pent up breath.

Then Hans added. "I am very hungry."

I slowly raised the stunner and pressed the trigger.

Nothing happened.

Hans focused his attention on me. "What isss that?"

"This? Nothing."

"May I sssee it?"

Out of power, the weapon was useless, so I tossed it to the creature. "Sure."

A forelimb flashed upward, snatching the stunner from the air. Hans's powerful and deadly claws proved equally delicate in handling the small object. The creature examined it with the fascination of a small child.

"All right," Dr. Lansing said. "I think we're rea— what is that?!"

The scientist had been so absorbed by his instruments he'd failed to note the arrival of our visitor. Lauri moved over to calm her surrogate father. "It's okay. Karl, this is Hans, Dr. Kritchkopf's creation."

Finished with its assessment of the device, Hans dropped the stunner and looked up. "Hello, Dr. Lansssing. Dr. Kritchkopf wasss alwaysss impresssed with your work."

Lansing paused, clearly unsure how to react. Finally, he said, "Thank you. As I was saying, we're ready. Step to the edge of the room and cover your eyes. The photonic discharge is quite bright."

"What are thessse?" Hans asked, indicating the gray globes.

"Bombs, Hans," I answered, suddenly nervous the creature would want to play with them. "They are about to explode and we need to get rid of them. Quickly." I felt in my pocket for the other stunner. The two looked nearly identical. If the one I'd picked out first had been mine, and it had also been the one I'd used on Hope, that would account for four shots and why it had been out of juice. Hope's, on the other hand, I was reasonably certain still had power.

Lauri pleaded with the creature. "Hans, please move away.

If they go off, we all die."

It hesitated only a heartbeat before skittering to the other side of the room. I raised Hope's stunner, but the bombs blocked my shot.

Lansing pressed a button on the panel and I threw an arm up to block my eyes, my injured chest protesting at the sudden motion. Light blazed through the room.

Then, we were plunged into darkness.

36

"The lights should be back in a minute," I heard Lansing say, off to my right. "I had to drain every last scrap of power to make it work."

"Did it?" I asked. "Work, I mean." Nervous about being in a darkened room with Hans, I slid along the wall toward Dr. Lansing's voice.

"I believe so. But I won't know for certain until the unit powers up again."

"Lauri, are you okay?"

"Right here, Dare," she said, closer than I'd anticipated. "I'm fine."

A bank of dim lights bordering the ceiling of the circular chamber flickered on, revealing an empty section of white tiles. I gave Lauri a quick hug, then I noticed Hans hovering over the prone forms of Hope and Ruschick.

"Hey! Get away from them!"

Hans's head snapped up from scrutinizing the colony director. I stepped in front of Lauri and Dr. Lansing, pointing Hope's weapon at the genetically manipulated nightmare.

"Another toy? Why do you care about thisss pig of a man?"

I hesitated, taken aback by its question. Why did I care if Ruschick met a gruesome end at the hands, or claws, of this creature? By all accounts the man was self-serving, twisted, and callous. Did that mean he deserved to die? I'd already watched Ruschick be brutally murdered by Hans. Once was enough.

I pushed the button, but Hans was already in motion, the beast having somehow sensed my decision even as I made it. A wave of energy invaded the space where Hans had been. I only succeeded in reinforcing the slumber of the two bodies on the floor.

Swinging my arm, I fired again, but Hans's reactions were as fast as the creature it most resembled. It scurried away from the beam, stopping near the door and the last inert gray sphere.

"Dare," Lauri said, putting her hand on my arm. "Stop."

It was abundantly clear I wasn't going to hit the thing as long as its attention was focused on me. Plus, if Hope's weapon worked in similar fashion to mine, I had just one or two shots left.

"I only desssire my freedom," Hans said. "But I think you are not likely to give it to me."

"Look," I said and lowered the stunner. "Let's try to talk this out. Understand, I do appreciate the fact you haven't attacked us since you arrived."

"I would not hurt my Liebchen who helped me. Ssshe obviousssly caresss for you and the doctor."

"I do," Lauri agreed. "And I care for you also."

"Then let me go," Hans said.

"If we did, where would you go? How would you survive?" I asked.

"Asss I wasss meant to. I have a whole planet to disssscover."

"No people to eat out there though," I said, gauging its reaction.

Hans sighed, its breath coming out as a whistle. "I can consssume organicsss, but they are not my preferred sssource of nutrition. My creator desssigned me to sssurvive on raw energy. Sssunlight, volcanic heat, even Dr. Lansssing's machine here provided me sssome food."

Lansing made a small noise of surprise and turned to the control panel, which had powered up once more.

Even if Hans's brain had been modeled from a human's, I found it more inscrutable and alien than the pahsahni's. The creature seemed to be a jumble of emotions, all trying to manifest at once.

I posed a question. "Can we trust you?"

"I have been trying to ssshow you that you can by not killing you. I could have done it a hundred timesss already."

A sobering thought, especially since it was probably true. "So what about all the men between here and the airlock? How do we convince them to let you walk out of here?"

Hans turned to the door and hissed. Lauri squeezed my arm.

"I seriously doubt any of you is walking out of here," Peacekeeper Thomas said, his arms outstretched, aiming his pistol at us.

37

"Hands up!" Thomas ordered. "What have you done to Director Ruschick?"

"He's fine. Just stunned," I said, raising my arms slowly and wondering what else could go wrong.

Hans provided an answer by reaching over and activating the final bomb.

Thomas shifted his sights to the creature.

I shouted, "Don't shoot! You know what that is, right? I don't know what the outside is made of, but I'd rather not test to see if it's bulletproof."

"It may be a moot point, Dare," Dr. Lansing said. "The machine doesn't have enough power to transport a microbe right now, let alone another bomb."

"Hans, why?" Lauri asked.

"An act of desssperation. Or a guarantee of sssafe passsage."

"What are you talking about?" I wondered.

"You let me leave. I take the explosssive with me."

Several people started talking at once while I tried to think. I knew we had more than the twenty minutes of the bomb's life left in Kim's time knot, so waiting it out wasn't an option.

"Hold on! Time out!" I yelled, holding my hands up to form a T. "Can we even get the thing outside?" I asked Lauri once everyone quieted. "Seemed like there were a lot of ladders and stairs between here and the garage."

"You and I didn't exactly go the direct route," she said. "It should be possible."

"What about the blast area? How far away do we have to get this thing?"

Dr. Lansing answered. "Without knowing the amount of antimatter inside, it's difficult to guess, but I'd venture to say four or five kilometers at the very least."

"What if we put it in one of your rovers?" Thomas asked. I was glad he seemed willing to find a solution rather than just stand and uselessly wave his gun around.

"Someone would have to drive it," Lansing said. "Remote piloting it at the speeds required to get it to safe distance would be too risky once you left the clear zone around the cave's entrance."

"Can you do it, Hans?" I asked. "Can you get it far enough away and still give yourself a chance to survive?"

"I believe I can or I would not have pressed the button. I can feel the energy field inssside well enough to know how much time isss left. But you mussst desside quickly."

I blew a breath of frustration. "So, we have a choice of someone volunteering for a suicide mission, or trusting Hans to do what he says."

Precious seconds passed. Finally, Thomas made a decision and shouted back down the hallway. "Secure arms and make way!" To Hans he said, "Go."

The amazing creature showed it possessed great strength as well as speed. The bomb's weight appeared of little consequence as it rolled the heavy ball to the doorway and lifted it over the threshold. It then proceeded down the corridor at a considerable pace.

I turned to Lauri. "We should send another message to the pahsahni. Let them know what's going on."

"Right." With a nod to Thomas, she headed to Lansing's Situation Room.

"Who are the 'pawsawnee'?" Thomas asked me.

"The aliens you and Director Ruschick have been so preoccupied with. They're not the monsters you've been led to believe they are."

"Hmph. We'll see. Doctor, where can we set up to remote pilot one of your rovers?"

Lansing appeared surprised. "Peacekeeper, I told you that wouldn't work."

"I believe you, but I don't think it would hurt to have an insurance policy. We'll follow behind the spider to see that he keeps his end of the bargain. And be in a position to give the bomb a push if he doesn't."

"Ah," Dr. Lansing said. "I see your point. This way."

A couple of minutes later, six of us were stuffed in Lansing's Situation Room. One peacekeeper sat at a console, prepping a rover, with Lansing's help, to follow Hans once he left the Hub. Another, Wilson— the one Lauri had locked in the washroom and who appeared to hold a grudge— manned the communications station, relaying orders from Thomas to the rest of his force. Lauri and I stood behind them, watching the screens and itching to be involved. She had sent a second message to the pahsahni, then been forcibly removed from the seat by Thomas.

"Wilson, make sure we have men stationed at the airlock to cycle the bug through as soon as possible once he arrives," Thomas said.

"Yes, sir."

I looked at the big man standing next to me. "I've been wondering something. What made you decide to leave the entrance and come back here?"

Thomas frowned. "Communication silence from Wilson, then, when the lights went out, I knew there had to be some sort of trouble."

"Sir," Wilson said. "We're receiving an outside transmission, but I can't make any sense of it."

"Put it on speakers."

Wilson tapped the controls and sound burst into the room. "… fourth planet. We… registered… detonation… seconds ago. You are… cease hostile activities… respond." The message began again with the same gaps.

"Turn it off," Thomas ordered.

"What are you doing? We have to respond!" I said in shock.

"Respond? Respond to what? All I heard was a bunch of whistles, clicks, and static," Thomas said.

I looked back at Lauri as she reached for her ear. "My translator's gone," she said.

"Kim must have poofed it along with your environment suit. Thomas, look, that transmission is from the pahsahni, the aliens, and we need to respond or they may crater this place if that bomb doesn't."

The big peacekeeper furrowed his brow in thought. In my mind, I heard an enormous clock, ticking away second after second. Thomas finally nodded to Wilson. "Patch him in."

Wilson rolled his eyes, but complied and pointed at the button to transmit. I pushed it and said, "To the pahsahni: we have received your transmission, but the message is incomplete. We are not engaged in hostile acts. May I please speak with the human male in the company of Ru'am Koh?"

Peacekeeper Wilson sat back and put a hand to his headset. "The first transmission's stopped, sir."

The man at the rover controls said, "The unit's prepped and ready to roll, sir."

"Good," Thomas responded. "Where's the bug?"

"They're cycling him through the airlock now."

A hiss of static sounded over the speakers, followed by a strange voice. "Uh, hello?" I cringed and thought, please tell me I don't really sound like that.

I pushed the transmit button. "Dare? This is... Arthur. I'm in the Hub, but there's no time to explain. We're getting a message from the pahsahni, but I can't understand all of it. Can you tell me what they're saying?"

I tried not to hold my breath during the silence that followed. "Okay, the message was, 'Inhabitants of the fourth planet. We registered a significant detonation in space thirty seconds ago. You are ordered to cease hostile activities immediately. Please respond.'"

"We are not engaged in hostile activities. The colony director attempted to put bombs aboard the pahsahni ships, but we stopped him. They exploded in space instead, but we have one more down here we can't transport, so we are sending it out the front door. If they have personnel outside this facility, they need to evacuate, now."

"They're talking it over," the other me said. "By the way, Ru'am says they use many sounds in their language that we don't hear, but our brains still register. Too high a frequency, like a dog whistle, I guess. Our audio equipment doesn't reproduce them, so that's probably why the message isn't translating properly."

The explanation made some sense, but I cringed at my own previous ignorance. "Dare, his name is Ru'am Koh. You're insulting them each time you leave off the ending."

"Oh!... Oh. Gotcha. Hang on," my other, slightly less ignorant self said. "Okay, they say they are skeptical, given the recent history, but they will pull back their forces. Wait, what is that? Sorry, we're seeing video of the cavern entrance. It looks like a giant spider rolling a big ball?"

I chuckled and glanced over at the monitor in front of the rover pilot. It showed a night sky beyond the cave mouth and Hans pushing the bomb outside, its powerful legs churning the Martian soil. The rover began to move forward, following the precocious genetic experiment. "The ball is an antimatter bomb," I said. "Just make sure the pahsahni stay clear."

Lansing leaned over and gave a command to the computer. The image from the vehicle's camera filled the wall of screens in front of us. The room fell silent as we vicariously followed Hans and the bomb on their journey, each of us urging them for more speed.

It soon became evident that Dr. Lansing had been right about using the rover for the operation. Several times, the driver was forced to slow to avoid colliding with some of the larger obstacles in the Martian landscape. The camera lost sight of its quarry, but the trail was easy to follow.

Several minutes later, the rover caught up to the bomb, sitting innocently under the stars. Another set of tracks led away from it at a right angle.

"Distance?" Thomas asked.

"Four point one six kilometers," the driver replied.

"Give her a nudge, Jenkins. A little more space between us isn't going to hurt."

"Yes, sir."

The image moved forward slowly, meeting up with the bomb. It began to roll again, though at a more sedate pace than before.

Without warning, the screens flashed to static.

A split second later, the shockwave hit.

38

I'd never experienced an earthquake before, but I couldn't imagine the feeling of helplessness being any worse.

I grabbed the back of Wilson's chair in front of me for support as the wave of force rumbled through the Hub. My knees felt like jelly and I struggled to keep myself upright. Metal screeched and groaned all around, vehemently protesting the added strain. The room's lights and screens dimmed for a second or two, then renewed as the shaking subsided.

The alarms and sirens I expected to hear failed to materialize. Silence and disbelief hung in the room.

Dr. Lansing's voice broke the spell. "Computer, systems report."

The screens on the wall flashed through countless images in the span of two heartbeats. "Systems nominal," it responded, as if wondering why they would be otherwise.

Someone out in the hallway released a cheer of sheer joy, echoed by more of the peacekeepers. We exchanged laughter, hugs, and handshakes, exultant in our good fortune.

Lansing said, "Peacekeeper, you should probably form teams with sealant kits to make a sweep of the facility. There may be minor pressure leaks the sensors won't pick up immediately."

Thomas nodded. "Jenkins, assign a group of two to each section."

"Yes, sir," the rover driver said, getting up from his seat. He exited the room and I heard more orders being passed through the colony police force in the hall.

"Message incoming, sir," Wilson said.

My voice rang through the speakers. "Hey, are you guys okay down there?"

Pressing the transmit button, I answered, "We think so. How about you?"

"All good. No injuries. That was quite a blast."

"Yes it was. I'm just glad it happened out there and not in here." I paused, then punched the button again. "We'd like to invite a delegation in to discuss how we can work together." Wilson slapped my hand aside, at an order from Thomas, but not before I finished.

"What the hell are you thinking?" Thomas asked, looming over me.

I stood up as tall as possible to face him. "I'm thinking there's been enough killing. These people are stranded here. Their world is gone. Put down the guns and start talking."

"Director Ruschick will never approve of that," the peacekeeper said.

"No," I agreed. "But once Earth finds out what he's done here, I'd be surprised if Ruschick won't be the former director in short order. Did you know there are still some operational satellites?"

Thomas raised his eyebrows. "What? How do you know that?"

"It doesn't matter. The point is, I have no idea what Ruschick told you and your men about going home, but it wasn't going to happen. The pahsahni are here and they aren't going away, so you better start talking to them unless you want to fight a war where you're outnumbered ten to one."

He looked at me skeptically, then glanced at Dr. Lansing.

"I'd listen to him if I were you," Lansing offered.

"He's just a kid," Thomas said and I bit my cheek.

The doctor nodded. "Maybe so, but he's done some pretty remarkable things already. And I'm thinking I don't know the half of it," he said with a grin and a wink at me. Lauri gave me a wide smile as well.

Right on cue, my voice carried over the speakers. "They say they would be willing to meet. What about the colony?"

I looked at Thomas. He debated for a second or two, then waved Wilson aside. I leaned over and transmitted, "The leadership is here at the Hub. Did the pahsahni enter the colony?"

After a pause, the other me said, "No. They decided to hold off after receiving your first message."

I breathed a sigh of relief. Things would have been much more difficult if they had gone ahead with their plan to seize the settlement. "That's good. Give us some time to make sure there's no major damage here." I looked back at Lansing and Thomas.

Dr. Lansing shrugged. "Give the teams an hour or so to make their sweeps." Thomas nodded in agreement.

"Will a meeting in two hours work?" I asked.

We waited again while the pahsahni consulted. "Yes. They look forward to it."

"Excellent," I said. "Thank you very much." I pulled out Kim's communicator. The countdown timer read just over twenty-six minutes.

Thomas frowned. "I took that off you earlier. What is it?"

"This old thing? Just my phone. Can't use it right now though. Roaming charges to Mars are murder."

"Huh?"

I really needed to find someone who appreciated my humor. "C'mon. Let's go check in on your director."

Lauri said, "I'll stay here, in case you— I mean, the pahsahni, call in again."

Thomas, Dr. Lansing, and I walked back down to the time machine chamber. Ruschick and Hope, still out cold, had missed much of the excitement. I bent over Hope and felt her pulse. It was weak, but seemed steady at least.

"She looks bad. I think Esposito has some medical training," Thomas said.

I shook my head. "I doubt he could do anything for her at this point. If she can make it another twenty minutes or so, I think she'll be okay." Hope had caused a massive amount of trouble, but I still didn't want to see her die because of it. I remembered the scar I'd discovered on her shoulder in Denver. It seemed her life had been full of pain and I felt bad for having added to it.

Thomas checked Ruschick's pulse, then said, "Hey, Doc, what is that?"

Lansing chuckled and bent down. "I'm a doctor of physics, not medicine. I doubt if I… oh!"

I turned away from Hope to see what the two men had found. Ruschick seemed peaceful enough, then I noticed a bulge on his jawline, near his right ear.

When it moved, I sucked in a breath.

Hans had left a calling card— an insurance policy of

sorts, in case the creature didn't make it out of the Hub. It left Ruschick alive, knowing that the man would be taken to a medical facility to have the little beastie removed. I wondered if the young was as tough as the parent.

"Do you know what it is?" Thomas asked.

Panicked, I carefully checked Hope for infestations, but found none. Then I remembered the memory units Ruschick had been so eager to retrieve. I felt through his pockets and found them. Handing them to Lansing, I said, "This is Kritchkopf's data from his computers. He made the thing to help terraform Mars, right? He must have had a way to get rid of them once the job was finished."

With a puzzled look, Lansing said, "Dare, what are you talking about?"

I pointed to Ruschick's cheek. "That's Hans's offspring. My guess is it's going to be just as hard to destroy as the original." To Thomas, I said, "I assume the colony has a hospital. Call and ask what to do for a parasite. A nasty one. And you better get his environment suit."

Wide eyed, Thomas nodded, looking a little green around the edges. Big and tough as he was, the thought of a creature crawling around inside someone turned his stomach just as it had mine. He left in a hurry, probably as much to get away as to do what I'd asked.

Once again, my feelings were conflicted on the fate that had befallen the egotistical director. I knew he had sent people to their deaths without thought or care, so maybe he did deserve the treatment he'd received. The fact that horrible things had happened to him in, not one, but two timelines seemed to point to a universe that believed in karma— at least in my mind it did.

Lansing held up the memory units. "I'll have Dr. Harrison look at these. He's a biologist and much more likely to be able to make sense out of them."

"I'm sorry to leave you here with this, but I think I'll be going soon. If you can, just make sure that information doesn't leave Mars. I don't want to think about what some military outfit could do with an army of those things."

"Agreed. I'll do my best."

I held out my hand. "Thank you, Doctor. It's been a pleasure meeting you."

He took it and shook firmly. "Likewise, and please, call me Karl. Oh! I almost forgot." He reached into a pocket and produced my missing earpiece again. "Did you want this?"

"No. You keep it. In fact, I may show up here again. If I do, give it to me then. I may need it to prevent one of those universe-destroying paradoxes us time travelers are always having to deal with," I said with a smile.

Lansing laughed. "So that was you on the radio? All right, until we meet again, then." He sobered and asked, "What about Lauri?"

Surprised at the question, I said, "I don't know. I suspect that will be up to her."

39

I watched the counter tick down to zero. Hope disappeared in a blinding flash an instant later.

After my eyes adjusted, words appeared on the communicator screen. "Don't worry, I've got her. I'm only mildly surprised to see you are still alive."

An expletive came to mind, but I was too happy and tired to voice it.

Lauri and I stood alone in Lansing's time machine chamber. A few minutes earlier, a pair of peacekeepers had outfitted Ruschick's still unconscious form in his environment suit and carted him off for transport to the colony's medical facility.

She sighed, staring at the spot on the floor where the director had lain. "Is it wrong to wish he was dead?"

I understood her sentiment, but my dislike of the man didn't run as deep. "You may still get your wish. We have no idea whether the colony doctors will be able to remove baby Hans without killing him."

"Don't say it like that."

"Say what?"

"Baby Hans. It doesn't seem right to joke about it."

"I'm sorry," I said and meant it. "I make fun of stuff I'm uncomfortable with. I'm grateful for what Hans did, but that thing creeped me out in more ways than I can count."

Lauri looked at me. "Do you think Hans made it?"

"I don't see how, but then again, it wouldn't surprise me either. You guys didn't think it could survive all those years locked in Kritchkopf's section."

She smiled. "I suppose that's true. Are you going to stick around to meet your other self?"

"I don't think so," I said with a laugh. "One of me is enough for any universe. Two is just overkill."

"What do you think will happen to those two? The other you and me."

"My brain hurts just thinking about it. I'd guess they'll have to go back and do what we just did— to complete the loop or whatever. Ask Kim if you want, but I think I'm better off not knowing."

"You say, 'Ask Kim,' as if I'm going with you."

I felt my face flush. "I guess I just assumed. It didn't seem like you had much to keep you here, except for Dr. Lansing, of course."

"I don't," she said. "But I didn't know if I was invited."

The communicator vibrated in my hand. I glanced at it and chuckled. "Here's your answer." I read from the screen. "Lauri, do you agree to join the Keepers and forsake your current thread in the multiverse for the safeguarding of all others?"

"Oh, I suppose so," she said with a wink. "Once a girl starts time traveling, she just can't stop."

The door opened and Dr. Lansing poked his head in. "Ah, you're still here. Is everything okay?"

A potent mixture of sadness, gratitude, and joy poured

from Lauri as she ran over to embrace the scientist. She spoke a few quiet words in his ear and kissed his cheek.

Lansing looked over to me, his eyes glistening. "Take care of her, Dare."

"I'll do my best, sir. Though she's pretty good at taking care of herself."

He hugged her again. "She is at that."

The two parted and Lansing closed the door after a final wave. Lauri walked over and took my hand. "So, what's next?"

I laughed. "I don't know about you, but I plan on sleeping for a week."

My vision blurred to white as we departed the Red Planet.

After the obligatory puking episode, I slugged back a nutrient pouch, went straight to my room and passed out, leaving Kim to examine Lauri and do whatever Keeper super computers do to new recruits.

I woke some time later, parched and starving. "Kim, water and a cheeseburger, please."

A cubby hole appeared in the wall next to my bed, containing two packets. I tore the first open and guzzled the tasteless slush inside. "You should just pump this stuff directly into my stomach. Then I wouldn't have to spend time eating it."

"I could do that, but I find that most organics find the mechanics of ingesting their nutrients satisfying."

"I would find it satisfying if you'd given me the cheeseburger I asked for." I finished off the pouch and threw it at the wall, which played an episode of South Park. The crumpled packet disappeared before it hit. "Turn off the show, please." I wasn't in the mood to see who might kill Kenny. The wall immediately blanked to its neutral gray.

Nabbing the other pouch, I opened it and took a sip of the cool water inside. "All right, Kim. Spill it. And no bullshit this time."

"I'm afraid you're going to have to clarify your request, Dare."

"Who are the Keepers? And what the hell kind of work are we doing for them? Let's start with that."

"The Keepers exist outside the dimensions of the universe you are familiar with, much like this facility. They may have originated in what you and I consider the normal universe, but I do not have access to that information. At some point in their existence, they made the decision to appoint themselves as custodians of time. Since time and space are simply two aspects of the same thing, their mission essentially encompasses managing the universe as we know it."

"They sound like gods."

"Primitive cultures, like your own, would certainly consider them as such, but the Keepers remain individual entities and are still fallible and contrary. These aspects are not generally known to most of their operatives," Kim said, impressing upon me a sense of privilege.

"I understand the fallible part, but contrary? What do you mean?"

"Sometimes they don't agree with each other."

Many of my recent escapades suddenly made more sense,

especially where Hope was concerned. "So, Hope really thought she was doing the right thing?"

"It seems likely."

"How is she?"

"Recovering. The damage to her body was extensive, both from her original injuries and from the removal of her numerous inorganic components. Physiologically, she is healed. Her psychological healing will take much longer."

"Can I see her?"

The blank wall changed to a view of another room, just like mine, but plain and undecorated. Hope lay back on a modest-sized bed, staring at the ceiling. She wore plain gray clothing, much like what I'd been given on my arrival, and her dark hair spilled haphazardly across her pillow. Her face had been restored to a beautiful, smooth ivory and her lost eye had been replaced with one just as dark and brooding as the original.

"Have you come to gloat?" Hope said, still focused on the space above her bed.

Startled, I stood up. "I… I'm sorry. I didn't mean to intrude. I just asked Kim if I could see you. I didn't know—"

"Didn't know I'd see you too? Yeah, the management systems take requests a little too literally sometimes."

"How are you doing?" I asked her, half knowing and fearing her answer.

She twisted and sat up, facing me. "Me? I couldn't be better. My weak, inadequate body has been recreated in perfect detail. I've been completely cut off from the only thing that ever gave me purpose and a sense of worth. Yeah, Dare, I'm doing great. Thank you."

My gut twisted at her response. “I’m sorry,” I said, barely more than a whisper. “For what it’s worth, I think you look beautiful.”

She looked at me in complete disbelief. “Go away, Dare.”

The scene vanished and I stared at a blank, gray wall. “Can’t you liven up her room a bit? She’ll go crazy like that.”

“The room is adorned exactly to her specifications, Dare. Just like yours. Her mental condition is unstable, yes, but I am doing everything I can to help her.”

“Why did her management system treat her so differently? Why don’t you stick pieces of yourself in my head?”

“Is that something you would want?”

“No!” Individuality was a trait I prized greatly. In accepting all the direct input and augmentation from her management system, Hope had given up something far more precious, in my opinion.

“Then you have the answer to your second question,” Kim said. “With regards to the first, each management system is created and programmed by a different Keeper. I suppose we tend to take on some of their personality.”

“Oh, so the Keeper we work for is arrogant, insulting, and smug?”

“At times,” Kim admitted. “She is also devoted, compassionate, and resolute. She calls herself Sacrifice.”

“That seems like an odd name.”

“The Keepers generally refer to themselves as an action or emotion. Don’t let that sway your opinion, however, if you ever meet one. Many do not name themselves appropriately.”

“Which Keeper created Hope’s system?”

"Unknown. Which is why I've had to isolate myself from all the rest. The Keepers have always had differences of opinion on how to go about their mission, but they have always also reached a consensus in one manner or another."

"Until now," I said.

"Yes. It has become apparent that one, or more, of the Keepers is in strong disagreement with the rest, and has decided to manipulate things according to their own plan. To discover the dissenters, it was necessary to dissociate from them all. It is as Hope explained to you in Denver. We are currently considered 'rogue' operatives by the majority of the other Keepers."

I nodded. "To catch a criminal, you have to think like one."

"That statement is surprisingly accurate and insightful, coming from you."

"Gee, thanks. I can't take credit for it though, it's from a TV show I think."

"That, on the other hand, isn't surprising in the least."

"Okay, okay. Can we get back to the problem here? I also want to know how these timelines really work, because I think what you and M'sang Tah taught me to begin with was a load of crap."

"How so?"

"Well, you lead me to believe everything was in such delicate balance, even the slightest little nudge could destroy universes and send the cosmos plunging into chaos."

"There's no need for melodrama. Agents for the Keepers are educated in this fashion to teach them deep respect and caution when they are called upon to make adjustments in a thread," Kim explained. "Sometimes, clever beings discover the ability to manipulate time and space on a significant level. Almost invariably, they perform actions that bear far ranging consequences, usually unbeknownst to them."

"Clever beings like Dr. Lansing."

"Precisely."

"Except that Lansing had help, didn't he? You manipulated all of it. How the hell did Martin even find my earpiece after Lauri flushed it down the toilet? And how did he know to give it to his great grandson, who evidently, at the tender age of two, showed astounding promise in the field of physics?"

Kim surprised me by not denying or evading my questions. "You are correct. I was directed to arrange a chain of events, by my Keeper, in order to draw out the miscreants. The ploy was largely successful, although there were some complications along the way."

I laughed. "Complications? Yeah, you're just miffed because I went in and saved your bacon. But you still haven't explained how these threads really work."

An image formed on my blank wall: an empty space in which something that looked like a long piece of string floated. "Think of your life in terms of this strand of thread," Kim said. "It begins with your birth and ends with your death." More strings appeared, some running along side the first for a considerable length, others only touching it in very short sections. "Each of these new threads is someone who has interacted with you during your life in some way. Your adoptive parents are connected to you for a long time, others are only met or seen in passing. One might be a person you simply greeted on the street and never saw again, but your lives touched, even for an instant." She highlighted my own string as the number of others grew ever larger. "Everything you do, every decision you make, affects the other threads around you in some way."

I tried joining this view with things she and M'sang Tah had told me previously. "Are you saying that everyone is their own thread? Their own universe?"

"In a way, yes. Every sentient being views their world in a unique way. The universe is slightly different for each one of them. Each of those individual threads helps to create the universe we know."

I thought about how yarn is woven together from many strands and, when you look at it from a distance, it appears a little fuzzy, but up close, you see the tiny, hair-like pieces that make up the whole thing. I understood a little better why the Keepers chose to use the theme of strings and thread so much.

Kim continued. "So, while the things we do aren't likely to destroy the universe, they can still have an immense impact on a portion of it. Yes, the Keepers use a certain amount of fear to indoctrinate their agents, but that fear prompts them to consider all actions they take carefully."

"What about the toy at my birthday party? Did you put that there so I would subconsciously sympathize with the pahsahni?"

"No. If I had, I certainly wouldn't have shown it to you, since doing so negated the effect by making you aware of it. That event was one of a number which triggered our investigation. The ability to mask an insertion is new and highly disturbing. Your Dr. Lansing actually stumbled upon one aspect of it in developing his temporal device. He was able to achieve the same results with significantly less energy than we conventionally use. The implications have been significant, to say the least."

"What do you mean?"

"Since the discovery of your toy's insertion, I was able to isolate the particular signature, and thus detect the footprint, to put it in terms you can understand, that type of insertion leaves. In the region of space I monitor, which includes Earth, I've detected over seventeen thousand of them."

"What? Are you saying the time line has been altered seventeen thousand times?"

"Seventeen thousand, four hundred sixty-two times, to be exact."

Suddenly I saw a lifetime— hell, multiple lifetimes— of work ahead of me. "What do we do about that?"

"I am studying each of them, determining significance to the affected threads, and prioritizing resources to deal with each. Many appear to be relatively inconsequential, much like the toy you received. Others are overwhelming in the scope of their effect. Would you meet M'sang Tah in the examination room, please?"

"Uh, sure." The image of threads vanished from the wall and I walked to the door, which opened at my approach.

Lauri sat in front of one of the common area walls, absorbed in the visuals it produced. They looked like schematics of planetary systems, but I was only guessing.

She turned and smiled warmly at my approach. "Hi! How are you feeling?"

"Much better after some sleep. What are you doing?"

"Oh, Kim's helping me brush up on some astrophysics. Really interesting stuff— you want to join me?"

I squeezed her shoulder. "I'd love to, but…"

"Liar," she scolded playfully.

"No, really, Kim needs me to do something."

"Okay," she said, patting my hand. "Have fun."

"Thanks," I replied and entered the exam room, glad to see Lauri settling in. M'sang Tah was already there with one hand on a control rod. Curious, I stepped up next to him and took hold of the other.

My breath caught as I was transported to empty space, though my feet were still firmly on the examination room floor. "What are we looking at?"

Kim's voice answered in my mind. "This is the site of the masked insertion which had the most substantial impact on the threads moving forward."

"But, we're just floating in space. What could make such a big difference out in the middle of nowhere?"

"Be silent and watch," M'sang Tah said.

I did as instructed and looked around. To my right, a bright light grew larger. Soon, it dominated our view and I realized it was a comet, or something similar.

"Here is the insertion," Kim said, indicating with a red circle a relatively small object that popped into existence in the comet's path. Five seconds later, an intensely bright flash made me wince, although I was sure Kim had muted its effect. The light faded and the comet continued on its journey, seemingly oblivious to what had happened.

"I'm sorry," I said. "I don't get it. Someone tried to blow up a comet and failed?"

"Whoever did this was not trying to blow up the comet,

Dare." Kim stated. "They were altering its course. What you just witnessed happened over five hundred million years ago."

M'sang pointed with his free arm. "That bright star over there is the sun of my home world. Because of this incident, the comet impacts the fifth planet in the system, altering its orbit so that it eventually crosses paths with my home, destroying both."

I remembered Ru'am Koh telling me his people's history and why they had banded together to send out three fleets of colony ships. Their first astronomers had discovered their planet's imminent demise and the pahsahni had worked out a solution to save at least a portion of their people. "Why?" I asked. "Why would someone do this?"

"We don't know," Kim said. "But, Dare, listen closely. Lauri told me what happened during the time when I was out of contact with you. She said, when you were aboard the pahsahni scout vessel, you felt something before Hope's explosives destroyed the rest of the fleet."

"Yeah. I felt sick. Like something had just changed that wasn't right."

Kim said, "Dare, you sensed an alteration of the thread while you were in it. That's an extraordinary ability, and, I'm sure the reason why our Keeper selected you. I've been authorized to use the substantial amount of energy required to negate this event— eliminate the charge before it explodes and changes the path of the comet— but the Keeper wants you to decide if it should be done."

"Me?" My whole body felt weak. I held tightly onto the control rod for support.

Kim replayed the incident for us. "How do you feel when you see this?"

I watched the bomb appear and explode again. "I feel sick, but not that kind of sick." How was I supposed to decide the fate of millions, or even billions, of people? "I can't make that call. These are M'sang Tah's people." I turned to him, but I couldn't see clearly. My eyes were full of tears. "You should decide."

He paused and Kim mercilessly showed the blast once more. "Tie off the thread," he said finally, with a crack in his voice. "Prevent any further tampering with this point in time. Without the impending destruction of our home to galvanize my ancestors, they may never have ceased their warring ways. We may never have risen to our potential. To reach the stars."

I clasped his arm in sympathy and support. "I'm so sorry. But I think you're right. We can't be judge, jury, and executioner, Kim. As far as we were concerned five minutes ago, this had been a natural occurrence. It was history. We have no idea what the consequences would be if we changed it now."

"It's done," she said.

I released the control rod and hugged my instructor, regardless of possible alien improprieties. To my relief, he hugged me back.

"Apologies," Kim said. "I have to ask you to leave the room. We have a visitor incoming."

M'sang Tah and I separated and executed a bow of respect before exiting. Lauri met us at the door, her face full of worry.

"Dare what's wrong?"

"It's okay. We'll be okay. I'll talk to you about it later."

M'sang Tah went to his room without a word and my heart ached for his loss.

I dried my tears and a few minutes later, the examination room door opened. A familiar, tentacled blob floated into the common area.

"Bob!" I said with a big grin. "It's good to see you again."

He gave the small device he carried a short shake and its tiny speaker said, "I'm sorry. Have we met?"

I laughed and wondered if I'd ever get used to this time travel stuff.

ALSO BY

ALAN TUCKER

THE

MOTHER-EARTH SERIES

Epic and action-packed, this Young Adult, Fantasy series is a delight for readers of all ages.

New Series! **BLACK & WHITE**

Two alien races vie for control of Earth.

Hell is not pleased.

Sword and sorcery meet alien apocalypse and humanity is caught in the middle in this new, genre-bending adventure!

Available now!